Pierre de Lano, Helen Hunt Johnson

The Emperor Napoleon III

Pierre de Lano, Helen Hunt Johnson

The Emperor Napoleon III

ISBN/EAN: 9783337350017

Printed in Europe, USA, Canada, Australia, Japan

Cover: Foto ©Andreas Hilbeck / pixelio.de

More available books at **www.hansebooks.com**

THE
EMPEROR NAPOLEON III.

BY

PIERRE DE LANO.

TRANSLATED
FROM THE FRENCH
BY HELEN HUNT JOHNSON.

NEW YORK:
DODD, MEAD & COMPANY.
1895.

71366

CONTENTS.

TO THE READER

DID I wish to write a preface to this third volume of the anecdotal history of the Second Empire, the numerous incidents which have accompanied and which have followed the publication of my previous works, would render the task easy.

Having, however, replied to my opponents in a special chapter upon the Court of Napoleon III., I will add nothing to what I have there said. In doing so I should but renew a discussion into which I do not care to enter. In arguments of this nature it becomes necessary, in order to affect public opinion, as well as to avoid the appearance of retreating before an adversary unjust through his own violence, to make use of the same vocabulary which he has chosen, to return his attacks — for a discussion is like a game of battledore and shuttlecock — to return his attacks, I say, with the same cold and intense passion, with the same ill-concealed anger as his own. None can fail to recognise in this a diversion hardly worthy of a writer; I prefer, therefore, to complete my work without resorting to recrimination. When all is still in the farmhouse, what does one care for the wind which howls round the barns stocked with wheat, and which is power-less to do more than shake the roof? There should, however, I repeat, be a preface of a peculiar nature which might serve to settle the controversies roused by my statements; but such a preface would have an interest alto-gether personal, and for this reason I limit to these few lines the introduction to my third volume upon the Second Empire. I have aban-doned every consideration irrelevant to my theme, that I may strive only for the achieve-ment of the task which I have undertaken, and for the faithful representation of a period which has all the charm, all the sustained inter-est, of a long romance; which has, too, all the terrors, all the convulsions, of an interminable drama. P. DE L.

PARIS, *February*, 1893.

NAPOLEON III.

I.

THE EMPEROR — HIS PRIVATE LIFE.

In writing my preceding works upon the Second Empire, I have allowed myself to be carried away by the element of strangeness, and also by the anecdotal interest of the materials which have helped me prepare my history; I have seldom had reason to be deeply moved, to experience that tremor of the senses or that tragic emotion which is fatally roused by an idyllic poem or by a bloody epic.

In certain chapters, however, relating more particularly to those events which occupied the latter part of the reign of Napoleon III., I have been unable to conceal the enthusiasm which then took possession of me; it seemed, as I understood better the personality of the Emperor, that I was in the presence of one of those heroes of romance or of drama before whom all subsequent heroes of romance and

7

drama in the literary world are insignificant.
This feeling is now strengthened in me as I
write these pages specially consecrated to Napoleon III., and the emotion which had hitherto
but touched me lightly has increased and taken
possession of my narrative. To whatever political party my readers may belong, my standpoint
must, nevertheless, be understood. It must be
admitted that the character of Napoleon III. is
more interesting to study, to watch, to puzzle
out, than the character of one — however psychological that character may be — who simply
comes and goes in the world like every other
man and woman, be he honest or a knave, art-
less or a dupe, a sceptic or a believer.

It is not without reason that I suggest a
resemblance between the Emperor Napoleon III.
and the customary hero of the modern novel.
The Emperor was indeed a hero of romance,
but a hero devoid of fictitious embellishment,
whose actual fortunes are developed and strung
together with all the interest, with all the
rapidity, with all the logic, of a good melodrama.

There is no reason to be surprised at the
attitude assumed by Napoleon III., or by the
peculiar character which he gave to his reign.
Though himself unconscious of it, the Emperor

was compelled to maintain, during the whole
course of his life, the gloomy bearing of an
actor in a leading *rôle ;* and despite his coldness, his reserve, and the accuracy of his observation, he was obliged to live his days like so
many chapters of a serial story, filling them
with incident and with change, and presenting
them to the public linked together by a kind of
" continued in our next," both enigmatical and
passionate.

In this attitude of the Emperor, and in the
peculiar aspect of his reign, there is nothing
unnatural.   Did not, indeed, this man and this
reign spring up in a moment, as if appointed
by destiny?   Was not the Prince Louis Napoleon thrust upon history with the opportuneness
of some legendary creation whose course is
immutably fixed, whose career irremediably determined?   Victor Hugo sang his name in
magic verse ; the works of M. Thiers celebrate
his uncle's glory ; the burden of Béranger's
songs, which are softly repeated by the people,
stirred the golden dust of the imperial bees
which perished at Saint Helena, but which
were revived, and are now buzzing round that
hive, the Invalides.   The Prince Louis Napoleon, urged by a force independent of his free
will, moved by a power stronger than his own,

under the influence, indeed, of that legend which prophesied the dizzy heights of the throne, longed to be emperor ; the demigod of that legend wished to realise in himself the sublime words of Victor Hugo, to perpetuate the glory of his uncle, to present to M. Thiers another episode in history, to fulfil the prophecy of Béranger. He was a man of Fate, the product of a combination of fatal causes; he was but what Destiny forced him to be ; he could not have been other than he was.

Rocked by the waves, the child of a sailor, when he arrived at manhood he, too, took to the sea. His ears filled with the groans of an empire in agony, whose voice lingered still as an echo, his imagination excited, despite an ostensible calm, by the power and beauty of a literature built upon his name, Prince Napoleon wished to revive a great epic, wished to be a Napoleon I. This was one of many dreams ; but he experienced neither Austerlitz, Waterloo, nor Saint Helena. Fate apportioned him instead, Chiselhurst, where men may die as upon that desolate rock, but from which one may, nevertheless, escape and still mount to glory. Fate apportioned him Chiselhurst, which is on the threshold of France, but from which he did not return.

I have already given a little sketch of the
Emperor Napoleon III. Never did a face reflect more perfectly a soul, never was a man
more fully than he the living, breathing embodiment of his feelings. The mind, the soul, of
the Emperor, still enveloped in visions of the
past, weary of the deceptions of which he had
been dupe, of the humiliations which he had
been called upon to undergo, seemed now to
falter before possible flight, as though stupefied
by the long sleep of his erring and almost
homeless boyhood. The bodily movements of
the Emperor were laboured, and gave an impression of indolence; he seemed to be weighed
down by a chronic fatigue which he tried to
drive away, but which always returned and
took possession of him. In public and during
official ceremonies he made a great effort to
overcome this depression, but its power was
often stronger than his will. He then became
a rigorous observer of etiquette, an impassive
sovereign who received unmoved the homage
of courtiers, of officials, of office-seekers; yet,
though he knew so well how to fill the *rôle*
of sovereign, he found the attitude which these
circumstances forced upon him wearisome because it deprived him of his beloved hours
of revery — revery called forth as much by

appeals to the past as by delusive visions of
the future. He was only happy when he had
escaped from critical observation, and could
once more assume his character of philosopher ;
when he was free physically, and mentally at
peace — a nobleman at home.

Those who but knew Napoleon III. among
the conventional surroundings of the court, did
not, in truth, know him at all. It is doubtless
interesting to study him in the public acts of
his life, but no less interest attaches to his more
intimate personality or to his life as a private
individual. As, day by day, the Empress grew
more trying and more deceitful, the Emperor's
heart and manner alike grew colder. Outside
the hours devoted to work, and when he could
escape from the anxieties which the unstable
policy of his ministers occasioned him, he was
always affable and kind, eager to make others
happy, and to bring good fortune to all, like the
head of a family whose constant thought is for
those whom he loves and by whom he is loved.
With a pleasant word for all whom he met, he
used to wander through the Tuileries, examin-
ing and re-examining, as in a museum, the
works of art which, through infinite patience
and the aid of connoisseurs, he had collected.
Often, too, he would pass from his own room

into the apartments of the Empress, a cigarette between his lips, and surprise her as she sat among the ladies of the court; smoking still, he would join in their idle talk, laugh at their remarks, then leave them as quietly as he had come, walking with that measured, swinging step which was habitual to him. Occasionally he would take a friend or an aide-de-camp and drive out in a phaeton, accompanied by one attendant only, and always keeping the reins himself. He preferred, however, to stroll upon the terrace of the Tuileries, along the banks of the Seine; there, with a confidential friend at his side, more often General Lepic, or General Fleury, he would walk quietly for long hours, gazing now at the river-banks, now upon Paris, in whose gardens troops of careless children frolicked merrily. At his own side, too, there often played a child who, however, was separated from the others, and whose recreation was controlled by official regulations. This was his son, whom he loved as a fanatic loves his God, for whom he lived after his fall, for whom he twice died when his effort to save the child's life betrayed him. The Emperor was troubled by the restrictions imposed upon his son. He would have loved to see him among the other children, mingling with theirs his shouts of joy

or his tears of childish grief, full of youthful
spirits, and like them, a joy to look upon.   He
longed to set him amongst these, but etiquette
required the poor, imperial child to sicken and
sadden among those friends whom alone conventionalities permitted him to love.

One afternoon the Emperor realised his
dream.   He took his son by the hand and
brought him into the public garden of the Tuileries.   There was some little excitement when
the Prince Imperial was recognised among the
noisy crowd of little urchins, whose parents
were seated near them under the great trees,
watching their noisy offspring.   The Emperor,
however, only laughed, and, bowing to the
crowd, pushed his son into the midst of the
children.   "Go," he said, "go and play."   The
bashful little Prince hesitated, perplexed by this
sudden liberty, by this unexpected contact with
human beings.   "Go, Loulou," repeated the
Emperor, "go and play with them ; you will
soon see how kind they are, and they will grow
to love you dearly."   That day Louis did indeed
play with the common children, while his father
watched him, his heart full of joy and tenderness.

When the Emperor returned to the Tuileries,
his face wore an expression of real content, that

content which may shine upon the face of a true-hearted man. At dinner he told of his little escapade, but a voice, that of the Empress, interrupted him sternly.

"You have acted most imprudently," said she; "why do you expose Louis to a companionship which he should never know, to the companionship of ill-bred children?"

The Emperor looked sadly up at the company. "Not all the children," he replied quietly, "who play in the garden are ill-bred."

He said nothing more, but the joy had suddenly left his face. On this occasion, as on many others, the young Empress had spoken tactlessly, and, not understanding his nature, had marred her husband's happiness.

I have already spoken of the lack of affection shown the young Prince by his mother. I have spoken of the way in which she brought him up, with a harsh, conventional care devoid of all demonstration and also of that tender simplicity which makes the love of parents so divinely human. I have also spoken of the Emperor's untold love for his child. It is impossible to emphasise too strongly this affection, or to contrast it too sharply with the cold indifference of the Empress. It would, in short, be impossible to overestimate the innate kindness of Napoleon

III. The consideration which he showed his child he would have liked to extend to all the world. This kindliness of spirit was not confined to his feeling for children; it characterised as strongly his relations with men and even those with his enemies. I will quote in support of this statement but one example, an example which is, however, convincing and eminently characteristic.

When Orsini[1] was condemned to death, and the question of pardon was submitted to the Emperor, the ministers insisted that the matter be referred to the cabinet. A council was called, and when Napoleon III. firmly asserted his right of pardon, in opposition to those who wished his life, a violent discussion arose between him and his counsellors. The council sat all night, and declared itself ready to hold permanent session. It was only when Napoleon III. saw that to persist in his determination would bring about a political crisis, that he yielded his privilege and sadly resigned himself to necessity.

[1] Orsini was one of the most desperate of Italian revolutionists. Considering the Emperor Napoleon III. as a great obstacle to the success of a general revolution throughout Europe, he, together with three accomplices, attempted his assassination on January 14, 1858. As Napoleon and the Empress were approaching the opera-house, he caused several bombs to be thrown under their carriage, which, exploding, caused many deaths, though the Emperor and Empress miraculously escaped unharmed. (Translator's note.)

I am not in this instance judging Napoleon III. as a politician, but rather as a private man. It would be a base injustice, an injustice of which I am, in the face of any circumstances, incapable, to conceal the truth.

Whereas all the sentiments expressed by the Empress were weak and superficial, the Emperor's affections and friendships were sincere and deeply rooted. The Empress had sudden and irrational attachments, which died on the very day that they were born. The Emperor, who was in every way the opposite of his wife in character, was slow to give his affection; but when once given it remained constant, and was only withdrawn under very exceptional circumstances.

The court was the scene of terrible jealousies, and of abominable animosities. In this assembly, on the one hand, of men and women newly initiated into grandeur, and an arrogant though subservient aristocracy, surrounded, on the other hand, by a foreign nobility and a sullen *bourgeoisie* with an uncontrolled thirst for pleasure, — in such a community, I say, plots, competitions, and rivalries were a natural and a logical result of circumstance. The political and the social worlds gave free play to their reciprocal intrigues; and as each mem-

ber of society cast aside all thought of the
future, an inordinate desire for present pleasures sprung up, and an entirely selfish enjoyment of them.

The Emperor, who was often appealed to
concerning these secret dramas, held himself
aloof from either side. He usually listened
patiently to the complaints, and to the claims
which were laid before him, but he forgot them
as quickly as they were heard. He did not
place in his friends thus slandered less confidence than before; and if he afterwards spoke
with them of what he had heard, it was only
that they might laugh over it together.

" Do not defend yourself," he said one day to
a friend who had been the victim of some jealous rival; " I love you all the more dearly
because unkind things have been said of you."

It was in this way and with such words that
he won the affection of his subjects, who, let
it be fairly stated, nobly retained for him, even
after his fall, an unalterable devotion. Certain
courtiers, however, by their constantly repeated
assaults, wearied the patience of honest men,
and finally compelled them to retire from the
council-boards, and to remain absent from the
Tuileries.

The attitude of the *habitués* of the court was

well calculated to distress those who were the
disinterested friends of the Emperor. These
arrogant noblemen and frivolous scoffers, encouraged and protected by the Empress, made
victims of their sarcasm, their abuse, and their
insupportable scorn, all persons who by some
special talent for letters, science, art, or politics, had attracted the attention of Napoleon
III. The courtiers considered the Tuileries a
sort of booty, to whose pillage they were exclusively entitled ; every newcomer was regarded
as an interloper, and his privileges carefully
restricted lest he should, perhaps, rob them of
their prerogatives, or win too much favor from
the Emperor.

In speaking of "pillage" I have used a strong
word ; but the Emperor's house was, indeed,
portioned out in equal shares by its guests and
beneficiaries. The indifference of Napoleon
III. to money was well known, and this indifference was with little scruple turned to their
own advantage by the courtiers. To impose
upon the Empress was, however, more difficult.
They stood in some awe of her own instincts
of economy, and also feared the terrible Pépa
who kept her accounts, and had an eye on her
expenditures, so that none might reap benefits
from this field, to whose good things the Em-

press had sole right. Gaining nothing in this direction, they, however, robbed the Emperor largely, and with little attempt at concealment. The Emperor was not ignorant of these thefts, but he feigned ignorance, silenced by his instinctive horror of bickerings and his inexhaustible sympathy for all those in need. He was not the only person, however, aware of this state of things ; General Lepic was one of the few men who could speak with perfect frankness to the Emperor.

" You are being robbed, sire," said he one day ; "if you do not put an end to this squandering, the Tuileries will soon cease to be yours at all."

The Emperor sadly shook his head without replying.

" It would be hard to find," added the General, "three thoroughly honest, upright men among those around you."

Severe as was this statement, truth was written upon the face of it — truth, emphasized by the fact that the very courtiers who openly robbed him, professed absolute devotion and were ready at any moment to sacrifice their lives for him ; it seems, indeed, as though they were almost unconscious of the disloyalty of their own acts, finding in their real affection for him an excuse for its violation. This is, it is true, a paradox, a sort of gambling with the affections.   I am, however, convinced that, had it been impossible to extract money from the Emperor, these men would, nevertheless, have remained faithful to him.   The morals of the court were peculiar to itself.   At the Tuileries good and evil were not, in the eyes of its chosen circle at least, measured by the same standards as in the world outside.

Not only did the Tuileries have a special code of morals, it also had a religion of its own.   The Empress, Spanish in all her sentiments, would have muttered a prayer at the same moment that she was watching a charade.   Her court, like herself, worshipped God in the Spanish fashion.   The men went with a devotion equally divided, either to mass or to their mistresses' boudoirs.   The women were at once frivolous and devout, and would meet their lovers, on issuing from the confessional, looking indifferently upon penance and upon the renewal of their sins.

There is an amusing story illustrating the religious practices at the Tuileries.

Mme. de Montijo, the Empress's mother, was extremely devout, and she never failed on seeing her daughter, to ask concerning the state of the Emperor's soul.

"How does he stand in relation to the good God?" she would ask. "Is he in favour with the Holy Virgin? Does he pursue the right course toward them, and is he careful in the performance of his devotions?"

The Empress always replied that he seemed to be on pleasant terms with the good God and with the Holy Virgin; that he went to mass and to confessional, and was always generous towards the Church.

This was perfectly true; Napoleon observed his religious duties with a faithfulness easily mistaken for true fervour. He was not, however, a believer, and only carried out these observances in obedience to the State, which required from the head of the nation an example of respect toward the Church. He also wished to avoid quarrels with the Empress and the loud lamentations which any other course would have called forth from his mother-in-law. He was not at heart religious, but he did not dare let it appear that he was not so, and through the intervention of his wife, he became the defender of Papacy at Rome. He showed great concern for the bishops, and made himself popular with all the curates. Referring to this purely surface devotion, which was made a real necessity to him, Napoleon III. once told an amusing story to a few of the intimate friends who were gathered round him in the privacy of his own study — the sole retreat where he felt himself at home and free.

When in the country with the Empress, so the story ran, at the time of a Church feast, Her Majesty persuaded him that good policy required his communing upon this solemn occasion. It was of course necessary that he should first confess himself, and as neither the prelate nor the priest — one or the other of whom ordinarily acted as confessor — were present, he was forced to ask absolution from the curate of the place. There was in Napoleon III. a love of mischief which found ready expression in innocent little pleasantries, not without wit, and which caused him infinite amusement. On this occasion the Emperor was seized with a desire to have a little fun at the expense of the priest who was about to shrive him. The poor divine was much agitated by the novel duty which he was called upon to perform, and had seated himself in the confessional with much trepidation, almost with terror. What, then, were his feelings when Napoleon III. began to speak! The sovereign had conceived the idea of accusing himself of all sorts of impossible crimes and follies. Each new confidence was interrupted by a sudden and persistent cough, which the priest, fearing to learn the further transgressions of his sinful penitent, had suddenly developed. This game was highly amusing to the Emperor, who, observing that the cough grew more and more severe, paused for a moment.

" You have a very bad cold, my good curate," said he. " I will wait till that painful cough is a little quieted, before continuing my confession. I am a great sinner, and want you to hear what I have to tell."-

The cough then suddenly ceased, but the priest grew more and more confused.

" If your Majesty," he said, " will permit me, I will grant your Majesty immediate absolution. That which has been already said satisfies my conscience."

Napoleon III., however, insisted upon full confession, while the curate expressed his preference for absolution.

" An emperor," he added with some shrewdness, " is, I see, unlike other men. I pray your Majesty, therefore, to permit a somewhat unusual treatment."

The Emperor, much amused and a little surprised at the wit which his confessor had shown, brought the proceeding to a close, and, on leaving the confessional, gave the curate a heavy purse for his poor.

It has been observed that the Emperor stood in great horror of the recriminations and lamentations, in regard to religious matters, of Mme. de Montijo, mother of the Empress. Nor was it only with regard to these that he had reason to dread the Countess. His fears were of long standing. If, indeed, any cause could have arisen before their marriage to separate Napoleon III. from the object of his passionate devotion, that cause would have been, without doubt, the mother of the future Empress. He was not ignorant of her past, of her doubtful morals, of her tendency to confuse good and evil, and to adopt a kind of virtue hardly deserving the name; he did not wish, indeed, that his young wife should hold too intimate relations with her mother, but he did not succeed in preventing these relations. When Mme. de Montijo was at Paris, she saw her daughter every day, and when she was in Spain a vigorous correspondence was kept up.

The Emperor, in marrying Mlle. de Montijo, had beyond a doubt given his name and his throne to a pure woman. Certain combinations of circumstances had at one time occasioned doubts in Napoleon's heart, which, though afterwards quieted by the dignified attitude of the young girl, had nevertheless left their traces behind them, such as might, perhaps, be left on the heart of any man accustomed to question his *fiancée* as closely as Napoleon did his.

Mlle. de Montijo confessed that she had loved before she had met him, which confession was true. Having visited with her mother many fashionable watering-places, having lived at Paris and at Madrid, in the midst of a lax society composed largely of foreigners, Mlle. de Montijo had frequently met men who had been impressed with her beauty. Indulged and encouraged by her mother, she had tied and untied several love-knots; it was the knowledge of this fact which troubled the Emperor, revealing, as it did, with how little scruple Mme. de Montijo had countenanced a doubtful line of conduct.

Mme. de Montijo is certainly a curious character, and must ever remain so. She is a good representative of that type of woman in modern life who takes little heed of conventionalities, and who, having a beautiful and a marriageable daughter, goes in quest of the desired husband. One encounters this type to-day on the shores of the Mediterranean. During the Second Empire resorts situated among the Pyrenees were in high favour, and it was toward that region that Mme. de Montijo directed both her steps and her hopes.

Possessing an income of a hundred thousand francs, she went to the shore in summer, usually to Biarritz, and spent the autumns and winters in Paris. Accompanied by her daughter, she frequented the *salons* which, thanks to influential friends, such as, for example, the Marquis de la Rochelambert, formerly French minister to Prussia, opened their doors wide to her. She was seen at the Comédie-Française, and at the Opera ; and she held, at her home in the Place Vendôme, receptions which were not without a certain notoriety. Politicians in large numbers frequented these *salons*, each attracted by the charms of the young girl, who, by her constant strategy, kept them always on the verge of hope. Mme. de Montijo was at this time very open-hearted and sincere. She had little objection to scandal, even to calumny, if these could be employed in bringing about a desirable marriage for her daughter — a marriage which should put an end to her adventurous wanderings, threatening now to become interminable. With a well-assumed artlessness, she was cordial to every one, but, the candidate out of sight, she would fix his exact value, and weigh him as a jeweller weighs an ounce of gold, and then without pity set him aside if he did not possess the fortune and the future prospects which her ambition, and also, be it said, her mother's heart, demanded. This mother did indeed love her child sincerely. Though she expressed her love in a way shocking to us because contrary to our French customs, such violation cannot prove her love to be less, or justify our doubt of it.

Mme. de Montijo would not have hesitated, had no favourable opportunity of marriage presented itself, to have her daughter become the mistress of some man of note, a prince or a minister. In this arrangement she would have thought only of her child's interests, and would have considered no personal advantage to herself which she might gain thereby. Her morals were those imputed to certain actresses' mothers, except that the Countess was neither avaricious nor selfish.

The reader will remember the letter which she wrote to her friend, the Marquis de la Rochelambert, after the marriage of Mlle. de Montijo with the Emperor had been arranged. This letter was sincere in its spirit, and gave expression to truly kind and natural feelings. At that time the Countess, overtaken by an unexpected joy, thought only of the probable fruits of that joy, and gave herself up to the pursuit of those maternal duties from which so much happiness was to result.

When her daughter became Empress, her position necessarily changed. The Emperor exacted of her a reserve which she could not hope again to throw off. In her inmost heart, she perhaps longed for her past freedom. She became sullen and tearful, and harassed Napoleon III., as well as her daughter, with multitudinous inquiries, demands, and complaints. She had an inordinate love of jewellery, and her purchases were all made known at the Tuileries by a bill which, together with a supplicating letter, was regularly submitted to the Empress. Had she been given free rein, she would have become a very great encumbrance; but the Emperor saw that she was kept within fixed bounds. Mme. de Montijo was, in short, neither altogether good, nor yet quite the reverse, and exerted but small influence on the life of Napoleon III. She was the unconscious instrument of an unkind fate, and in the family life of the Emperor she played the part of many a plebeian mother who has been fortunate enough to have a beautiful daughter. A nobleman one day sees the daughter and marries her; but he carefully hides his mother-in-law. It is a common story in many a family among the aristocracy, and it is that of Napoleon III.

I have in my previous works told many anecdotes, and stated some facts which give a truthful picture of the home-life of Napoleon III. Judging from an external view of my statements, this home-life was not, in appearance at least, altogether unsatisfactory. Despite appearances, however, and the affectionate letters which the sovereigns, during their infrequent official separations, exchanged, the union was not happy. It had been hastily made under the influence, on the one side, of a violent passion, and on the other by a line of cold, calculating argument and deliberate determination. It suffered the inevitable fate of all such unions. Calm and satiety follow the first feverish hours of joy, and fill the man with a consciousness of disappointment and of mistaken hopes. He sees that what he has purchased through many a folly, many a sacrifice, has given him but a material and a transitory joy, the most superficial, the least enduring, of all joys. He sees that there is a spiritual barrier between him and his wife, that she can respond to no feeling of his, understand nothing that is dear to him; and bitterness then replaces love in his heart. In the presence of his cold reserve, the wife, who, though never having loved, is yet accustomed to affection, to companionship, and to admiring flattery, rebels,

and, under the sting of a wounded and an heart-
less vanity, becomes moody, irritable and nervous, finally giving way to a feeling of honest
jealousy. Such is the romance of Napoleon
III., such, also, the romance of the Empress
Eugénie.

They had, nevertheless, three years of unalloyed happiness, which began on January 30,
1853, the day of their marriage, and lasted till
March 16, 1856, when the Prince Imperial was
born. After this time all intimacy between the
Emperor and the Empress ceased. Napoleon
III. deserted his wife, and bestowed his affections upon whoever called them forth.

It might, perhaps, have been possible at that
time for the young wife to win back the love of
her husband, but despite the power which, during their courtship, she had possessed over the
Emperor's heart — the letters which she had then
written him and which he had found so charming, were dictated to her by Merimée — notwithstanding her power at that period, she showed
herself essentially tactless in the relations of
married life. Of a cold, unimpassioned temperament, she had nothing to offer but false
protestations of love; she thus became powerless to keep the affections of her husband, who
could no longer doubt that in the first exalta-

tion of his feeling, in the blindness of his hope,
he had given far more than he had received.
His wife no longer satisfied him ; and he left
her without remorse, as a lover deserts an un-
feeling mistress, pursued by the cruelty, the
egotism of a lonely, an unreciprocated love.

With a little conjugal tact, the Empress
might certainly have lessened for herself, as
well as for the Emperor, the loneliness of their
domestic life. She might have aroused in her
simple-hearted husband, if not a new love, a
feeling of remorse which would certainly have
checked the increasing coldness between them.
She, however, was no diplomat. Beset with
pride, she but followed its promptings, and
harassed the Emperor with complaints and
reproaches, which wearied him and drove him
more than ever from his home. There thus
arose a daily warfare between them. Napoleon III., gentle by nature, tried to avoid discussions, and fled from his wife's anger and her
accusations, dreading, indeed, to be alone with
her. He lived in constant terror of conten-
tious scenes, which seemed endless, and which
filled him with disgust of his own home. There
was no retreat in the palace where she would
not find and follow him. In his own study,
the one place where he might hope for repose,

he was only half safe. It often happened when he was studying or, perhaps, talking to some visitor, that a door would be slyly opened and the Empress's head disclosed through the crack, her face wearing an anxious, hard, and inquisitive expression. If it happened that the visitor were a woman, he was certain to receive, after she had left, a multitude of reproaches, and was compelled to endure a sulky face for many succeeding days.

The Emperor was fond of women, and by nature irresistibly attracted to them. There is, however, every reason to believe that he would have sought their society less, had he found at home that companionship and that tenderness for which he had doubtless hoped. A separation or a divorce could alone remedy this state of things ; but these, as I have elsewhere shown, were forbidden the Emperor, and it was with no hope of realisation that he dreamed of this expedient for recovering his liberty, and also that serenity which was at once necessary to his personal happiness and to the pursuit of his imperial duties.

The Empress had a fatal influence upon the political as well as the private life of Napoleon III. We must even believe that the anxieties which she occasioned him at home were not

without influence in bringing about a certain
lack of force and a weakness of will-power,
whose result was the omnipotence of the
Empress, and which also helped to lay at
home and abroad the foundations of a despic-
able policy, the formal expression of an authority which emphasised the weakness of Napoleon
III., to increase the discontent of statesmen and
strengthen the claims of the people. These
causes contained, indeed, the germs of the war
of 1870. This is undoubtedly the psychological
analysis of the Second Empire : psychology is
not always a romantic word.

In order to escape a certain kind of criticism,
and also that I may avert any possible misunderstanding as to the purpose of my work, I
have already stated that I make no pretence
of writing the history of the Second Empire,
according to the sense in which the word history is usually understood. My object is to set
before the public, in their more intimate relations, certain persons and events which characterise that epoch, and to trace their course.
If there are some who have preferred to mis-
understand my thought, there are surely others
who have grasped it. I cannot, however, too
strongly emphasise my purpose or establish
my position, wishing, as I do, to avoid all useless discussion and criticism.

It is in accordance with my original idea that I have spoken of the private life of Napoleon III. Still in harmony with it I will complete the sketch.

The somewhat monotonous amusements afforded the Emperor in his private life at the Tuileries are well known, and also the ingenious efforts of wise and devoted friends to lessen their dulness.

When the public heard that there were charades at court and amusing *tableaux-vivants*, the *habitués* of the palace took alarm at the sudden amazement and the severe criticism of the people. It was, therefore, decided that the newspapers should, as far as possible, be kept ignorant of affairs relative to the private life of the Emperor and Empress. It was even agreed that foreign papers which gave accounts of imperial life at the palace should be confiscated on the frontier. It will be remembered that the Empress, sharing the indignation of the courtiers, wrote a letter concerning a much-talked-of charade acted at Fontainebleau, in which she gave vent to her bitterness.

There is a document not less curious, which reveals this universal dread of publicity, and gives a just idea of the attitude maintained by the court to the people. This mean, paltry, and

arrogant spirit is represented as fully as possible in this document, which was but intended
for private reading.

" All the papers," says the author of this note, "have
published accounts of the hunt which, in honour of her
Majesty, the Empress, will be held at Saint-Cloud. They
also describe in full the proceedings which are to take
place in Compiègne. The *Petit Crayon*, after consulting its council of state, has decided that such matters should not be made public. The following are its
reasons : —

" Should one read the *Moniteur* of the time of Napoleon I., such a simple statement as ' The Emperor
hunted ' would alone be found. In this we have a good
example.

" Again, the infuriated enemies of the government,
who find in every circumstance an opportunity to destroy,
undo, dissolve, and annihilate, have here a fine pretext
to continue their work; for there is deeply rooted in
France a foolish impression that all monarchs who have
been hunters have made but poor rulers. There are
thousands of stories to this effect which, on the long
winter evenings, are circulated in the corn-sheds of the
peasants. The first Napoleon knew this, and saw that
the *Moniteur* stated but the bare fact : ' The Emperor
hunted.' In many cases even this notice was omitted.
A suffering people is jealous of everything; it feels that
its interests are alone to be considered, that its burdens
are too heavy to bear !

" We consider, furthermore, the descriptions published of her Majesty's toilettes quite beyond the bounds
of decency. She is, in all truth, the victim of sufficient

slander, without our furnishing the material for more of that scandal which pursues its pitiless work under cover.

"This, moreover, is not all. Frenchmen are born poachers, and their envy is aroused by any one who is able to hunt under their very eyes and without them. This is a strange but a true fact. Let us, then, imagine the news spread among thirty-six million poachers, which is what we are, that the Emperor and Empress, instead of inventing means to lessen their miseries, have hunted and killed some thousands of pheasants, etc. This would be but to nourish envy, and to open the gates to calumny.

"The *Petit Crayon* is convinced that accounts of the hunt are furnished by some foolish fellow to one of those sly foxes who are continually prowling round in search of a victim for their hatred. There are many enemies to be found in the court itself.

"The *Petit Crayon* begs that journalists shall not be allowed at Compiègne, and believes that its advice is good. The world will then no longer be supplied with accounts of the imperial hunts and diversions."

These lines are written in pencil, as the pseudonym of their author would suggest. The chirography resembles that of Merimée; it seems probable that he who gave such good advice to Mlle. de Montijo before her marriage should be responsible for them. We must not, of course, exaggerate their importance; but I think they will not prove quite useless to those who, after me, may seek by philosophical analysis to understand the character of the Second

Empire. I can form no estimate of what the future's verdict will be, but can only hope that to it this curious epoch which occupies and often perplexes my mind, occasioning me, by an accumulation of perplexing facts, doubt and surprise — I can only hope, I say, that to it this strange period of the Second Empire will be easier of comprehension than it has been to me.

What, indeed, is not confused and incoherent in the court of the Tuileries, in the surroundings of the Emperor and the Empress, whose union was itself a defiance of all reason?

We have seen in the preceding paragraphs how great was the fear at the Tuileries of anything which might place the public in contact with the affairs of court, of anything, indeed, which could lessen the authority or the prestige of those who wielded the power, and who, at their will, might create a nation's happiness, or call forth its tears. It is strange to find these courtiers, these monarchs, who were made indignant by accounts published of their amusements and by the revelations of their daily life, rushing with a thoughtless inconsistency to the representations of the operettas which at that time were in the height of the fashion. The diabolic Offenbach had invented these to the great satisfaction, not only of the people, — the people which felt its power and its pride greater when in the presence of those stage heroes grotesquely royal or divine, — but also to the satisfaction of the men and women of the court, who, blinded by a stupid vanity, did not hear the laughter of the people, or perceive that it was but amused by General Boum and the Grande Duchesse, because these were conventionalised types of what they knew to be realities ; because under the Second Empire it obtained no chance to look upon the great ones of this world, except when these were masked, or else disguised in the transparent tinsel of the carnival. The populace did indeed christen with real names the puppet faces of the opera. There is here a subtle suggestion to be noted in studying the history of the Second Empire.

Jacques Offenbach appeared at a moment of great psychological interest. Like a skilful handler of a magic-lantern, he threw a strong light upon the minds of the people, inspired them with a sense of their own rights, with strong hatreds, fierce scorn, and sweet hopes of deliverance. He moved in the midst of a great living parody. His long, Mephistophelian shadow crept in and out among a crowd of disjointed beings, and is felt in the vortex of a

whirling mass of humanity. He played the
part of sorcerer; he presided over the orgies
of pleasure; he was the delirious leader of an
orchestra composed of laughter, folly, and extravagance, of light and sensual loves; an
orchestra whose first strains were those of an
infernal life-march, whose last a noisy chaos of
sound, after which came silence and a great
void.

I remember a few years ago, just after his
death, standing beside Offenbach's coffin.
"That corpse," said a man near me, "is
the corpse of the first socialist of our day;
it was he who, in reality, put an end to the
Second Empire — that Second Empire which
was deemed to be eternal."

The speaker was right. The work of Offenbach was a high trump card slipped into the
hand of the Empire's opponent. He, more
than any, hastened the overthrow of official
prestige. In adorning with gilt braid the
cuffs of his General Boum and of his fiery
Achilles, in placing the captain's plume on
the head of Corporal Fritz, Offenbach committed a revolutionary act. The Empire was
crumbling under the sonorous shock of his
musical cadences, while the footlights in his
theatres shone with the reflection of Roche-

fort's *Lanterne.* He laughed no less than did those whom he amused by his own drolleries, dreaming, perhaps, as little as they that the clashing music of his quadrilles and of his boleros should some day be accompanied by the terrible bass of the cannon.

He prepared with strong spices and with vinegar the colossal salad of kings and emperors, of princes, marshals, and functionaries, a salad which the future was to devour. While from the heights of the legislative tribunal the " Five " were hurling into the midst of the people words that roused the country, Offenbach used his conductor's baton as a cudgel with which to deal formidable blows upon the heads of potentates.

He was Molière set to draw the bow upon a squeaking fiddle. More than once the shadow of that other honest scoffer must have laughed in the presence of these operatic revolutionists, and shaken the bells on his fool's cap by way of applause and approval.

This century is accused of giving birth to a sceptical and a pleasure-loving generation. Such a verdict fails to take into account the applause which Mlle. Schneider, the first interpreter of Offenbach, called forth when, with her father's famous sword, she made her superb thrust at the person of prince and commoner alike. This sword had a sharp edge, and Mlle. Schneider used it marvellously well in cutting down old theories.

We must not, however, attribute to Offenbach's destructive and democratic work an exaggerated importance. Though with every drawing of his musician's bow, he overthrew some prejudice and shattered some idol, to ascribe to him an undue influence upon the events of the Second Empire would be to give way to a childish enthusiasm. Jacques Offenbach created a fashion for scoffing, and made a whole generation dance the death-dance of doubt and irreverence; it would, however, be but foolishness to believe that the notes of his fife or the thunder of his drum resounded beyond his own generation. His name is, nevertheless, forever linked with the history of the Second Empire; and in that final shock which overthrew the Tuileries and its court, is heard the ring of his prophetic voice. He is a curious phase of the psychological life of the imperial world; he was one of those infinitesimal atoms which, when accumulated in vast numbers, formed the fearful avalanche that swept the Emperor and his court into the fathomless abyss of destiny. It was essential from the standpoint of justice to mention him here, essential that a place should be given him by the side of the many persons who, like worms and butterflies, swarmed in the Second Empire; it is but fair that he should be accounted one drop in that great sea which, at times calm and again tossed in storm, rocked the life of Napoleon III.

In private life the Emperor was a man like other men, sharing the faults and the characteristics common to all. He was, however, distinguished from other men, be they kings or simple citizens, by a deep and a sincere love of humanity, by a spirit of true kindliness. It would surely be ignoble to forget the high sentiments by which he was so often animated, and to consider only his faults. I know no sinless man. Professional moralists are often less sinless than are those to whom they preach. I, therefore, have no desire to imitate them in their denunciations or to give way to any indignation concerning the irregularities of the Emperor's private life. These irregularities had no direct influence upon the politics pursued at the Tuileries, if, indeed, exception be made of two or three of the women who at one time or another were mistresses of Napoleon III. These women were no more a vital part of the Emperor's life than were meteors in the

far-off firmament, meteors whose light illumined the immensity, but which were then
forever lost within the night.

There was a charming custom in olden days
of covering with rose leaves the heads of lovers
and of their fair mistresses. Without requiring
such homage for Napoleon III., I would yet
beg indulgence for his frailties, and wish that
their revelation might be met without indignation, but rather with that smiling philosophy
which, more than anger or reproach, is in
harmony with the French character.

II.

THE EMPEROR CONSIDERED AS A POLITICIAN.

WE are familiar with the attitude assumed by the Parisian world toward Prince Louis Napoleon Bonaparte during his presidency. Descendant of the greatest name of the century, heir of a legendary history, the Prince was yet the object of raillery and of systematic scepticism. No confidence was placed in him; he was, indeed, hardly considered seriously; his appointment was accepted in the absence of anything better, with the feeling that some other man would soon take the place which he then occupied. This attitude of the people is curious, but more curious still is the reception which Prince Louis Napoleon Bonaparte received when, in 1848, he presented himself as candidate for deputy. An atmosphere of absurdity seems to have surrounded the person of the applicant. The uprisings at Strasburg and at Boulogne, even his captivity and his escape, were set forth in a humorous article, and ridicule followed him wherever he went.

The upper classes of society, the political world — and in this world were included those of no social rank, Bohemians, and even the un-principled — alike turned from him. The populace, made vaguely anxious by the mention of his name, hoped to gain nothing from him, listened indifferently to his appeals, and dared place no faith in that great awakening which he prophesied.

Prince Louis Napoleon Bonaparte was alone, absolutely alone, in 1848, surrounded only by strangers, by common workmen, and small merchants. The truth of this statement, if we except the army, which was ready to enter the field for his cause, is fairly staggering. The electoral committee of the Prince was composed, when, after his first election he arrived in Paris from London, of two shoemakers, a coal-dealer, a hair-dresser, and an upholsterer. Those who, in the nature of things, should have marched in the van, those who should have cheered him, taken him by the hand and presented him to the people, these and the survivors or the descendants of that aristocracy which had been created by his uncle, — even these, I say, seemed to have forgotten his coming, seemed to ignore his very existence, prudently keeping them-selves out of his way and apart from one who

was deemed of little use, and of far too compromising a nature.

Prince Louis Napoleon Bonaparte was alone in
1848 ; he had neither friends nor money. There
was, however, one man of power at his side, a
man of true intelligence, and one whose devotion is unequalled, who believed in him, watched
over him, and worked for him. This was M. de
Persigny ; and when, in later days, the Prince,
who had then become Emperor, gave him his
unalterable friendship, it should be remembered
that this friendship was but natural and, one
might say, obligatory.

We have seen how little respect his electoral
committee could hope to inspire at the time of
Napoleon's arrival in Paris. This committee
held its sessions in a small office situated at the
back of a dark passage-way ; but despite its
extreme indigence, it had, nevertheless, assured
the triumph of its candidate.

Some time before the election, M. de Roth-
schild, having positively declined to furnish the
imperial candidate with funds, the poor members of whom the committee was composed
were obliged to collect pennies in any quarter
where they could, in order that the name of
their Prince might be placed on the walls of the
capital. They frequented the faubourgs, spoke

to the people in their own language, and only returned after having increased the number of their adherents, and having won rare promises concerning the vote which was to decide a nation's destiny. The committee was not, in reality, without some apprehension concerning the result of this vote. Its machinations, however, had been more clever than it knew. In stirring the ashes of the Imperial Epic, they had won the hearts of the women. It may also be affirmed that it was the women — the women of the people — who brought about the triumph of the Prince.

The story of this triumph is indeed a curious bit of history, like the parody of an old-time farce. Labourers' wives, moved by the remembrance of Napoleon I., and also by that of his son, who, a melancholy shadow, wandered far from him, and by the knowledge, too, of the efforts made by Prince Louis to regain the throne, embraced his candidacy with great zeal, inspired by one of those irrational enthusiasms which are characteristic of all women, plebeian and patrician alike; and they, by the side of their husbands, conducted a fierce campaign in his cause. They were almost ready, like their sisters of long ago, to lay down their lives for their hero.

The common woman has considerable influence over him whom in vulgar phraseology she terms her "man." This expression is not, however, without its poetry.

On the day before the election, all Paris, and, indeed, all France, was laughing at the candidacy of Louis Napoleon Bonaparte. He was made a subject of mockery, nor was his election ever for a moment considered as a possibility. When, however, the ballots were counted France stood by in consternation. The Prince was elected by a majority of more than eighty thousand. Precedent had been stronger than prejudice. The most refractory bowed down before it, and were ready to accept its consequences. From that day the Prince became a power not to be ignored. From that day, too, the Prince, in his innermost heart scorning — though he succeeded in concealing this scorn — the leaders of different political parties, and also the upper classes of society, had but one aim, that of winning the confidence of the poor, of entering into the heart of labourer and peasant, of gaining the sympathy of the army which, in the decisive hour, was to secure the victory.

Encouraged by his first success, he now became bold. He resigned his deputyship on

September 7, 1848, but was re-elected, not only in Paris, but also in several of the departments. This act was, on the part of the Prince, a test of public sentiment.

Despite his dizzying onward march, however, despite even his election to the presidency of the Republic, Prince Louis Napoleon Bonaparte, nevertheless, remained a man morally isolated from his surroundings. It was not until after December 2, 1851, that courtiers and office-seekers gathered round him. They then became very numerous, and the Emperor forgot their former self-interested doubts and their cowardice; he, like another prince in history, forgave, if not the injuries done him, at least the selfish indifference of those who had not at one time believed in him, but who now so suddenly offered their most ardent sympathy.

There is a curious incident relative to the election of Louis Napoleon Bonaparte. The very day after the election, the Count de Morny was recommended to the Prince as a man whose royalist and liberal tendencies would be of great value in the new political *régime*. The Prince, however, looked displeased by the mention of his name, and struck it resolutely from his list of friends. M.

de Morny was not unknown to him, nor did he doubt his ability, his energy, or the strong support which he was capable of offering him; but he was vexed and embarrassed by the blood relationship existing between himself and the Count; he could not forgive his brother's unseemly and too conspicuous crest, upon which the branch of Hortense's house was subtly but conspicuously suggested. An easy reconciliation was, however, effected between these two men, with the consequences of which we are familiar. Despite the repugnance which, before December 2, Prince, Louis Napoleon Bonaparte had shown toward M. de Morny, he, nevertheless, on becoming Emperor, granted him every indulgence.

Though the Prince in his own heart attached but little importance to the support of those influential personages who were leaders of various political parties, though he had told his partisans to depend wholly upon the people and upon the army, he did not, on the other hand, altogether despair of rallying about him a few men of authority from other quarters.

The political agitation which he felt about him at the Elysée led him to believe for a moment that there was a response to his ap-

peals, that the people were flocking round him,
not from idle curiosity or with a courteously
concealed indifference, but with the sincerity
of an higher purpose and the firm intention
of actively assisting in his labours. He was
soon brought to see the vanity of his hopes.
When finally convinced that nothing could
change the hypocritical hostility which pursued him, and which was now but quieted as it
were, by a temporary truce, he resolved to act.
He made the appeal which is made by all
adventurers, all seducers. " He who loves,"
he said, "must follow me!" In the year 1851,
moreover, the parties became bolder, more
clamorous, and more formidable. Having believed that the duration of the Prince's presidency would be brief, they were now tired of
awaiting its end; they were troubled by its
evident vitality. The strength of the opposition was each day increasing, each day making
itself more manifest. The Prince, who at this
time had a quick perception and a ready mode
of action, wished to temporise no longer. He
assembled his friends, and with their aid put
at nought the projects of those who could not
hide the hatred with which he inspired them.

The Coup d'État of December 2, 1851, has
occasioned many discussions to which I care to

add nothing, be it either of praise or blame. In view, however, of the time which has elapsed since this event, and despite the various judgments which it has called forth, I do not hesitate — bearing always in mind that genesis which, in every century, is common to the events which determine social evolution — to ask that question which a thousand times already has been asked : Was the Coup d'État of December 2, 1851, a crime?

I do not lose sight of nor ignore the fact that on December 2, 1851, the laws of the country were violated. What historic or social revolution has ever been accomplished along the lines of law? In relation to politics, what is the exact significance of the word crime?

The Coup d'État is to be regretted inasmuch as it placed the destiny of a people in the power of one man, and compelled it to pay homage to a military force with but little intelligence; a force which, by a slavish submission to an implacable power, accomplished its annihilation. Viewing it, however, from a purely human standpoint, when we examine the Coup d'État philosophically, we cannot fail to see in it all the characteristics of a revolution ; and a revolution can be accomplished only by a logical and almost mathematical course of violence.

The Second of December undoubtedly caused liberty and progress to take a step backward. It would, however, be childish to believe that, even had it been inspired by the spirit of progress and liberty, it would have found a peaceful development. It is with nations as with some women, one can only hope to influence them through violence.

There is a faith prevalent to-day in the advent of a social era which shall be built upon justice and an humanitarianism faithfully observed and peacefully accepted by all men. I, together with those who are distressed by the servitude and the sufferings of certain classes, with those who believe in a supreme and an universal pity, have faith in this new era, and even believe that we are nearer it than is generally supposed; an era when the world, liberated from its bonds and from its oppressors, shall step forth into the future free. Contrary, however, to the hopes of certain eager and generous souls, of certain too visionary minds, we may safely affirm that this coming revolution will be accomplished no more peaceably than the preceding ones have been, that revengeful but fertile hatreds can alone give birth to the relative happiness of humanity.

This theory is, I think, applicable to the Coup d'État of December 2, 1851, which was,

I repeat, a revolution which inaugurated a new social era. This theory is, indeed, so true, it expresses so justly the exact nature of things, that when later Napoleon III. hoped to rebuild his Empire by giving it free institutions, he failed absolutely in his efforts of reform. He failed because in 1869 and 1870 politics did not possess that impetus which is necessary to social evolution, because he hesitated in the practical application of his ideas, because he did not dare to carry out his wishes.

The second of January, 1870, demanded the same energy and force which had contributed to the success of the second of December, that energy and force which are the final consecration of all earthly labours, which are the necessary foundation of all building that is to endure into the future.

Prince Louis Napoleon Bonaparte had in 1851 reduced to silence the liberal opposition; in 1870 the ministry, represented by M. Émile Ollivier, should have crushed the dynastic opposition, and thus have secured calm for its deliberations, and means for successfully determining its line of action. It is true that the very underlying principles of the government would have been imperilled by such an act of authority, but politics, like the more insignificant affairs of life, are controlled by an inexorable logic. It is in the course of this logic that we can vaguely see new eras arise, whose storms and calms must, however, remain unknown to us.

There are two entirely distinct elements to be studied in the political policy of Napoleon III.; one concerns affairs of the interior, the other the attitude of the Tuileries toward foreign nations.

Though the interior policy of Napoleon III. was distinguished by absolutism, it cannot be denied that, despite the intrigues going on about him, despite the covetous spirit of his ministers and their rivalries, so well described by M. Roulland, this man knew admirably well how to carry out his own wishes so long as his personal control over the government lasted, knew how to impose upon the country an administration keenly attentive to the expression of his wishes. The prefects, indeed, of the Second Empire remain celebrated in the annals of officialism, as do the women of this period in the annals of love. The men of the Second Empire administered laws and loved their mistresses with an equal ardour; the one office was, indeed, often closely allied to the other. The women who, regardless of their social rank, filled so important a *rôle* in the private life of Napoleon III., exerted also an indisputable influence upon the course and destiny of his government.

Every prefecture, no matter of how small consequence, was like the court of the Tuileries in miniature. The mistress of the house held her *salon;* and those women about her who either for their beauty, their wit, or their frivolity were most remarkable, received frequent summons to Paris on days of public festival. The official and the private gates of the palace were both open to them, and from these they would issue with the envied prestige of personal distinction.

M. Janvier de la Motte is a type of the prefect of the Second Empire who has received, and deservedly so, the most censure, but who was, nevertheless, one of the most popular men of his day. M. Janvier de la Motte acted unjustly toward tax-payers, introduced into his prefecture renowned members of the *demimonde*, and quarrelled with the magistrates. In his rounds, however, he knew how to speak to the people in their own language ; he went into their cabins, inquired the condition of their cows, asked the prices that their eggs and their butter were bringing, was interested in the

health of their wives, and invariably compli-
mented their children ; while they, in return for
so much courtesy, judged the Emperor by the
suave manners of his representative, and at the
time of election voted for the official candidate.

All the prefects did not pursue a similar
course. There were some who, less familiar,
less ready to place themselves on grounds of
intimacy with the people, were more successful
in retaining their prestige. M. Janvier de la
Motte was, however, valued by all as a power
to manage the humble classes, and as a means
of procuring work from labourers in the cities.
It was thus in winning the constant sympathy
of the masses that the government of Napoleon III. maintained its apparent unity, and
could, with so little cause for discomfiture,
afford to neglect the occasional adversaries which
from time to time dared present themselves.

It is important to state here that, while the
prefects served Napoleon III. with zeal and intelligence, the ministers, on the other hand, who
followed each other in quick succession round
him, forgot the welfare of the dynasty, and
thought only of their own hopes and interests,
of their hatreds and their retaliations. The
majority, indeed, maintained this careless attitude in the fulfilment of their duties — an at-

titude which made it easy for others to usurp the real power; slaves to their own selfishness, these ministers failed to see the abyss which they were preparing under the very feet of their sovereign.

The most pernicious among them was undoubtedly M. Rouher, who could do what he chose with the Emperor, and direct his judgment into any channel; but he met with great favour and encouragement from the Empress. Napoleon III. had cause to regret having given this counsellor the title of vice-emperor, and had the public any sense of justice, it would realise that this man — whom I shall consider in a subsequent chapter — was responsible for those disasters which form an epilogue to the Second Empire far more than were the unfortunate liberals of 1869 and 1870.

Despite many statements to the contrary, the political, liberal, and social work of Napoleon III. was immense, and strongly resembles the govermental theories of Prince Napoleon.

Imbued with the spirit of the Revolution, and possessing a thorough respect for its principles, the Emperor, though he repudiated all parliamentarianism, was nothing of an autocrat; he consented, from the very beginning of his reign, that those prerogatives which by the constitution were awarded him — i.e. right of initiative, right to sign treaties of commerce, right to declare war — should be modified by an electoral body especially authorised to vote upon taxes and laws. It may be objected that the deputies of the Second Empire were firm partisans of the Tuileries, and that official candidacy insured a power against an apparent legislative independence. Official candidacy gave the Emperor, it is true, a certain support necessary to him for the accomplishment of his wishes; it would, however, be unjust to suppose that Napoleon III. abused this privilege, and it would be still more unjust to deny that he was more than necessarily careful to establish between his power and the electoral corps an understanding based upon the purest liberalism. This is shown by his sending to the Bourbon Palace ministers authorised to discuss public affairs, as well as in his acceptance of the ministerial responsibility, and in his choosing his very ministers from members of Parliament, without obliging those among them who were elected to resign the commission which they had received from the people.

The Emperor, with a wisdom which claims recognition, was careful not to confide to the

Senate the legal prerogative of recognising
danger threatening the State.   A Senate composed for the most part of men thirsting for
power, could hardly be an impartial judge in
political matters.   The Emperor knew that the
public always invalidated, and with reason, a
sentence passed by an assembly of men whose
interest it was to flatter or to serve the government of which they were the strongest supports,
a government which made favourites of them,
and paid them for their services.   He, therefore,
in order to avoid criticism, as well as to give
greater authority to future verdicts, instituted a
Supreme Court composed of magistrates who
were counsellors in the Court of Appeals, and
also chose by lot several jurymen from among
the general counsellors of the departments.

Napoleon III., more honest and more courageous than his courtiers, who had an instinctive horror of book and newspaper, re-established
the liberty of the press.   Continuing still on
the path of reform, he proclaimed freedom to
hold public gatherings, facilitated co-operation,
and, in overthrowing the penal laws made before his time, freed labour from the authority
of labour unions.

The Emperor had truly at heart the welfare
of the poor.   He decreed that when disagree-

ments arose between employer and employed, the former should no longer be acquitted upon his simple statement of the facts ; he therefore insured, better than the Revolution had done, the equality of all men before the law ; he condemned all jurisprudence tending to the repression of labour unions, he protected workingmen's associations, commercial or civil ; he made laws for the societies of mutual aid, and established a superannuation fund.

Here, surely, one does not recognise the work of a tyrant, of a man absorbed in his own interests.   If the reader will, after this brief exposition of a policy which has too often been censured, call to mind the different character sketches which I have given of Napoleon III., he will, I think, acknowledge that I have not yielded to a mere feeling of personal sympathy in trying to set forth, as I have, the real character of this man in whom was an inexhaustible spirit of true kindliness, or in endeavouring to do him the justice due to the head of the nation.

A separate volume would be necessary, were I to discuss at length and to analyse the policy pursued by the Emperor Napoleon III. My design is but to sketch its general outline.

In exposing, a few pages back, the Empress Eugénie's participation in affairs of state, and in sketching the character of the political and of the diplomatic world which surrounded Napoleon III., I have developed certain of the strangest and most important features, both of his internal and of his international policy; and I have based my account upon unpublished letters of ministers and ambassadors who were received at the Tuileries. It has been my special purpose to show the attitude of the court toward foreign nations and toward the representatives of certain powers; I have also spoken of the Empress's infatuation with some of these, and have emphasised the sad reproaches made her by the Emperor on this score.

In the midst of adulation and of triumph, the Emperor Napoleon III. could not fully forget that lack of sympathy, that reserve and defiance, which Europe had shown him at the time of his succession or, more truly, after his Coup d'État; he could not completely ignore the hypocrisy and the egoism of the foreign courts; he would have wished more dignity and more reserve shown the diplomats accredited to Paris, that they might find no pretext for familiarity. Those round him, however, seldom paid any

attention to his wishes. They were whirled in
a mad vortex of folly; and the Emperor himself stood so close on the brink of this whirl-
pool, that, despite his sorrow and his efforts
to escape he was seized, and his course determined by it.

Did not the Emperor who, in his foreign
policy, pursued, as we know, a dream — the
dream of national unity — did he not see that
this policy, this inevitable vacillation, would
give a fatal blow to the governmental edifice,
that edifice which had been raised on the Second
of December by an arbitrary act of authority?
To this fact he was undoubtedly blind, as he
made no effort to avert that great collapse
which threatened during the whole course of
his reign. Had he been less harassed by private cares, had he been free from the disturbing
influence of an unintelligent and a self-seeking
court, he might, perhaps, have perceived more
clearly the symptoms of that evil which was to
overthrow his work; he might then have better
directed his public policy.

The ideals which he had formed, and which,
in the present state of things, were far too
visionary, and whose realisation would have
been most dangerous, were, nevertheless, beautiful ideals and worthy, though their develop-

ment was too rapid for the peace of France, to
be considered and pursued by the present generation.

The theory of national unity, which leads to
the violent but the real emancipation of the
classes, was in the mind of Napoleon III. the
same humanitarian and social problem which in
its logical and inevitable development to-day
occupies the strongest and the most imagina-
tive minds.

European diplomacy — particularly that of
Italy and of Prussia — availed itself of this
visionary scheme to conciliate the sovereign.
They deceived him with gracious and insin-
cere words. Let us, however, not fail to render
homage to the generous and the high-minded
sentiments of the man who, mastered by his
universal sympathy, allowed himself in the simplicity of his heart to be misled.

Prussian diplomacy reaped its own benefits
from the dreams and utopias of Napoleon III.
Less self-seeking than the Italian diplomacy,
however, it sought to reward the Emperor for
his graciousness and for the good-will which
he showed in all questions of international
policy, by offering him on several occasions the
strength of its alliance. He, however, was
averse to such alliances ; they seemed like a

kind of co-operation in behalf of conquest; and the Emperor, who had not at all a warlike nature, and who never fought except from necessity, or out of a certain feeling of sentiment, rejected these offers. By a cruel and a singular fatality, it was through accusing him of warlike tendencies, of pursuing the policy of a kind of imperial ogre, that, at the final and the decisive moment, the sympathies of Europe were turned against him.

Prussia announced after the interview at Biarritz, that, in the words of Count Bismarck, "nothing could be done with the Emperor." From that time it watched attentively for a moment when it might play with Napoleon III. as a cat plays with a mouse. Having assumed a warlike policy, it now awaited an opportunity to compromise the Tuileries. When Prince Bismarck thought that the proper moment to act had come, he shut himself up with M. Benedetti, our ambassador to Berlin, and dictated to him the famous project by which Prussia engaged, in exchange for a stated liberty of action, to allow France to take possession of Belgium. M. de Benedetti, at Prince Bismarck's courteous request, committed into the hands of the Prussian minister the compromising pages which he had just written; it was this scrap of paper, this lie so difficult to disprove, which the cabinet at Berlin waved in the face of all Europe when war broke out.

France cannot know the profound emotion which this revelation caused in Belgium. The feeling was intense, and turned this little nation against ours, nor has a friendly spirit ever been revived. It was evident to me, when in Brussels a short time ago, that the hostile feeling roused at that time was not in the smallest measure appeased. Belgium believes, or, more truly, chooses to believe, that France once sought by an act of violence to annex it; if, indeed, our neighbours, from an instinctive dread of Germany, fear to rejoice too openly over our disasters, they, nevertheless, consider our defeat in its results as an escape for them from a great danger which threatened.

It is natural to ask why, if Napoleon III. disliked the very idea of war, he entered into it with Russia; why he undertook the Italian campaign against Austria; why he organised the expedition to Mexico; and, finally, why he so unfortunately entered into hostilities with Germany.

The Emperor had a secret motive in his war with Russia, a motive which he concealed under the pretext of an international policy, and this

was to form an alliance with England. Beside
this, Napoleon did not like Russia. Strangely
enough, he seemed to have forgotten the cruel
treatment which his uncle had suffered from
the English, whereas he felt a hatred toward
the Russians which cannot be intelligently explained by the ignominious and famous retreat
of the French army. He neglected no opportunity to express his antipathy to Russia; yet,
notwithstanding the private letters which I have
published, and which prove that he loved England no better or, at least, that he never forgave Waterloo or Saint Helena, he continually
affirmed, for state reasons which remain problematical, feelings of cordiality and of regard
for the latter. Beside the personal feelings of
animosity which we have sought to analyse, it
is important to add that Napoleon III. considered the commercial interests of the French
people to be more closely related to those of
England. This was undoubtedly the cause of
his determined advances to England, and of his
scornful indifference at this time to all other
European alliances. I do not say that the Emperor, socialist and humanitarian that he was,
had not against Russia, or rather against its
autocracy and its institution of serfdom, a, so
to speak, sentimental prejudice. If, however,

we accept this hypothesis, how can we account
for his indulgence toward England, with its false
liberalism, the cruel working of its laws, and
the condition of subjection in which it keeps
its colonies ?

The Emperor Napoleon III. is a sphinx, an
unanswered riddle ; he will remain to history
the living synthesis of a subtle philosophy.

We cannot too strongly emphasise the fact
that, in the mind of Napoleon III., the war with
Austria was the fulfilment of a promise. Bound
by previous agreement to the liberal party in
much-divided Italy, he wished to free himself
from former pledges by giving that nation, once
for all, an active evidence of his sanction. The
thought of releasing Italy from the Austrian
yoke, the thought of becoming the high priest
of its independence and of its unification,
seemed a faint realisation of his ideal. Thus the
war was undertaken more for the satisfaction
of a desire long cherished, but never, as yet,
practically applied, than for the sake of faithfully fulfilling a vow. Did he also think of an
alliance which, at some future day, should be
useful to him, and prove an ample recompense
for his kindly efforts in Italy's behalf, the ample recompense for a campaign which promised
no practical results ? It may be that he did ;

just as he dreamed of a confederation of the Latin races, a confederation which should be so strong in its feeling of unity, and so built upon mutual interests and sympathies, that at the critical moment it might checkmate that confederation of northern nations whose voice was already heard in imperious appeals and loud claims.

The letters of Prince Metternich have thrown light upon the Mexican expedition; they represent it as the realisation of a beautiful romance, of a charming fairy tale, and also as the Empress Eugénie's revenge against Italy in the interest of Austria. This campaign was, indeed, instigated by the Empress through the urgency of her friend, Mme. de Metternich. It was a long time before they consulted the Emperor at all concerning the plans which they were making; and when, at last, the Empress decided to reveal their scheme, after having already involved Napoleon, after having used his name on her own authority, it was too late for him to withdraw the promise which he was reported to have given, without occasioning scandal in the court, and provoking displeasure which would have brought with it serious consequences.

It was not, however, without remonstrance that Napoleon III. allowed himself to be dragged into this enterprise, of whose absolute futility he was even then convinced. There were long, painful, and violent conferences on the subject between him and the Empress; it was, so I have been told, after a most impassioned scene, that the Emperor, abandoning any further discussion, resigned himself to destiny.

" Why should I," Napoleon asked his wife, " why should I go to war with Mexico? Why, under the pretext of recovering a trifling debt, should I pick a quarrel and involve my country and my soldiers in an inglorious and a profitless enterprise? My name is trafficked with, intrigues are formed around me, and you are the willing accomplice of these penny-newspaper sensationalists and sharpers."

The day after this scene, M. de Morny, whom the Empress informed of the Emperor's remonstrances, and of the danger menacing the " Californian dream," went to Napoleon and restored in some degree his peace of mind, compelling his agreement, and extracting from him the promise to offer no further opposition to the expedition.

M. de Morny had a colossal fortune to gain in this Mexican enterprise; and the fortune was worth an argument to him, as was Paris worth a mass to King Henry. He argued, and his eloquence overcame the Emperor's objections. Indeed, preparations were so far commenced in Paris and in Vienna that it would, I repeat, have been impossible to retract at this late hour without occasioning most unfortunate complications.

This rapid analysis of events, with whose realisation and results we are familiar — events which official documents, destined to remain long ignored, will eventually explain and pass a fairer judgment upon — this analysis, I say, shows that, incontrovertibly, the power and the caprice of this man, supreme in authority, will hold awful surprises for the future, and perhaps involve the safety of nations. The Emperor Napoleon III. possessed both power and will, but he unfortunately confided in the Empress; and as a man may, according to the feeling of the moment, love or betray his mistress, so he, despite his many admirable qualities, yielded to present impulse and to that instinctive egoism which rules all men, citizen and prince alike, in the affairs of life.

The famous words, *L'État, c'est moi*, have perhaps their excuse, their logic, even their grandeur, though they are the expression of an abominable despotism, when spoken to a society not yet established, and which is still a mys-

tery to itself. They are shocking, even criminal, when uttered in a community of free men
conscious of their strength, their vitality, and
their intelligence, moved by the consciousness
of a common duty to be fulfilled, inspired by
the noble doctrine of universal sympathy, and
borne irresistibly on toward a long-promised
Elysium, toward a destiny irrevocably determined.

Having briefly recapitulated the warlike enterprises of the Second Empire, it would seem
natural to complete this page of history by relating those incidents, unknown to the public,
whose results were to render inevitable the
Franco-Prussian war of 1870. This would
seem also an appropriate place to speak of the
events which are connected with this campaign, and to analyse their strange genesis.
In this chapter, however, which is especially
devoted to the personal study of the Emperor, I will say nothing of the war of 1870.
Before treating, as I shall do in another
chapter, the problem so intimately connected
with this war, I pray that the reader will
permit me to complete my sketch of Napoleon III.

I have already told an amusing anecdote

showing the religious feeling of the Emperor; and I have said that, in pursuing the favourable policy which he did toward the Papacy, and in showing so much concern for the French clergy, he but yielded to the entreaties of the Empress. I repeat that the Emperor was not at heart religious, and was not, in reality, cordial in his feeling toward the priesthood. He feared the influence of the Church upon the State; and as the clergy, for its part, did not hesitate to show constant hostility to the sovereign and to his government, he would only too gladly have welcomed an opportunity to check the authority which these adversaries constantly assumed, emboldened as they were by the approbation of the Empress.

The bishops knew well the attitude of the young Empress toward ecclesiastical affairs, and stood in little fear of the Emperor. Encouraged by the concessions made them, and becoming day by day more confident of the inviolability of their position, they grew more and more arrogant, more and more exacting, and more difficult to please.

The position occupied by the clergy under the Second Empire is peculiar. Notwithstanding the support which Napoleon III. gave the Papacy, to the detriment even of French interests, notwithstanding the indulgence which during the whole course of his reign he showed the bishops and the factious priests, the clergy never for a moment recovered from the antipathy with which from the very first they had regarded him; the idea of showing any real gratitude for his generosity never occurred to them.   It was a dangerous generosity, and cost us more than one disaster, making at last between Italy and ourselves an impassable gulf.

The majority of the bishops were very velvet-pawed with the Emperor when they presented themselves in Paris, or when they received him in their cathedrals; but they opposed him energetically, spitefully, and slyly at other times, and never for a moment ceased the opposition which they had taken up against him.

Some among them, as, for instance, Mgrs. Pie and Dupanloup, did not hesitate to provoke open revolt against the imperial power, and from this continual conflict arose a national anarchy which should have been vigorously repressed.   As soon, however, as Napoleon III. spoke of reproving and bringing to terms some arrogant prelate, the Empress, who had emissaries and spies of the orthodox religion scattered everywhere, was informed of the intention; and then there were reproaches, tears, and menaces in the Tuileries — expressions of the wild rebellion of a woman whose caprice and whose superstition had been violated.

The Empress had never truly at heart the welfare of the imperial dynasty, the future of her husband, or the interests of France. She was autocratic, dangerous, and mischief-making; she followed her personal wishes, regardless of their non-conformity to the demands of the nation and to the security of governmental institutions. She made marriages and she created bishops, nor was her judgment always the wisest. Among the prelates whom she thus, despite the instinctive repugnance of the Emperor, inflicted on the Tuileries, M. Bauer should be mentioned — that strange man who came to her from Queen Isabella of Spain, and whom she appointed moralist of the court and worthy hireling of her chapel, bestowing upon him the honourable title of Monsignor, that authoritative *passe-partout* in the world.

M. Bauer was indeed a strange man. A baptised, if not a converted, Jew, he had travelled and preached all over Europe, as he was afterwards destined to preach in the elegant court of the Tuileries; suddenly he appeared in Paris under the patronage of Queen Isabella, who presented him to the Empress. This abbé,

whose popularity was so great and so sudden,
was unique in his profession; it is said that,
before assuming the priest's garb, he had tried
every occupation — had been a painter, a commercial traveller, a photographer, and a monk.
The mystery attached to his person did not at
all displease the Empress, who had a strong
taste for romance; and, willing or not, this prelate found himself established at court, where
for a time he occupied the position of favourite.
He arrived in Paris in 1866; and three years
later, at the time of the opening of the Suez
canal, the young Empress took him with her
on the first solemn day of the festivals, that he
might bless the sea. He, like so many others,
was lost to view in the war of 1870. It is said
that after the storm had ceased he wished to
continue his sacerdotal functions and to occupy
some pulpit in Paris; but the archbishop forbade his continuing in the ministry, and he
disappeared, or rather withdrew, from the religious world. He consoled himself by a regular attendance at the opera; he resumed his
civilian's dress, and was an assiduous visitor at
the dancing-hall.

There were, however, priests who were not
interlopers among those who mingled with the
courtiers of the Tuileries. Royalty received

eminent men of the Church whose sincere affection for the imperial family cannot be doubted.
Such was the Bishop of Nancy, of whose experience with the Emperor I have already
spoken; such, also, was Mgr. Donnet, of Bor-
deaux, a thoroughly intelligent prelate who was
more than once received at the palace. There
is an amusing story told of him also.

Cardinal Donnet, so the story runs, having
on one occasion been delayed quite late at the
Tuileries, rose to leave when some women attired in low dresses for the evening entered;
Napoleon, however, insisted on detaining him.
Having exhausted all his arguments in vain, the
cardinal pointed to the group of women which
surrounded the Empress.

"Does not your Majesty see," he asked,
"that I am put out by the *shoulders?*"

Napoleon smiled.

"Pardon, your Eminence," he replied, "you
should rather feel that you have a warm place
in our *bosoms.*"

The cardinal, amused by the unexpected and
somewhat irreverent pleasantry, forgot his excessive austerity and willingly remained a few
moments longer. Such affability between the
Emperor and the clergy was, however, unusual.
There existed between Napoleon III. and the

bishops a lack of sympathy which no circumstances served to lessen.

Pius IX. never forgave Napoleon III. for refusing to support, in open warfare, his pontificial claims upon Romagna, which had been separated from the Papal States ; and he imbued the French clergy with a spirit of revolt and of opposition that found daily expression, and which rendered all friendly intercourse impossible.

This opposition was felt most strongly at the time of legislative elections. It was not unusual then to see priests of the most humble parishes take part, through the instigation of bishops, in the political campaign, and uphold the liberal who was opposing the official candidate. In the departments nearest Paris, where opposition always gains a strong hold, where the people are ever ready to support the enemies of all government, this attitude of the clergy was more marked and became more aggressive.

A sort of fatality, a sort of false pride, caused the Emperor to hesitate at the thought of an open rupture with the Papacy. Made bitter and indignant by the ingratitude of the Court of Rome and of the clergy, he more than once conceived the idea of freeing himself from the religious tutelage which was so burdensome

to him.   He always wavered, however, at the
final moment ; and when, as a reproof to Rome
and the bishops, he determined to support the
movement which was then agitating France in
favor of the Gallican Church, a movement led
by Mgr. Darboy, he only succeeded in rousing,
as was his wont, fierce hatred and bitter resentment against himself.

The Emperor was too often the dupe of
his own generosity, of his own good humour.
Statesman that he was, however, he should
have known that no power could compel the
obedience of the clergy unless administered
with bold and pitiless authority.   A statesman
should have realised that no power could hope
to conquer the resistance of the Church to the
institutions of modern society.

It required twenty years of opposition and
warfare, during which time the civil power was
continually in arms, to repulse the demands of
the Church, and to overcome the opposition
of the clergy to the established government.
To quiet that anarchy which hastened the fall
of the Second Empire, a pope was needed who
should also be a strong politician, and who
should command his bishops to accept republican laws.   We should not accord the clergy
more credit than is its due in this submission.

The treaty which it signed, and which was, indeed, forced upon it, is only nominal, and through it one hears to-day the mutterings of anger and of threatened revenge.

One of the most curious pages in the history of the Second Empire is certainly that which concerns the titles of the nobility. Like his uncle, Napoleon III. attempted the dissolution of the ancient aristocracy, and sought to surround himself with newly created dukes and barons, hoping to win from them gratitude on account of this social advancement.

The Emperor, indeed, to speak truthfully, with his eccentricities and his unacknowledged socialism, attached but a relative importance to the nobility, and was not pursued, as was his uncle, by the wish to give to this social caste the prestige, if not the privileges, necessary to it, if it is to retain its power and win the respect of the masses. He looked upon the nobility as a decorative institution, as a useful stimulus to his government, and as a power which should add a certain dignity to his own office. For these reasons he re-established the law which maintained an aristocracy in the Empire ; for this reason he instructed his Keeper of the Seals to draw up a paper designed for the pacification of the rebellious nobility of birth, in which were explained the revision of titles, their authenticity, and the regulations of judicial proceedings which should be exercised against those who might take a name or a title not belonging to them.   Before he definitely determined upon this resolution, Napoleon III. wished to consult the most prominent men in the Empire ; many most interesting facts have been furnished me in regard to this affair.

The sovereign summoned MM. Rouher, de Morny, de Persigny, and Count W., — who is the author of the information to which I this moment referred, — and having explained to them his project, awaited, as was his wont, their comment in the councils.   There then arose a characteristic discussion among the four men.

M. Rouher, who had not yet become vice-emperor, that fierce mountaineer and convert from democracy, tossed his head and only replied in monosyllables, and in thoroughly non-committal words to the Emperor's questions.

M. Rouher, in consequence of his descent, cared little for the nobility.   In his respect for authority, however, he did not altogether scorn the institution ; and while, personally, he took little account of its existence, he acknowledged it a necessary part of governmental machinery, and a strong check upon the people in their efforts toward freedom. Actuated by such principles, he expressed his feeling : —

"I believe," said he, "that the nobility has had its day ; that modern society will act foolishly in looking to it for strength in the future ; I believe that the State can no longer find support in any privileged caste; that its one support must be a principle of universal equality, and that the world must belong to the man who does most to make it. I also believe, however, that the people need constantly to see a light above them, a shining *something* which they cannot reach. The populace has little reverence, and its absolute submission to authority is necessary to its effacement ; it must not be brought near to power. In creating a nobility loyal to the Empire, that is to say, in creating a new social caste, one which will form a closer link between the people and the governing power than does the official class to-day, and which will be more able than it to prevent any dangerous contact between the classes, a peaceable and a neutral spirit toward political affairs will be insured in the masses ; governmental prestige will be augmented thereby and the threats of the rabble checked. For these reasons the Emperor's project is excellent."

M. de Morny said little; he had already been converted to Napoleon's theory, and he contented himself now with a few witty remarks in which was once more displayed his elegant scepticism.

" To be noble," said he, adapting to his own purpose the celebrated words of a woman of rather loose morals, " to be noble is little trouble and much pleasure. So create your aristocracy. Those whom we shall adorn with plumes will be neither more nor less stupid now than when they were plebeians; and if among them there are some clever enough to wear their titles with dignity, all the better, we shall gain just so much from the rabble. The nobility is not absolutely necessary to the Empire; France has already that of the Faubourg Saint-Germain, which is constantly fighting it, but with which it may on occasions grace itself. . . . Many nobles to-day," he added, after a pause, " are, alas, so poor that one can hardly distinguish their nobility through the cloak of their poverty. If we create nobles, let us be sure that those whom we thus honour shall have, beyond all things, a field of gold as the base of their armorial bearings."

M. de Persigny had seemed very impatient while MM. Rouher and Morny were speaking. When his turn came, therefore, he expressed himself with great spirit. M. de Persigny, like M. Rouher, was an autocrat, but a more upright and a more generous-hearted one than he; the thought of resorting to these expedients to quiet the people was repugnant to him. He was a man who played his hand openly, who in a duel bared his breast to the enemy; if, despite the humanitarian dreams which haunted him, he was willing to see the people crushed, he would wish it done in open warfare, without hypocrisy, without ambush. Though he felt that the populace must be kept in its own place, he had no wish to humiliate it; he desired, on the contrary, to see it happy, and perhaps organised into a social body whose needs should be met and whose existence insured. The theories of M. Rouher, therefore, which put a sort of halo round the abasement of the people, he found most displeasing, and M. Morny's scepticism irritated him. Himself a parvenu, he had always remained simple-hearted and unpretending; a nobility, that is to say, a class, placed by an official stamp, and a little pageantry, on a higher level than the rest of humanity, could hardly expect much mercy from him.

M. de Persigny is well known as a violent
speaker; he put great force into his language,
and his reply to MM. Rouher and Morny was
vehement.

"The nobility," he cried, "is a ridiculous institution, and has never been of use to the
governmental power. It has burdened the
nation with its conceit and its folly, and has
done it no good. The Empire has nothing
to gain by the creation of dukes and barons,
in the exhibition of asses carrying relics. You
think as I do, Rouher, and you are not honest, you are but flattering the Emperor when
you say that the nobility will add a prestige
to his authority. As for Morny's little speech,
that is not worth considering. Morny talks the
same nonsense to us as to the women; he is
a dandy and loves to pose. Frippery and hum-
bug do not take the place of ideas; they may
succeed with women, but they will not do in
politics. I discard your noblesse, ancient or
modern, and you will be wise to follow my
example; for, if that is your only defence, I
will give little for your lives on the day when
the populace begins to fight and you have need
to buckle your armour on. . . . Look higher,"
he added, with a quick gesture. "We are
paid for that. Unite the people; establish

them in peace under the intelligent guidance of authoritative leaders, and resign to others foolish and sneaking methods."

M. Rouher had remained calm and attentive during this harangue, while M. Morny had nervously stroked his chin. The Emperor, annoyed by the opposition offered his project, and himself still fully convinced of its wisdom, interposed and again established peace among his councillors.

"We are talking to no purpose," he said quietly, "and I think you have hardly understood my meaning. I do not wish, in creating a nobility as my uncle did, to put a barrier between myself and the people, or to deprive them of their rights. My object is but to honour and recompense, by this means, those who have served me."

"For that, sire," replied M. de Persigny, "for that the nobility is not at all necessary."

"Ah, Persigny," said the Emperor, "be reasonable and a little less obstinate; at heart you are not so bad, after all!"

The awful councillor smiled; no one understood the sovereign better than he, and he knew now that no argument would change his determination. Like a dog, therefore, obedient to the voice which rebukes it, he became humble, almost sad, and said nothing more.

Count W——, having no motive for opposing the Emperor, and perhaps finding this conversation rather futile, approved the project without reservation.

It was thus that the formation of a new nobility was decided upon ; it was another act by which the Second Empire became a feeble imitation of that of Napoleon I.

Destiny, too, has its caprices. Of the four men who on this occasion surrounded Napoleon III., M. Rouher alone remained a plebeian ; but he was the most powerful among them.

In his political policy Napoleon III. was continually led by visionary hopes ; continually under the influence of an illusion, of a mirage ; continually in pursuit of a goal to which he could not attain. Himself a fatalist, his days hung in the balance of fate. He conceived an idea, and then, like a man who, speaking a foreign language, cannot find the right word to express his thought, Napoleon III. searched in vain for means by which to put his idea in execution. He was kind, yet he drew forth tears ; he loved the people, but he involved them in trouble. In fairy-tales one reads of will-o'-the-wisps leading travellers astray, and bringing them to the verge of great abysses. A will-o'-the-wisp flew before Napoleon III., who watched and followed it with all the simple-hearted faith of a child. A dreamer and a mystic, he was the victim of dreams and mysticism ; he pursued them fatuitously, as though predestined to do so. If some day the character of Napoleon III. shall inspire a drama, he will be represented as a wandering shadow never at rest — a figure passing through life enveloped in mystery, or, perhaps, as a condemned being.

III.

PRINCE NAPOLEON.

It is well known that Prince Napoleon, son of Jerome Bonaparte, at one time King of Westphalia, and first cousin of Louis Bonaparte, President of the French Republic, was violently opposed to the Coup d'État of December Second ; it is known, too, that his political independence very nearly occasioned a serious rupture between him and the man who afterwards became Napoleon III. After the Prince had openly declared his liberal views, a certain coldness arose between the two cousins and kept them apart. This coldness, however, was not destined to last; when Prince Louis Napoleon became Emperor, he summoned his cousin and offered him, if not his full confidence, at least a strong affection. These men had henceforth a true attachment for each other ; and despite all that was said to make the Prince appear ridiculous and odious in the eyes of the Emperor, despite even the unconcealed hostility of the Empress toward

him, Napoleon III. gave his cousin continual
evidence of esteem, and ever expressed for him
sentiments of profound friendship.

State reasons sometimes compelled him to
disavow or to blame publicly the utterances or
the acts of the Prince ; in private, however, he
atoned for this severity, and drove from his
cousin's memory expressions of an authority
which might have wounded him, and whose
tendency would have been — so irrascible and
combative was his temperament — to drive
him to a more active opposition, which opposition was, however, on his side less a rivalry than
a political dandyism. One anecdote will serve
to illustrate the cordiality which existed between
the Emperor and his cousin, and will prove that
their public dissensions were superficial.

One evening Prince Napoleon was at the
Tuileries ; and having that day given expression
to certain seditious sentiments, which had
forthwith been repeated to the Emperor, he
was taken aside by his cousin and reproved.

" I hear, Napoleon," said the Emperor, " that
you have been at your old tricks again today."

" Have I really been as revolutionary," the
Prince rejoined, laughing, " as I am reported to
have been ? "

" Revolutionary," muttered the Emperor, " is

a word which may signify anything or nothing. No, you have not been revolutionary, you have been imprudent. I have in you," he added, after a pause, "a terrible cousin, Napoleon. You make me a great deal of trouble — a great deal. My ministers are displeased by my conduct toward you. In reality you and I agree about many things, but I cannot let them know that. Ah, Napoleon, you have a great advantage over me, inasmuch as you may express your thoughts without fearing to shock the world."

Prince Napoleon had indeed this privilege which was denied the Emperor; he could, on occasion, though without official sanction, sow seeds of freedom among the people. It was true, too, that the Emperor's secret feelings were often closely allied to those of the prince.

Prince Napoleon was not blind to his cousin's innate kindness of heart, nor to his rare intellectual qualities. He frequently discussed with the Emperor schemes which the latter, unknown to his ministers, took pleasure in elaborating, and which, had he been more resolute, or, let us say, tyrannical, he might have put into execution. If, therefore, there was always a certain restraint between the Emperor and his cousin, this restraint was but the result of the scornful attitude of both courtier and minister toward the Prince, and of the Empress's avowed enmity for him.

I have already spoken of the Empress Eugénie's strong dislike of the Prince ; and since the publication of the pages in which I emphasized this animosity, partial and self-interested writers have sought to disprove my assertions, and to show us a Prince Napoleon and an Empress Eugénie traversing the imperial reign as enemies, it is true, but representing the Prince as the instigator of all the trouble, and the Empress as a persecuted woman. To accept such a revised version of facts, and to credit for a moment this perversion of history, must require a truly credulous spirit.

Though the character of the Empress inspired Prince Napoleon with a kind of antipathy, with anger at times, and again with pity, he would doubtless have preferred, under the force of existing circumstances, to have cultivated a sort of intimacy with her ; and though a feeling of friendship were out of the question, he might at least have borne with her in patient indifference. Such a course would have been possible had the Empress shown him any sign of friendship, or even of a negative regard, but became hopeless, since in her heart there was no sentiment which could call forth the slighest cordiality from her cousin.

The Empress was not ignorant of the fact that, at the time of her engagement to the Emperor, the Prince was one of Napoleon's counsellors most vehemently opposed to the marriage; the memory of his opposition and his scorn at that time prevented any feeling of friendliness now.

At the news of the Emperor's violent passion for Mlle. de Montijo, not only did the old King Jerome violently remonstrate with the Sovereign, but Prince Napoleon hurried to him in the hope of successfully representing the folly and the danger of such an alliance.

The Prince knew Mme. de Montijo and her daughter, and considered them aristocratic adventurers; it seemed to him that the Emperor must realise how he was demeaning himself in marrying a watering-place belle. Though the Prince, when a personal matter was under consideration, committed so many political imprudences, he had, nevertheless, a pretty clear judgment; more than once during his cousin's reign he pointed out the evils from which the Empire was suffering and suggested their remedy.

At the time of the Emperor's engagement,

inspired by a kind of presentiment, he felt the
danger threatening, and expressed himself freely
to Napoleon. He called upon him, and in the
strength and the sincerity of his convictions, and
the despair with which he was filled by the
thought of the contemplated union, he addressed him in the second person, contrary to
the custom which, since his cousin's accession,
he had adopted.

"You cannot," said he, "think seriously of
marrying Mlle. de Montijo. She is, I know, a
beautiful woman, capable of inspiring a violent
passion. Love her, if you will, but do not
marry her, do not make her Empress. What
will the nation say? What will all Europe
say? Your own unhappiness and that of
France will result from this union. I implore
you to break the engagement. You are fascinated by Mlle. de Montijo. That is natural, for
she is a creature to charm a king. Make her
your mistress, pay dearly as you will for this
folly, but let the romance end here."

The Emperor took no more notice of his
cousin's warning than he did of that of his
many friends, who also saw in his marriage
with Mlle. de Montijo an act which must occasion both domestic sorrow to the Emperor, and
political trouble to the state. He smiled at

the Prince's remonstrances as he had done at those of others. Touched by the magic wand of a fairy, of a wicked fairy who brought bad luck to all whom she visited, he yielded to its enchantment, and was both incapable and unwilling to escape.

Mlle. de Montijo, having become Empress, had not sufficient nobility of character to forget the Prince's former opposition, and she entertained for him an hatred which neither the fall of the Empire, nor exile, nor even the death of her husband and child, served to appease.

Though this hatred had a fatal influence upon the future of the imperial dynasty; though we feel it to lie at the root of many disasters in the reign of Napoleon III.; though it drew wrath upon his coffin, and lied concerning the miserable and mutilated remains of the Prince Imperial, can we, I ask, even in the face of all this, blame her too mercilessly for the feeling? Is it just to blame Mlle. de Montijo for becoming Empress of France, for having been beautiful, for having known how to master men's hearts, and also how, under the enchantment of her smiles — which were like those beautiful flowers in which is hidden a subtle and deadly poison — to watch unmoved the failure of their joys and their hopes?

That fictitious story whose truth some have sought to establish, and which claims that Prince Napoleon persecuted the Empress, is based upon several assertions which it is necessary to mention here and to disprove.

Prince Napoleon, this story says, hoped that the Emperor would never marry, and that his own inheritance, there being no direct heir, would be thus assured. This secret hope blasted, he vowed fierce resentment against the Empress. One evening, it is further said, at a dinner given in honour of the Empress at Compiègne, he gave way in public to a sudden manifestation of this resentment, and when Napoleon III. asked him to offer the first toast to her, he bluntly refused to do so.

No statements could be more false than these. When Prince Napoleon opposed the Emperor's marriage with Mlle. de Montijo, it was purely with the feeling that an affair of sentiment like this attachment should take into consideration the social rank of the woman who inspired it, and find some other conclusion than that of an official marriage. He urged that the Emperor of the French could make many alliances in Europe, even in France, more worthy than that with a woman whose reputation was somewhat compromised, whose beauty had been paraded on every side, and had rendered her a too notorious character.

That the anecdote concerning the toast is purely fictitious, is proved by a letter which I have received upon this subject from one of the most influential and most respected members of the Court of the Tuileries. This same letter denies the assertion that the Prince had solicited for himself the hand of Mlle. de Montijo.

"It is not true," writes the authority whom I quote, "it is not true that Prince Napoleon ever declined to drink the health of the Empress on the occasion of her birthday celebrations. It cannot be denied that he often failed to conceal his sentiments, for he was frank and open-hearted by nature, hated dissimulation, and was unable to hide his true feelings. He knew, and the fact caused him pain, that, with the exception of the Emperor and of two or three friends, every one at the Tuileries hated him, and that his every word and gesture were misinterpreted. We can hardly blame him for not enjoying these surroundings. The Emperor was annoyed by all the idle gossip circulated about his cousin, but was powerless to prevent it. His own affection for the Prince was criticised at court and made the subject of foolish ridicule.

"The story that the Prince had himself wished to marry Mlle. de Montijo, is absurd and unworthy of consideration. Such an idea was never entertained at court; and if the Prince was at one time fascinated, like so many others, by the beauty of Mlle. de Montijo, he was certainly never in love with her, and still less dreamed for a moment of marrying her.

"The Empress, aside from any personal dislike, hated the Prince, because she recognized in him a superior mind, and feared his influence upon the Emperor.

"After the death of Napoleon III. she rejected the Prince as tutor to her son and as director of his education. Had she, however, retained him, I cannot doubt that he would have proved a faithful adviser, and would have mitigated, in some degree, the sorrow which overcame her. When Prince Napoleon was suggested to the Empress as director of her son's studies, she replied that he would bring misfortune to the poor child. Was it not, alas, rather by her persistence in an implacable hatred, that misfortune was brought upon the Prince? Was it not this which, in truth, ruined the future of the imperial dynasty?"

Events prove the accuracy of these assertions, whose author was, I repeat, one of the most important personages at the court of the Tuileries, one of the most devoted friends of the Emperor; during the whole course of the imperial reign, he watched hour by hour the wearying annoyances with which the incessant bickerings of the Empress poisoned the sovereign's life.

It was at the express wish of the Empress that, after the death of Napoleon III., the Prince was dismissed from the royal family. After the death of her son, the Empress, with a discourtesy hardly in keeping with that solemn moment, requested him to leave Chiselhurst immediately after the funeral solemnities. He wished to express his sympathy for the Empress, but was refused admittance to the presence of the lonely woman. He realized then, how, even in the presence of her dead son, this mother could not forget her petty bitterness and resentment, and he left her inhospitable roof. He understood also the plot which was being formed even at the grave of his cousin, by which he should be deprived of his indisputable claim as the head of the dynasty, and he then and there relinquished his title to the succession.

"I have no place at the Tuileries," he said to those who were surprised at his sudden departure, "and I have no duties to fulfil here."

I well remember, one day at Versailles, at a time when the Chamber of Deputies held its sessions there, when Prince Napoleon, representing the people, appeared in the tribune at a moment when there was a debate on the question of public worship; in an allusion to the Emperor's policy toward Rome, he cried, pointing toward the Empress, that if it were permitted him to speak and to divulge the secrets of the late Emperor's reign, he would satisfy

Parliament as to the cause of the policy which he had pursued, and give it an idea of the fatal and the pernicious influence exercised by the Empress upon the councils of Napoleon III.

It may be that Prince Napoleon was on this day overcome by a natural resentment for that hatred of which, for so many years, he had been the victim, and gave way, therefore, in that moment to a desire for revenge which he found in accusing, for the first time in his life, the Empress Eugénie of all those evils which fell to the lot of France and of Napoleon III. I am ignorant as to whether, among the papers bequeathed to his heirs, there were documents in which the accusations as yet but hinted at were definitely set forth, and which should serve to exonerate him in the judgment of the future. Were there such papers, his heirs doubtless made haste to destroy them. He is dead, but in death itself the hatred of the Empress pursued him ; she won from him his own son, he who might have filled with sweetness the last hours of the dying man — in whom, too, was the chance of political restoration.

Prince Napoleon had the mask of the Cæsars ; we may, indeed, despite the many errors of his life, attribute to him many of their moral and intellectual qualities. Tall and large, with the

figure of an athlete, he was wont to walk through
the streets with a certain solemnity of manner
which made him appear a stranger to all his surroundings. To see him pass thus with his head,
which was shaped like that of a Roman emperor, slightly bowed, conjured up a vision of one
of those patricians who, at the time of circuses
and of heathen rites, wandered through the ancient city enveloped in a flowing peplum fringed
with royal purple.

His character is more difficult to describe
than is his appearance. Though his judgment
was both keen and accurate, a kind of nervous-
ness and a certain lack of balance led him to
commit many errors fatal to his reputation and
to the fulfilment of his own wishes. Democrat and autocrat at once, he at one moment
aspired toward an universal freedom, and at
the next showed himself absolute in authority.
Such inconsistencies as these rendered him
often incomprehensible to his most intimate
friends, and, if I may use a simile, placed him
in the position of a navigator driven between
two seas, the one calm, the other tempestuous,
but prevented by some evil fate from embarking upon either.

The same inconsistencies were apparent in
his domestic life. This professed democrat

entertained his visitors with all the dignity
which his social rank justified; he established
in his home a most severe etiquette, so that it
was said in the royal household that the court
atmosphere was far stronger at the Palais-Royal
than at the Tuileries.

Prince Napoleon had many and great faults,
but he possessed in equal measure qualities
which made him one of the most remarkable
men of the century.

A brilliant conversationalist, he loved, as did
the Emperor, to provoke opposition and to seek
argument for the simple joy of displaying his
powers, that he might, by a sort of coquetry,
by almost feminine artifice, triumph over the
arguments of an adversary, and leave him a
thorough convert to his own views. For some
inexplicable reason, that grace and charm which
distinguished the prince in his more intimate
relations were lost entirely when he appeared
in public. There was in his bearing at such
times an unconcealed scorn for all those who
were about him; he would, by his unpleasant
manner on such occasions, make enemies of his
former converts.

His contempt for politicians, with whom he
was necessarily thrown in close contact, and for
the masses, whose cause he publicly advocated,

was genuine and ingrained ; it was the occasion
of many misfortunes, which saddened his life,
and filled his days with controversy and with
disappointed hopes. His thoughts, always far
loftier than his conduct, and adverse to many
acts which through a fatal tactlessness he committed, dwelt among high ideals — ideals which
remind one of those which filled the mind of
Napoleon I.

A certain uncompromising and almost dis-
courteous manner, either natural or assumed,
kept at a distance those who, though not partisans of his policy, would, nevertheless, have
gladly pleaded his cause with the Emperor at
a time when calumny sought to undermine the
affection existing between the cousins. The
prince was never consciously unkind ; his heart
rebelled with childlike simplicity against all
that is morbid, deceitful, and bitter in life, and
he regretted the evil he had done, and the ridicule and insult which he had heaped on others.
If a friend pointed out to him the tactlessness
or the injustice of his conduct, he listened with
interest to his remonstrances, confessed his
mistakes, which he immediately hastened, with
no false pride in his heart and no ostentation or
princely condescension in his manner, to repair.

There is an anecdote which illustrates admirably his true kindliness, a kindliness which the prince would have taken pleasure in constantly exercising, but which was often concealed by the force of circumstances.

One day at Compiègne, M. Billault, a minister without a portfolio, who, with MM. Rouher and Magne, had been appointed by the Emperor to defend the policy of the Tuileries before the Chambers, M. Billault, I say, happened to pass the Prince, who was talking at that moment with a friend, and bowed deferentially. It is well known that M. Billault was a frequent visitor at the Palais-Royal, and there is, indeed, a story which assigns to the strong affection which the old King Jerome always entertained for him very natural reasons. M. Billault, therefore, having made his obeisance to the Prince, the latter looked at him blankly, and did not return his salutation.

The lady with whom he was talking could not conceal her surprise, and asked Prince Napoleon frankly the cause of his action, which, insignificant as it seemed, might yet occasion serious trouble.

"Did you not see, Monseigneur," she asked, "that M. Billault bowed to you?"

"I saw, certainly, that M. Billault bowed to me," was the reply; "but I prefer that no

friendly relations shall exist between us, and
no courtesies be exchanged."

"Do you forget, then, Monseigneur, that M.
Billault is a true friend to you, that he is a
man of rare gifts, and was much loved by your
father?"

"According to my convenience, I forget
everything or nothing.   Billault made yesterday such a weak speech in the Chamber, a
speech so flat and pithless" — it had concerned
the question of Rome, a subject which always
excited the prince to much vehemence — "so
flat and pithless, I say, that I place no more confidence in the man.   I will have no friend whose
political views are controlled by the Empress."

"Ah, Monseigneur," replied the woman,
"you are unjust.   We must admit that M. Billault spoke as he did yesterday to please the
Empress, and is somewhat too ready to conform
to her wishes; but he loves you, notwithstanding this, and you should realise that he who is
chosen by the Tuileries as one of their first
instruments in this Roman question, could not
have spoken differently.   Can a musician in an
orchestra play other than the notes belonging
to his score?   Lay aside your resentment, then,
and give him your hand.   He will be touched
by your apology, and will feel more than ever

cordially toward you. You have not so many friends, Monseigneur, that you can afford to neglect those who are brave and faithful."

The Prince listened attentively to these words, remained pensive a moment, then rose, his face wearing an expression of great sadness.

" You are right," he said ; " Billault is not his own master, and I owe him an apology."

With that gracious cordiality, therefore, by which his manner was at times distinguished, he went in search of the minister, and expressed to him his regret for the recent evidence of ill-humour which he had given.

This anecdote shows how ready was Prince Napoleon to obey the impulse of the moment, and it also gives us insight into the causes of the imperial policy toward the great Roman question ; it throws light upon those secret agencies which kept this problem in a state of continual danger and conflict. The woman whose argument with the Prince we have this moment quoted, was thoroughly conversant with affairs of state, and was among those who exercised the strongest influence upon the Second Empire.

I have already stated that the Emperor and Prince Napoleon felt a strong attachment for each other, and that all the stories are false which represent these men as bitter enemies, as rivals ready at any moment to fall upon and to harm each other. Prince Napoleon had constantly to undergo, during his cousin's reign, the hatred of the Empress, which hatred inevitably called forth the ill-will and the prejudice of her courtiers. Had the Emperor possessed the courage or the power to interpose between the Prince and his enemies he would have found in this man an useful instrument; he might have put a restraint on his many unwise actions, and made use of his gifts for the imperial cause; a political understanding between these two men, an harmony of purpose which the public should have recognised and respected, would have given the government a firm foundation and have insured the future of the imperial policy. The most serious charge brought against the Prince was that in his speeches he openly and systematically opposed the Emperor's projects. There is, however, a curious fact relating to these speeches of which it is well to remind the reader.

Prince Napoleon — I am in a position to verify this statement — never expressed an opinion officially without first submitting his remarks to the Emperor for examination and

for approval. Previous to his speaking in public, the Prince invariably gave the Emperor a
written version of his address, which the Emperor promptly returned him. If he found
therein the expression of some sentiment opposed to his own, Napoleon III. simply suggested that a little revision here and there
would be advisable. Such suggestions were,
however, never given as a command, nor did he
ever condemn any part as evil or dangerous.

The Prince always deferred to the Emperor's
wish, and revised his manuscript in a way to
satisfy him. It, however, sometimes chanced
that at the time of delivery he would astonish
his cousin by an unexpected violence, and by
spontaneous outbursts quite foreign to the text
which they had prepared together. The explanation and the excuse for this lie in the
fact that between the time of his conversation
with the Emperor and that when he delivered
his speech — this is a fact to be noted and
borne in mind — that in the meantime, I say,
intrigues, scandals, annoyances of every kind,
had been instigated by the Empress ; there
was a foolish and profitless delight taken in
provoking his excitable and rebellious nature ;
he was persecuted despite his submission to the
wishes of the Emperor ; despite his own meek-

ness of spirit, was persecuted and hunted down like a goaded beast in the arena which longs for the undisturbed peace of his own lair.

The indignation of the ministry and of the entire court at the time when Prince Napoleon delivered his famous speech in Corsica will be remembered. This very speech, strange as it may seem, this speech which called forth such bitter criticism in the *Moniteur,* and was sought by some as a pretext for exiling the Prince, had been read by the Emperor, and returned by him to his cousin without modification, without comment.

"Their purpose is," said Napoleon III. to one of his most intimate, one of his most dearly loved friends, "their purpose is to influence me against my cousin, that I may drive him from the Tuileries, and add one more indignity to those which are now heaped upon him; that I may close alike my heart and my home against him. I will never accede to these wishes. I will never look upon the Prince as an enemy. When not in my presence he seems to disapprove of my actions; but when with me he is all that he should be. He is my friend, and there is no hypocrisy in this attitude; he is alike sincere when he expresses an attachment for me, and when, driven to revolt by the bitter hatred which pursues him, by the contempt of which he is a victim, he rises in arms, it is not against me personally, but against the men and also the women who surround me. I forgive his resentment; in his place I do not know how I should act. When humanity attempts indifference to abuse and to insult, it finds itself confronted by a force which it is powerless to overcome. At heart Napoleon loves me, and I require from him nothing more than this. Why should I, by withdrawing my sympathy, add another cause of bitterness to the many which he already has?"

The Emperor took comfort in feeling that the Prince was no hypocrite, and his judgment of him in this respect was certainly right. Prince Napoleon scorned deceit, was loyal in all the relations of life, was open with his adversaries, faced obstacles bravely, though at the risk of doing himself harm, and despised subterfuge and compromise. In these virtues is power sufficient to influence the destiny of a nation.

The Prince was, however, neither popular at court nor in the world of politics, nor yet with the masses. Whatever the gifts and the intelligence of a man may be, of however honest a nature he is, he cannot counteract the influence of slander, nor hope to extricate himself from the meshes which calumny weaves round him. Notwithstanding his strong moral and intellectual force, Prince Napoleon thus became the victim of falsehood.

He understood the theory of government, but the law-makers would have nothing to do with him ; he toiled for the people whose interests he had at heart, and, in return, was ridiculed by them. He was more of a prince, more of an aristocrat, than are many princes and aristocrats, yet he was despised by the upper classes. He was a democrat, but the democrats never gave him their confidence ; in short, he was opposed, envied, feared — feared in the face of raillery and scorn, because none could fail to recognise his intellectual superiority, and was like the abortive progeny of a gigantic dream, a dream of the Cæsars, upon whom a wicked spirit has cast the evil eye.

Prince Napoleon's *rôle* in the Second Empire was that of a malcontent, of a fault-finder, and almost of a factionist. Yet he not only loved the Emperor and was loved by him, but held views on many questions which were in harmony with his. His liberalism, even his radicalism, were not incompatible with those vague socialistic dreams which haunted the sovereign's mind, while his theories of national unity were peculiarly satisfying to the Emperor's ideals. The consolidation of Germany was not at all alarming to the Prince; but he would have wished it accomplished by an understanding with France, and he was among those who most regretted the failure of M. Bismarck's mission when that statesman went to Biarritz, hoping to win the co-operation of the Tuileries in the fulfilment of his political schemes.

The Prince's feelings of sympathy and of accord with the Emperor were, alas, often concealed by the ill-temper, the irritability, excited in him by the annoyances which he was called upon to endure at court, and also, we must admit, by his temperament, somewhat like that of a spoiled child, and by his tendency to commit indiscretions, repeated time after time. A strange fatality prevented his availing himself of his opportunities, and forced him to speak when he should have been silent, and to be silent when he should have spoken. It was, however, more especially the attitude of hostility which the Prince always assumed outside the Tuileries, and when surrounded by the splendour of the Palais-Royal, which served to

belie his real feelings of accord; the political
counsellors whom he chose, and the friends with
whom he surrounded himself during hours of
recreation, contributed also to the same end.

His court — for the Prince held a court of
his own — was made up of men opposed to the
Empire; this assembly of politicians, of journalists, and writers, who were all enemies of the
Tuileries, furnished the Empress daily with a
plausible pretext for making both the official
and the domestic life of the palace unendurable
to her cousin.

The Emperor himself never seriously feared
the friends whom Prince Napoleon chose.

"No, no," he was wont to say, when these
men were represented to him as dangerous,
"no, no; they are but an herd of neglected
sheep, which need a little care; a few good
seats in the Senate will make that right."

It must not be thought that Prince Napoleon,
in gathering about him men of this nature, had
any desire to make a display, or to fill the *rôle*
of Dauphin *in partibus;* nor did he seek, in an
interested and forced allegiance, to gratify any
feeling of vanity or of false pride; he even
failed to see in it an opportunity of increasing
fortune, or of facilitating an opposition to his
cousin's government. He had, on the contrary,

a horror of courtiers and of money transac-
tions. One anecdote will illustrate his strong
sense of honour in affairs of finance, and the
fear which he had of money not his own.

After the war of 1870, Prince Napoleon
expressed a wish to establish a paper which
should support his views. A rich friend and
enthusiastic admirer, approving his project and
appreciating the difficulty in the way of its fulfilment, — Prince Napoleon's means did not permit the expenditure necessary to such a scheme,
— consulted with him on the subject, and offered to lend him, unconditionally, the required
sum, with freedom to return the amount as
should be convenient. The Prince, delighted
to put his plan into immediate execution, accepted directly the money of his generous
patron. As soon, however, as he came into
possession of the desired capital, he grew
uneasy.

"You know that M. X——," he said one
day to a friend who asked the cause of his
anxiety, "you know that M. X—— has lent
me the money necessary to establish the paper
of which I have long dreamed. It is this generous loan, this borrowed capital, which worries
me. The money I shall use is not mine; it
may, of course, increase, but it may, on the

other hand, be lost. As I should not be able in the latter case to return what was given me, surely I have no right to use the amount at all. This money troubles me, it burns my fingers, I cannot keep it. I feel that I have no claim upon it, and I shall return the loan to-day. If I find that a paper is absolutely essential, I will sell some land which I own near Prangins, but it shall not be said that I have speculated with the fortune of another."

The Prince acted as he said he should ; he returned the money to M. X——, and to establish the paper sold a part of his own property, that he might be a debtor to no one.

This conduct must be acknowledged honourable and praiseworthy, and should not be forgotten in our estimate of Prince Napoleon. It gives to his character, which is the object of much controversy and much persecution, an element of loftiness demanding our esteem. I know that the public will never appreciate the chivalrous nature of Prince Napoleon, — that public which finds little interest in simple and unromantic acts, which enjoys only scandals and the apotheosis of the successful villain, or the awful ruin of the honest man. I foresee the astonishment of such a public when it reads these lines. We have become accustomed to look upon the Prince as upon a grotesque figure, around which are grouped ridiculous and unpleasant stories.

Of Prince Napoleon there remains in our memories to-day only that absurd nickname which caricaturists and penny-a-liners created, and which serves to call forth laughter at the very suggestion of his personality. This sobriquet did more to ruin his hopes and to weaken his authority than did even the objectionable reputation given him by the world of politics; he was constantly before the public in the character of a tragic actor who awakened only amusement.

Prince Napoleon is represented as revelling in low orgies, whereas his dinners, at which were present the *élite* among writers and artists, had the charm and the brilliancy of social gatherings in the time of the Renaissance. He is represented as a man without ideals, whereas — this fact cannot be too strongly emphasised — whereas, in this Second Empire, which had no sympathy with culture or learning, he stands forth as an enlightened protector of arts and letters, as a lover of the beautiful, and as a man of an almost creative mind. His mask of the Cæsars, the mask which Nature had modelled after that of

Napoleon I., should have impressed the people by the majesty which was recognised in that of his uncle. The public, however, did not see this mask; did not recognise in this man the risen figure of him who was *the Emperor*—we write the title without epithet—it made this silhouette of the Cæsars the object of ridicule as though it had been the comic apparition of a Chinese ghost.

The war of 1870 broke out while Prince Napoleon was travelling in the north of Europe, and filled him with despair. As soon as he knew of the events which were following each other with appalling rapidity, he returned to his own country, and hastened directly to Saint-Cloud, where, as I have already said, the Emperor, the Empress, and the whole court had removed.

When the Prince presented himself before Napoleon III. there followed an animated scene, no account of which has ever been given, and of which I am about to speak.

The Prince, carried away by his excitement, became vehement as soon as he entered the Emperor's presence.

"We have declared war, have we," he cried, "war, for which we are totally unprepared! In

what condition are we to enter on a campaign?
This is a war against a powerful nation, one
which has not trusted to mere chance; against
a nation, I say, which will crush us."

"Yes," muttered the Emperor, "this will be
war indeed."

"If I have been rightly informed," continued
the Prince, "it is the Empress who has brought
this upon us. It is Eugénie and the pernicious
men who obey her who have involved us in this
trouble. I told you long ago, sire, that this
woman would be your ruin and that of France.
Your reign is strewn with the havoc which she
has wrought."

The Emperor rose, and turning ashy pale,
faced the Prince.

"Napoleon," he exclaimed, "Napoleon!"

"Forgive my frankness, but do you not see
that the Empress and those who surround her,
those whom she inspires with her own hatred
of your government and with her desire for absolutism, — do you not see that these are filled
with joy by the prospect of war, and, be it successful or the reverse, hope to gain from it the
one result, the end of your present policy, and
the restoration of the Empire of December
Second?"

"Napoleon," said the Emperor gently, "your

words are rash ; your presentiments, which, alas ! perhaps correspond with mine, lead you to speak more strongly than you feel. You are unjust toward Eugénie ; she has faith in our victory ; let us believe as she does and be hopeful."

The Emperor paused for a moment, then went forward and took the Prince by the hand.

" What does it avail," he added, " to regret what has already occurred ? War has been declared, and we cannot now change our decision."

" So be it," returned the Prince, " so be it ! Let us, however, make haste to pack our possessions, for we are already beaten."

Having thus expressed himself, he left Napoleon III. alone with his melancholy thoughts.

The following day the Prince gave an account of this scene to the Marchioness de ——, and it is she who repeated it to me.

On that day the Prince expressed to Mme. de —— almost the same sentiments which he had done to his cousin.

" We are lost," he said. " We are entering the field without an ally, and we cannot hope that Italy or Austria will come to our aid. Italy is not prepared to do so ; and my father-in-law, Victor Emmanuel, could not, at the very earliest, collect his troops in less than a month or two. What reason have we to suppose that

Austria will care to help us? Did we come forward in her behalf after Sadowa? Did not
Prince Metternich himself tell you that his
nation would remain a simple spectator of the
struggle about to take place? Oh, the Empress
and her party knew well how to bring affairs
to the desired climax! One fact, however, as-
tonishes me; that is, that Ollivier should have
so easily fallen into the trap which was laid for
him. Why did he, who is so patriotic, so wise,
so reserved, allow himself to be ensnared like a
fool? You may be sure that there is some
snake-in-the-grass, of whom we shall hear later;
but, however that may be, we are lost."

There is a certain ambiguity, perhaps, result-
ing from the accounts which I have given of
scenes and conversations concerning this war
problem. In a subsequent chapter, called "The
Declaration of War," I will explain more fully
the meaning of Prince Napoleon's words, and
will speak of those intrigues organised about the
Emperor, for the purpose of creating between
him and the King of Prussia an inevitable cause
of hostilities, and of making all reconciliation
impossible to the Cabinet of January Second.

After the fall of the Empire and the death of
Napoleon III., and during the short life of the

Prince Imperial, Prince Napoleon maintained a strict reserve and calmly awaited developments. Banished, as I have said, from both the domestic and the political circle at Chiselhurst, he now devoted himself exclusively — though without severing the ties which bound him to his devoted friends at home — to the education of his son; he travelled back and forth continually between the Boulevard d'Antin, where he lived in Paris, and the home of his brother-in-law, King Humbert of Italy.

When, after the death of the Prince Imperial, he was brought to realise that the Empress's hatred had in no wise abated, and that intrigues were still formed among her courtiers and in those parts of France which were obedient to her, by which he should be excluded from the direction of all that concerned the Bonapartes — when he realised this, I say, the Prince assumed an offensive attitude, and presented himself before the people as their leader, though he concealed under absolute submission to the will of the people his real hopes and claims.

The evil fate, which, however, pursued him in politics, prevented his having at any time what could be truly called a party, a firmly established party, that is strong in its feeling of unity and able to withstand its adversaries;

having, therefore, been elected deputy, he found himself practically isolated in Parliament.

I can remember him at this time when, in his loneliness, he seemed like some wild animal that has taken refuge in an obscure place to watch for the desired prey, or, not finding it, to die. He sat in the right wing of the Assembly, but on the top row of the amphitheatre, near a doorway leading into the lobby. He was seldom in his seat, but wandered back and forth between the Assembly-room and the lobbies, and appeared only interested in the more vital questions of the day.

I have mentioned elsewhere a discussion upon religious observances in which he took part. It was, I believe, the only occasion when he spoke in Parliament, and his attitude on that day is most curious.

When he mounted the tribune, his large, athletic figure seemed almost to strike awe into the Assembly; a low murmur passed round the room, but was soon followed by cries of " hear, hear!" after which deep silence filled the hall.

The Prince, apparently unmoved by this questionable reception, whose meaning might be approval or insult, addressed himself to the deputies in language of familiarity such as he would have used in talking to a few friends in

a drawing-room ; in his attitudes even, and
in his gestures, there was an air of hail-fellow-
well-met.

His thumbs in his trousers-pockets, his other
fingers outside, he spoke for several hours, at-
tacking vehemently the Catholic party, and
upholding the rights of civil society against
the religious world ; he called forth shouts of
applause from the left wing, while the conservatives hissed angrily. Even the latter, however,
forgot from time to time their indignation and
listened attentively, secretly admiring, it may
be, his eloquence. His whole discourse was
marked by rare oratorical beauty, and those
who were fortunate enough to hear him on
that day can but acknowledge and admire his
great gift.

He was too often regardless of his power to
charm, and, carried away by enthusiasm in his
subject, became violent. Each word clearly
enunciated, the accents of his rich, sonorous
voice fell upon the ears of his adversaries
with its message of studied and faultless logic.
His scornful gestures, the shrug of his broad
shoulders, told now little weight he attached
to their arguments and to their interruptions.
When he had finished his speech, and, having
descended from the tribune, was returning to his

place amidst shouts of applause from the republicans, he was suddenly forced to pause in the
semi-circle. The conservatives, roused to indignation, had risen from their seats with loud
exclamations, and were advancing toward him
with threats and menaces.

There now followed such a scene as had
never before been witnessed, and which will
never escape my memory.

Against this human avalanche which barred
his way, Prince Napoleon took his stand at the
foot of the tribune, squared himself and waited
the attack; his great frame trembled with fury,
his eyes flamed, his nostrils and lips quivered.
Some of the deputies were already upon him,
doubling their fists in his face; he was being
borne from his position by the on-pressing mass,
when, with a great shake of his mighty shoulders, he stepped forward, and, throwing himself
against the opposing force, made an opening
in the ranks of the enemy and in two or three
strides gained his seat. Resuming his place,
he then crossed his arms on his chest from
which his breath came like the blast from a
blacksmith's forge, and looked scornfully upon
those who had sought to insult him; he smiled
and played the part of a Cæsar indeed, — *Cæsar
imperator.* In that moment he showed the

representatives of the nation a vision of the
Prince who might have reigned over them; of
a tribune who, having himself issued from the
people, might have laboured in behalf of the
people, had they but given him their affection.

When the decrees relative to religious assem-
blies were signed, Prince Napoleon was no
longer deputy, and having no right to speak,
came out in a famous letter approving the legal
measures about to be taken against Catholic
associations.   The stir and controversy excited
by this letter are well known.

I had occasion to interview the Prince at
about this time, and was received by him in the
Boulevard d'Antin.   My mission related to various provincial journals, and we discussed the
question together.

The Prince wished to win to his cause certain
organs of the press representing the departments.   I told him frankly that the letter
which he had just written made any such co-
operation impossible.   He listened attentively
to what I said, and, as I ceased speaking, rolled
a cigarette, then walked up and down the
drawing-room for several moments.

"Monsieur," he said at last, "Monsieur, the
meaning and import of my letter have been seriously misunderstood.   There is nothing anti-

religious meant by it, nothing hostile to freedom. It approves and demands the execution of laws which should be the same for all citizens, and whose enforcement I should compel had I power to do so. You say that the provincial press, the moderate press, that is, cannot, after this declaration signed with my name, support me. Certain papers have, indeed, taken a well-defined position, and the fact has given me pleasure ; these have among their readers many Bonapartists, royalists, and church-going republicans, and if these journals should praise me, if they should venture to suggest that I am not a great patron of curates, they would not be believed ; as a consequence, their subscribers would go elsewhere, and they would be ruined. This is sad, yet were I to write my letter once more I should still express myself as I have done. The moderates, nevertheless, know very well that I am the enemy of all persecution, that I uphold liberty of conscience and the Concordat. They are, however, like frogs which cry out for a king ; I offer myself in this capacity, but they reject me, fearing that I may devour them. It is not I, however, who shall enjoy this tidbit. Another will arise and claim it ; then, when it is too late, the frogs will wish for me."

I could but maintain my position, and consequently turned the conversation into other channels. The Prince, who was in a conversational mood, spoke of affairs and of men of the times. There was one little sketch which impressed me as peculiarly charming.

"Gambetta," said the Emperor, "is at heart a kind fellow, and wishes only peace. He has not the cruelty which is so often necessary in politics. He is a sentimentalist, as all fat men are. He will come into power, he will be prime minister; but he will be like the lion in love; he will allow his claws to be cut, his fangs to be removed. Oh, he will be politic enough. As for M. Jules Ferry, he is a different man. M. Jules Ferry has a temperament as cold as that of the surgeon who, unmoved by the cries of his patient, cuts deeply into the flesh. He is made to govern. It was he who created Article 7, and prepared the decrees, nor has he spoken his last word. Will his end be triumph or ruin? What will be the result of his final message? I do not know. To whatever extreme, however, he may be led, this man will certainly never allow himself to be buried alive. He is a lean, fierce bull."

After a pause, the Prince added a remark which I have quoted in the first chapter of "The Court of Napoleon III."

"I will not speak," said he, "of M. de Cassagnac. He is a very worthy pontifical Zouave."

One of Prince Napoleon's last political acts was to cover the walls of Paris with that manifesto which cost him several weeks of imprisonment in the Conciergerie.

When, after this experience, he returned home, he was greatly disheartened, and for a time dropped out of public notice. Then his eldest son, Prince Victor, deserted him, and by this act drew forth, in behalf of Prince Napoleon, the sympathy, if not of statesmen, at least of all fathers.

An accurate account of the scene which resulted in a final rupture between him and his son has been given me by an intimate friend of the Prince, and I repeat it here just as it was told me.

The general reasons for this rupture are known, but the public is ignorant of many distressing details in connection with the occurrence. With whom in this affair lies the responsibility, the blame? With the father, or with the son?

I believe that both were victims of competition, of ambition, and of ill-will, strangely out of harmony with their own natures. I believe that this father and son were alienated, as it were, against their own wills and by the mighty force of circumstances.

Prince Victor had been appointed by the Prince Imperial as successor to the Empire; and so it chanced that, some time after the death of the unhappy boy, the Bonapartist faction divided into two camps, one of which rallied round Prince Victor, the other round Prince Napoleon.

M. Jolibois and all those who remained of the party which, during the Second Empire, had been known as that of the Empress, rose in arms. M. Jolibois led the anti-Jeromist faction, and aided by a few too-fervent friends, succeeded in persuading the Prince that, in the interest of the cause and in loyalty to the wishes of his dead friend, he ought to break with his father. As Prince Victor seemed adverse to such an act, M. Jolibois and his adherents next attempted a little strategy with Prince Napoleon, by which they sought to bring about an abdication in favour of his son. It is hardly needful to state the reception which this proposal met.

The conspirators then changed their tactics. They returned to Prince Victor, and declared that under no circumstances ought he to remain

under his father's roof. The young man suffered still a few qualms of conscience ; but when
finally it was said that the future of the dynasty
depended upon his decision, and that in it, too,
lay the chance of a speedy restoration, he acceded to his friends' wishes and endorsed their
conduct.

Prince Napoleon remained for some time
ignorant of these circumstances, but at last a
moment came when his son could no longer
conceal his plans. After breakfast one morning, the Prince remarked to his father that he
had resolved to live henceforth independently,
and must ask his consent to a separation.
Prince Napoleon only half understood his son's
words.

"I have no opposition to make to such a
plan," he said ; "you are young, and I perfectly
understand your wishes, and even approve of
them. I will see that apartments are found for
you quite separate from mine."

The Prince tossed his head.

"Thank you, father," he replied, "but that is
not what I mean by being free. It seems to me
wise, in the interest of my cause, that we should
be entirely separated ; and for this reason I have,
I confess, already rented an apartment. . . . I
have need to be alone," he added ; "my party

demands this separation, and it is my duty to obey my friends' wishes."

Prince Napoleon could hardly believe his ears.

"Your party," he cried, "your party; of what party are you speaking? Our cause is not divided; my party is also yours. What is the matter," he added in a fatherly tone, "are you in need of money? Are you wearied by the monotony of this life? I will increase your allowance, I will leave you absolutely free."

The young prince did not, however, swerve.

"Thank you, father," he protested; "but it is not that which I want. Our separation is all that is necessary."

"Ah, I understand now," exclaimed Prince Napoleon; "I understand; there are those who wish to make us enemies, and they place you in a position opposed to mine, in the position of my adversary. This conversation has been required of you by certain colleagues. You are doubtless bribed by Jolibois. Go, sir; I do not seek to detain you."

Prince Napoleon rose, and, leaving his son, withdrew to his own room. This is the last hour which the father and son spent together. Prince Victor was henceforth his own master and the leader of his party.

I can but feel it well-nigh impossible that he should fill his father's place, who, though he fell behind in the race after power and was guilty of many political errors, yet remains in history one of the most remarkable minds of our day.

The exile in which Prince Napoleon spent the last years of his life seems to have wrapped his memory in oblivion; the tomb where his remains are laid conceals his very name from the world. Men of arts and letters cannot, however, forget that this man gave them his devoted interest and knew how to appreciate their works intelligently. Politicians can scarcely overlook his statesmanlike qualities, — qualities which sought an higher plane for their exercise than that of the small quibbles of the hour. Philosophers, a class of men whose companionship he loved and sought and to whose message he eagerly listened, would indeed be ungrateful did they ignore his memory.

Men of letters should remember, too, that Prince Napoleon was himself a writer of some little power. His book entitled, "Napoleon and his Detractors," which was written in reply to a work by M. Taine, is a masterpiece. That circle of gifted minds, of whose companionship he was so fond and so proud, surely owe him respect and admiration.

In behalf of the general public — that public whose interest was chiefly excited by his final suffering and by that domestic drama which took place at his death-bed — I allude to the moment when Prince Victor asked his father's blessing, and Prince Napoleon, already a dying man, rose on his pillows and cried, " Begone, begone !" as though he were uttering a fearful anathema — in behalf of this public to whom Prince Napoleon has always appeared in the character of a damned spirit pursued by avenging angels, of a sinner driven without the gates of Eden, I repeat that he was a man gifted with all the qualities necessary to a ruler, but became the plaything of an evil fate which forbade the exercise of his powers. He was like the heroes of fairy tales, to whom are given every good gift, but who are made impotent to use these gifts by the mysterious spell of some malicious genius.

That evil fate which hung over all his race, over all who bore his name, did not spare Prince Napoleon. With a personal malignity, it even denied him what it gave others, both the crimson glory of the battle-field which is like the splendour of the heavens at sunset, and the tragic horror of defeat which is like the darkness which covers the earth before a cataclysm.

It destined him to mediocrity, and forced him to travel a road which led to no glory. Fate apportioned to this man, in whom was the spirit of an ancient hero and the nature of a Cæsar, the existence of an unfortunate modern gentle-man. Chained to the earth, he spread his eagle wings longing for flight, and became an object of ridicule. He was regarded as a kind of mask, fit for the carnival, a poor, painted thing, at which our hearts may well cry out in shame and anger.

IV.

TRAGIC SHADOWS.

Two men filled tragic *rôles* in the Second
Empire, and fixed their sinister hopes upon
Napoleon III., as the technical traitors of the
drama are wont to fix theirs upon some object
of hatred.   These men are Prince Bismarck and
Count Cavour.   Two women exercised a fatal
influence upon his life and upon his Empire,
and these two stand forth in history like one
figure with a double face.   They rise like living
images, on each side of his tomb, evil spirits
from the nether world.   These women are the
Empress Eugénie and the Empress Charlotte of
Mexico.   While Europe looks on expectant and
submissive, Bismarck and Cavour dare to cherish
the hope of overthrowing the Emperor.   While
Europe bends her knee before the magnificence
of Napoleon's name — that name in whose syllables resound the rebellion and the glory of the
century at its birth, in whose syllables ring out
the hosannas which shall be sung for victories
still to be gained — these men, Bismarck and

Cavour, cherish a hope, which, in the eyes of the people, had they known it, could but have appeared extravagant and absurd — the hope, I repeat, of crushing the Emperor.

While Europe looks on aghast, a woman appears who is jealous of the power and the authority exercised by Napoleon III., and who resolves, without considering the consequences of such a determination, to turn to her own advantage this power and this authority. With no malicious purpose, for this would be too terrible an accusation, but rather in a careless unconsciousness of evil, she weaves her meshes round the Emperor's feet ; this woman is the Empress Eugénie. The Roman venture was a partial realisation of her dreams, dreams from which she woke, at the close of her imperial reign, to find herself bathed in tears and blood.

A second woman appeared upon this stage, a stage whose background is the great world ; and this woman is the Empress Charlotte. Like a creature just escaped from Eden, she stepped forth radiant in beauty, a woman hardly awakened yet to life and love, bathed in sunshine and crowned with flowers. She stood there in her nudity, the innocent victim of a danger which she did not recognise, and into the midst of which she was cast by a power not her own. The thunderbolt fell, and she still stood upon the great stage, a sad phantom. Like a terrible spectre, she haunted the Emperor's life and thoughts, a melancholy companion, a vision of sin from which he could not escape.

Bismarck and Cavour made use of very different methods in pursuing their policy with Napoleon III., though it was their common purpose to win, if not his conscious co-operation in their schemes, at least an unacknowledged sympathy with their ideals, which should reflect upon his whole governmental policy.

Count Bismarck used Napoleon III. as a tool, with which he would, however, dispense when it ceased to be useful; but he never converted him to his theories. To him the Emperor was a sort of sphinx; he never felt sure what he might gain from him in the unforeseen course of events. These circumstances, which placed the Emperor in the power of Prince Bismarck, were of greater force in overthrowing Europe than was the personal genius of the Prussian minister.

Count Cavour pursued a totally opposite course. He knew marvellously well, and with a sort of mathematical precision, what he might expect from one of the Emperor's visionary

mind and humanitarian dreams ; and day by day
he sought to direct the Emperor's policy into
certain well-defined channels. More subtle and
less violent than Bismarck, who, with his ogre-
like personality and his voice like the growl of a
bull-dog, was too apt to inspire fear, Cavour understood Napoleon's nature, and encouraged his
aspirations. We may, indeed, safely affirm, if
philosophical deductions are permitted, that, had
the Emperor been freed from the bonds which
united him to Italy, had he felt himself independent, and unhampered by debt, he would still,
at the instigation of Count Cavour, have laboured
for the territorial and political emancipation of
this nation. When we consider the progressive
development which he wished for Italy, and that
fine enthusiasm which drew him toward her in
the struggle for greatness and unity, it even
seems probable that he would have dealt none
too gently with the temporal power of the Pope,
had he not been checked by fear of the Empress's wrath, and of a rupture with his habitual
counsellors, as well as with the party in power
of which he had need for a support which he
could not at that time hope to find elsewhere.

The consolidation of Germany followed that
of Italy. In the history of Europe, Prince Bismarck appears as the corollary of Count Cavour.

Both men sealed the glory of their countries
with the blood of France. They divided between themselves the Emperor's spoils, the one
storming his heart, the other his mind. Both
visited France, though under differing circumstances ; both received admiration and homage.
The beauties of the court welcomed them,
courted their smiles, and kept their sayings
fresh in the memories. Those young girls
even, of humble station, who read hour by hour
to the Empress, shared, so one of them has confessed, the universal infatuation, and had their
dreams, too, of the great men who had passed
so near them.

The Tuileries was at this time possessed by
a strange enthusiasm for what is foreign. The
courtiers of both sexes were indifferent to everything French ; they cared nothing for the miseries and the joys of their own country, for the
persecution of the masses, or their hopes of
freedom ; whereas, for affairs transpiring in distant lands, they professed strong interest and
concern, and directed their attention toward
them with that inexplicable lack of forethought
which is common to ignorant minds.

M. Cavour appreciated this tendency in the
French people even before Prince Bismarck did
so, and reaped from it his own harvest. During

Prince Bismarck's visit to Biarritz, and later, when in 1867 he came to Paris for the Exposition, and to take part in the imperial apotheosis, after which the star of the Bonapartes set, he, too, became aware of it, and found therein a powerful advantage.

I remember a strange legend told me as a child, the legend of a distant country through which there wandered an evil spirit without abode, and which suddenly appeared where it was least expected; they told me that it haunted wedding-feasts, family reunions, and places of public rejoicing. Its visit was followed by the ruin or the death of those on whom it had fixed its eye, nor was there any power which could save the victims thus condemned.

This story filled me with terror, and I used to hide my head upon the breast of her who told it me. I am reminded of the story now, and not less frightened by it, when I remember how, in 1867, in the midst of laughter and of universal joy, while a hymn proclaiming the glory and the power of the Empire was being sung, while humanity had given itself over to the folly and mad extravagance of love, and kings, with their subjects, feasted and drank together at one gigantic table; when I remember, I say, that in the midst of this there rose a man, Prince Bismarck, whom I can but liken to the evil phantom of the legend, a man who fixed his gaze on each object, each human being, and by one sweeping glance brought death upon all.

The Italian problem had, during the reign of Napoleon III., a genuine though somewhat misleading popularity, and is even considered to-day as the brilliant prologue of a national idyl ; so strong is humanity's affection for an object by which it has once been charmed, so untouched is it by the remembrance of harm which has come to it through that object. If we put aside the great Italian struggle, there remain in the history of the Second Empire two forces which exerted a fatal influence upon the Emperor and his epoch. These were Mexico and Sadowa.

At the beginning of this chapter I alluded to the unhappy woman in whom the Mexican disaster seems to find its synthesis. She passed through Paris, triumphant and joyous, on the way to her new home, filled with pride by her husband's recent glory ; she returned there, as I have already related, as a fugitive, almost as a beggar, an expiatory victim suffering unjustly for the folly — I dare not call it crime — of the Empress Eugénie and Mme. de Metternich. This woman appeared before the Emperor, whom she accused of her sorrows, like a lifeless statue of Despair, like an image of pending judgment. From this hour her memory dwelt with him, an awful companion.

I have given an account of the terrifying scene which took place at Saint-Cloud in the presence of the whole court, when the first symptoms appeared of the insanity which afterwards attacked this poor woman.

There is a scene more dramatic than this, whose actors were the Empress Charlotte and the Emperor Napoleon III. It took place some days later at Saint-Cloud, and has a tragic and inexpressible grandeur, a horror infinitely pathetic.

Many times during her stay in Paris the Empress Charlotte had requested an interview with the Emperor, that she might explain to him the motives of her visit to Europe, and plead for the continuance of the support which he had promised her husband, Maximilian, but which he had subsequently withdrawn.

The Emperor was not ignorant of the character of the interview which she sought ; but he had resolved to relinquish the Mexican campaign, and to accept its profits and its losses as they had come to him. He therefore evaded as long as possible the supplications of the young Empress, but there came a time at last when he could no longer refuse her audience.

Under the influence of the Empress Eugénie's enthusiasm, and through the diplomatic intrigues secretly conducted by Mme. de Metternich and officially by the Prince, her husband, Napoleon III. had perhaps himself become convinced that a certain glory would redound to him through this Mexican campaign, by which a monarchy was to be established on American soil. He sustained the campaign, and preserved his faith in its outcome, just so long as the mirage of success kept his eyes turned away from the actual. When, however, he perceived that the Emperor Maximilian could never win the affection of the Mexicans, who are a people opposed to every foreign element, when, in short, he saw the error into which he had fallen, he withdrew to his tent, and uttered the words of the ancients, *alea jacta est.* It was not, perhaps, a very generous course of action ; but the logic of government is often cruel, and fails to take into consideration generosity and sentiment.

When, therefore, Napoleon III. granted the Empress Charlotte the audience which she

awaited with eager anxiety, he had already prepared his reply to her arguments, her tears, and
her anger.

Very nervous, very excited, with a half-wild
look in her eye, the Empress Charlotte awaited
with mingled feelings of hope and fear the
arrival of the Emperor. She dared to hope;
because it seemed to her that Napoleon III.,
after raising a throne for her husband, would
be unwilling that the whole work should be
destroyed. She could not but fear; because,
by his evasive words, his disheartening actions,
and the pity which he showed, the sovereign
had made her understand that her story had no
longer any interest for him. She suffered from
hallucinations, and was now again haunted by
a fear which had taken possession of her at
Saint-Cloud, that of poison which she should be
forced to drink.

When the Emperor was announced, she went
forward to meet him, and speedily cut short all
preliminaries by introducing immediately the
subject which lay so near her heart.

"Your Majesty is perhaps moved at last,"
she said, "by the cruel fate which has overtaken my husband. May I hope that your
Majesty will grant him assistance?"

The Emperor remained silent a moment,

then spoke with an accent of great deference
and of sincere regret.

"My action in Mexico, Madame," he replied,
"is at an end, and I cannot renew it. Were I
inclined myself to do so, my government and
the Chambers would oppose such a course."

"You are Emperor, sire."

"I am Emperor, madame, and my commands
are respected and obeyed when they are in harmony with the glory and the interests of France;
but " — he became much excited — "I shall not
use the power of Emperor to plunge my country into imminent danger, into an interminable
war from which France could gain nothing."

"A short time ago, sire, you spoke differently."

"A short time ago, madame, I had hope."

"Ah, you had hope?"

"Hope that Maximilian would avail himself
of the assistance which I gave him, and win the
love of the people; that he would learn to understand their needs and their natures, and be
able to carry on by himself the work which we
began together."

"And now?"

"Now I have no longer this hope."

The Empress shuddered, rose, and took one ·
or two steps across the great room; then she
passed her hand over her forehead.

"This is terrible," she muttered, "terrible."

Once more she seated herself near the Emperor and resumed the conversation.

"Sire," she said, in a supplicating voice, "Sire, it is said that you are kind, that your heart is touched by those who are in misfortune. My husband and I are both victims of misfortune; have pity, therefore, upon him and me. I implore you, sire, give us your support, and our hearts will love and bless you."

She took the Emperor's hand, and brought it to her lips as she stooped to kneel. Napoleon III., however, checked this movement, and, full of compassion, bent over the woman who supplicated him.

"You speak, Madame," he said, touching her fingers with his lips, "as though your husband were in danger. It lies with him to avoid this danger. Let him retreat with my troops, and leave behind him the dream of an empire; it was an unfortunate dream."

The Empress Charlotte drew herself up with pride.

"What is this, sire?" she exclaimed. "You counsel my husband to fly, to commit an act of dishonour and of cowardice?"

"A general, madame, is guilty of neither cowardice nor dishonour when, after having lost a battle, he capitulates. Is not the Emperor Maximilian in the position of a defeated general? Let him act, therefore, as such a general would. Fine phrases have little sense or utility. You are suffering, madame; you are much unstrung. I pray you calm yourself."

The Empress had risen, and was no longer listening. "Never," she cried, with growing enthusiasm, "never will Maximilian accept such proposals. He will never seek escape, never turn his back to the rebels who try to rob him of his crown. No, he will, if necessary, die for the cause which he has espoused and I will die with him."

Again the Emperor spoke.

"Madame," he said, "I beg you to examine more coolly the arguments which I have presented, and the advice which I have given. The Emperor Maximilian's future and your own depend upon your doing so."

Still the young Empress stood there, gazing, it seemed, into space, or at some danger visible to herself alone; she had no appearance of listening to Napoleon's words, her lips were moving as though murmuring some chant.

"He will die, he will die, and I shall die with him. They will put us into the same tomb; we shall lie there together, and we shall love each

other, love each other still, despite the cruelty
of man. We shall be exalted, and the future
shall sing our glory."

The Emperor made a movement of dismay
and alarm. He remembered the attack from
which the Empress Charlotte had suffered at
Saint-Cloud, and he feared a similar one now.
He touched her arm gently, and made her sit
down. She obeyed unconsciously, and gazed at
him for some moments with no sign of recognition in her manner, and then seemed suddenly
to recover herself.

"Ah, you are the Emperor Napoleon III.,"
she said at last, "that all-powerful Emperor
who raised my husband to a throne; and I
am a wretched woman who implores mercy
for a victim who you have condemned."

Her voice then changed, and assumed a tone
of severity.

"You have, then, made your final decision?"
she added. "You will leave us to our own
resources with no hope of assistance from
you?"

"I have told you, madame," replied he, awakened to a consciousness of his painful position,
"I have told you that I have no longer power
to assist the Emperor Maximilian."

A second time she rose; standing motionless, she fixed her sad and earnest eyes on Napoleon III., who, embarrassed by her gaze and by a kind of magnetic influence which resulted from it, bowed his head. Suddenly, and without having spoken a word, the Empress Charlotte became desperate, and threw herself upon her knees at the Emperor's feet ; and before he could check her passionate supplication, she clasped her hands and pleaded with him as the faithful plead with their God in whom is their last hope.

"Sire," she said, and the tones of her voice were like caresses, "Sire, the Emperor Maximilian has enemies in that country, enemies who do not know what it is to forgive. Unsupported, he is powerless against them and must become their victim. I have taken this journey to save him ; he awaits my return with loving impatience, with the anxiety, too, of a condemned man who counts the hours which separate him from death. Sire, you have loved ; surely the remembrance of your happiness must open your heart and mind to the feelings of others. I love my husband, sire, and he loves me ; we are everything to each other. I entreat you to have mercy upon him and me. I entreat you not to sacrifice him to the pride of a rebellious people. From him who more than once has granted life to the criminal, I, sire, dare entreat the life of an honest man, the life of the Emperor Maximilian."

The wretched woman paused, exhausted; a great sob shook her frame. She had put her whole soul into her prayer; she collapsed with its last words.

Gently the Emperor sought to raise her and to offer some consolation. He felt that this heart-rending scene was prolonging itself uselessly, and hastened to bring it to a close.

"Madame," he said, "I will do all that lies in my power to secure the safety of, and the happiness of, both yourself and your husband; but I cannot, alas! deceive you as to the attitude of my government in this affair. France will no longer support Maximilian on the throne of Mexico."

He had hardly spoken these words when he started back in horror. Empress Charlotte had risen, one may better say leaped, to her feet, and stood tall and majestic before Napoleon III. Her lips were drawn, and her look was that of a mad woman, at once terrible, and superbly beautiful. Thus facing him, she flung out her words of despair, of fury, and of hatred.

"Sire," she cried, "it is said that you are good; it is a lie! It is said, sire, that you are a magnanimous sovereign; it is a lie! It is said that you are great; it, too, is a lie! You are, sire, an evil man. You are an Emperor without authority; a ruler without ideals. You are ruthless fate, and we are your victims. You are the author of evil; you favour its existence. Evil, however, returns to its source; it will find you, sire, and at no distant time. You and your throne shall be swept away by a mighty force which you do not understand!"

Her frenzy increased as she spoke, and finally took full possession of her. She stretched out her arms with a wild gesture.

"Move back," she cried three times, "move back, move back! Sire," she then added, "it is my turn to say that nothing more may be expected of you."

The Emperor had risen as though struck by a thunderbolt. For a moment he had been filled with anger by the violence of the young Empress; but looking upon her despair, he had forgiven her wild language, and calmed the feeling of rage which had taken possession of him. It was seldom that the Emperor's anger was aroused, but when it was it knew no bounds. In this instance, however, he recovered self-control, and listened without a word, without a gesture, to the imprecations and the curses which were flung at him. When at last Empress Charlotte, in the final climax of her despair, drove him from the room, he bowed his head in profound commiseration and withdrew.

When once more within the palace, he retired to his own apartments and forbade admittance.

The Emperor Napoleon III. feared the fulfilment of these evil prophecies, and was much disquieted by the words of the woman who had thus foretold his doom. It was a relief to find himself alone, and able to look calmly forward into the future. Who knows but that, by an effort of the imagination, that future seemed still to smile upon him? Who knows but that, in the terror of his soul, he, in that hour, saw the star of the Bonapartes begin to set?

The events which preceded and which followed the disaster at Sadowa are of a less personal nature, and belong more properly to politics so called.

On two occasions, both in 1864 and 1865, Prince Bismarck conferred with the Emperor Napoleon III. upon the existing state of affairs in Europe and upon the advantages to be derived therefrom. Neither of these audiences,

however, whose purpose was to bring about
an understanding with the Cabinet of the Tuileries, met with results favourable to a united
action between France and Prussia against
their neighbours.

In 1864 Bismarck attempted to soothe the
disappointment and the uneasiness which the
defeat in Denmark had caused Napoleon III.
He returned to Berlin, having succeeded fairly
well in his mission, and able to bring back the
assurance that France would at least allow
events to have their course without, for the
moment, intervening.

After his visit to Biarritz in 1865, Bismarck
felt less confidence in the Emperor's neutrality.
His previous interview with the sovereign had
encouraged the hope that he could without
much difficulty secure him as an ally in the
cause which he had espoused. The Emperor,
however, maintained a questionable position,
made but a few comments on the general prosperity of European nations, and refused absolutely to commit himself. I have related
elsewhere the conversation between Bismarck
and Count Walewski, after the famous visit
in Biarritz. As a result of this conversation,
Prince Bismarck ceased altogether to regard
Napoleon III. as a power upon which they

might rely for assistance. As soon as he began to consider the Emperor a person whose influence could be turned to no advantage, he immediately became in his eyes an obstacle in the way of his own policy, of which it would be well to get rid. Prince Bismarck's efforts with the Emperor were, as we know, renewed, and with better success, by M. de Goltz.

It now became important that Napoleon III. should bring about an understanding between Austria and the Cabinet at Paris in regard to the Italian question, by which the complete independence of Italy should be secured. This was a time in which to realise without bloodshed the famous words once pronounced by Napoleon III. in the interest of the Italian people: " Free," he had said, " to the very shores of the Adriatic."

Victor Emmanuel, voluntarily or involuntarily, did not allow the Emperor to carry very far the negotiations which he had begun through the mediation of Prince Metternich. Solicited by Prussia, he pledged himself in case of a disagreement between the Cabinet at Vienna and that of Berlin, to declare war with Austria. This secret treaty, made known at Vienna by an act of indiscretion on the part of the government, put an end to all conciliatory negotiations.

Austria felt its security threatened, although it had given every proof of good will in the affairs which were now agitating Europe, and had declared itself desirous to settle them peacefully. It therefore abandoned all parleying, and intrenched itself behind what it called its rights, that final argument which savours of war and which all nations urge in the hours of political crises.

It was at this time that Prince Bismarck, fearing the effect of these international problems upon the policy of Napoleon III., invented as an hypothesis the annexation of Luxemburg and of Belgium to France, as a compensation for his neutrality and a balancing wheel to his power. It must, however, be stated that the Emperor never seriously considered these propositions, and was uninfluenced by them on the eve of the Austro-Prussian conflict.

The Emperor, who was opposed to war, found himself placed in a most trying position. Face to face with the disagreement between the Cabinets of Berlin and of Austria, it was impossible for him to check the bloody consequences of that disagreement without himself taking a positive stand, and making it clear to Prussia that he desired no European war. This would have been an extreme policy, exempt

from all subterfuge and all intrigue; it would
have been a bold game, but it did not impress
Napoleon III. as compatible with the authority
which he had assumed; for, if his ultimatum
should in this case be treated with scorn, there
would remain but one course for him to pursue,
that of exchanging his *rôle* of counsellor for
that of belligerent.

Subsequent events have proved that the Emperor should not have hesitated to enter into
war with Prussia. We are, however, never able
to judge fairly of a circumstance till that circumstance is past; it is futile to philosophise
upon possible results of a course which might
have been pursued, but which, nevertheless, was
not the one chosen.

Should a war between Austria and Prussia
become inevitable, there were at least two consequences which must result therefrom, in
which the Emperor had every reason to rejoice;
these were the confirmation and organisation of
Italy's independence, and the weakened power
of Austria and of Prussia; this last result would
procure for Europe a long season of peace, and
permit France, not only to collect her forces, but
to prepare without interruption for future complications which were almost sure to arise through
the agency of Bismarck's troublesome genius.

The Emperor's arguments seemed to be of
the strongest ; and he was regarded by the people as their supreme mediator, as the builder of
their future destinies.

Public opinion was, in 1866, after the Austrian defeat at Sadowa, entirely in sympathy
with the Emperor ; it was indeed even more
violent than he in the expressions of an unre-
flecting hatred of Austria and a childish enthusiasm for Prussia and its needle-guns.   The
Emperor was, therefore, urged by public opinion
to pursue the course which he had adopted, and
forced by it to maintain his attitude of arbiter
in this problem which involved, in reality, the
reconstruction of European policy.

Among the politicians who at this time surrounded the Emperor, there were those who
did not feel the same assurance, or see in the
violent development of events the same cause of
satisfaction, as did the people at large.   Some
counselled him not to settle, by a Solomon-like
judgment, the conflict which had broken out at
Sadowa.   Others advised him to arrest Prussia's encroachment upon the whole of Germany,
to check her demands, and, in case his arbitra-
tion were not successful, to take up a position
on the Rhine.   Others felt that the *rôle* of
arbiter which was offered the Emperor gave

sufficient dignity to the attitude of France in this matter, but would, nevertheless, have wished the Cabinet in Paris to require, as conditions of peace, guarantees from Prussia against the return of present difficulties and against the disastrous results of that ever-increasing influence which her victories throughout Europe secured to her. The scheme for the annexation of Belgium having been set aside, it now became necessary to formulate the demands which should be presented to Berlin.

The Emperor, still pursuing the ideal of the unity of nations, and cherishing those humanitarian dreams which were its natural fruit, made few remonstrances against the project for Germany's unification, a project which, nevertheless, was not without its disturbing complications. It was decided that no objection should be made to this unification, and that France should simply present to Berlin the claims made by the Cabinet of the Tuileries in its own interest.

These claims were formulated as follows : The reinstatement of French boundaries as defined in the clauses adopted by the Powers in 1814 ; the annexation of Luxemburg and of Mayence, and the preservation of the kingdom of Saxony in its entirety. It was decreed that Count Benedetti, our ambassador in Berlin, should be charged to support these claims, and to submit them to the consideration of Prince Bismarck.

When Count Benedetti, charged with instructions from the Cabinet of the Tuileries, arrived from Vienna, where he had explained to the Emperor Francis Joseph the humiliating conditions of peace and presented himself before Bismarck, the Prussian minister was billeted at the King's headquarters in a small town on the way to Vienna. An armistice had been arranged in order that negotiations could be pursued, and the Prussian army was awaiting the results of this armistice, ready at any moment to resume its march against the Austrian capital.

Count Benedetti found Prince Bismarck favourably disposed toward his mission; he made known to the Prussian minister the result of his visit in Vienna, and said that he had found the Emperor Francis Joseph, though not prepared to yield his position entirely, yet resigned to a cessation of hostilities under the conditions which have already been stated; the confederation, that is, of the northern states of Germany independently of the authority of Austria, and the surrender of Venice to France, which nation would cede it to King Victor Emmanuel.

Bismarck was much encouraged by this success, and the interview would have been in every way most friendly had Count Benedetti spoken only of the conditions just enumerated. When, however, our ambassador made it clear to his interlocutor that France required as a recompense for her share in the disintegration of Europe, and for her absolute neutrality, the annexations of which I have spoken, and the guarantee of her own security in the future, Prince Bismarck's joy was somewhat abated. With his impulsive temperament, and that instinctive violence which he had never been able to conquer, Bismarck assumed an indignant attitude before the claims presented by Count Benedetti, resented his demands, and replied that he could not pronounce upon them without first consulting the king. In a moment, however, he resumed his character of diplomat.

"It is difficult," he added, in a most suave manner, and with that smile again upon his lips which a moment ago had disappeared, "it is difficult to discuss at one time every item involved in so serious a matter; there is ample opportunity for satisfactory arrangements to be made, and I have no doubt that our views will be in perfect harmony."

Having received these vague and halting assurances, Count Benedetti withdrew.

When, a short time after this interview, our ambassador was able to report to the Emperor the partial failure of his mission, it was already too late to subdue the pride of Prussia, and to impose upon it the conditions supplementary to peace, for which it had at one time stipulated.

Bismarck, who knew how to make the best use of time, had, in the interim, secretly enlisted the sympathy of various states with the new political *régime* which he was about to establish; and these states, which a few days before had stood in the relation of belligerents against Prussia, now declared themselves satisfied with the conditions set forth in the treaty of peace which had been submitted to them. It is probable that they would have rebelled against the renewal of a war which had already weakened their power; but the prospect of obtaining the privileges and the glory of a separate nationality did not appear to them altogether undesirable. They had, on the other hand, nothing to gain by a war with France, and would not readily have consented to it.

It was upon an intimate knowledge of these facts that Bismarck relied in concluding peace with Austria. The Cabinet of the Tuileries,

however, failed to appreciate them, and neglected to assert its claims in the imperative
manner which circumstances required.

Prussia having by a hasty peace freed itself
from Austria, and intrenched itself behind a
national power as strong as German pride could
demand, now directed hostilities against France,
and refused absolutely to accede to the propositions presented by the Cabinet of the Tuileries,
as formulated for the second time by Count
Benedetti. She even declined to discuss these
propositions, or to permit any annexation to
our territory or any change in our existing
borders.

These new complications produced great consternation in the political world of France. It
was as though the Tuileries had been struck by
the first blast of a mighty storm, which had
awakened those who were sleeping in peaceful
oblivion ; it was like one of those squalls which
spring up in open sea, and toss vessels hither
and thither, sweep their decks, and fill with
terror the hearts of those on board.

There was, however, no time to be lost in the
expression of fruitless fear. It was important
that prompt resolutions should be taken ; and
the Emperor, who a few weeks previously had
opposed war, was now made uneasy by the

state of affairs, and felt that the welfare and the dignity of France depended on decisive action. He therefore recalled Count Benedetti, who hastened directly to Paris.

Prussia had granted our demands no consideration whatever, and it became necessary to determine immediately upon our course.

The period which now approached was full of ill omen, full of tragic possibilities, and is memorable in the life of Napoleon III. as one of the most crucial periods of his reign, as the beginning of a long moral agony.

He was urged by the minister of foreign affairs to declare war against Prussia, even at the risk of incurring the hostility of united Germany, and of seeing Austria abandon his cause, and watch, impassive, the defeat of France; at the risk, too, of being forgotten by Italy, which was covering itself with laurels easily won, and which, in the strength of its unforeseen success, — a success born of defeat, — was already becoming indifferent to the policy of Napoleon III. Urged, therefore, by M. Drouyn de Lhuys to declare war against Prussia, without waiting to strengthen his resources, which had been exhausted, or nearly so, by recent campaigns, the Emperor Napoleon III., under the influence of his own anger and of the indignation excited in him by the treachery of Prussia, resolved to march upon the Rhineland.

When, however, he gave the command to prepare for war, when he communicated his intentions to his counsellors and to the captains of his army he was brought to a startling realisation of public sentiment upon the question.

A sudden terror had taken possession of those round him. Politicians shook their heads, and muttered that France, not in reality seriously threatened, was, on account of a little wounded pride, entering a campaign which involved the heaviest risks. Military men discussed the question among themselves, and were at variance as to the possible results of such an enterprise.

Our armament was compared with that which Prussia had recently had an opportunity to test ; it seemed doubtful whether our forces would be able to resist a probable invasion. A committee was appointed to examine the military condition of France as opposed to that of Prussia, before a definite conclusion should be reached ; and the Emperor inferred from this action that his counsellors feared the responsibility of advising war, and evaded his appeal.

He stood alone — alone with his faith in some kind providence, abandoned by the rightful supporters of his throne and of his dynasty; alone in all France, which he was about to involve in war against Germany. He did not dare take upon himself the responsibility of an action upon whose results depended the glory or the dishonour of his country; and bowing his head in the humiliation of defeated hope, he resigned himself to inaction, with a bitter sense of disappointment.

It was, however, agreed that the position in which France was placed by the sudden development of Prussia's power required the nation at least to feign an unity of sentiment, and to direct its attention toward means whereby the triumph of its claims might at no distant day be assured.

Henceforth, however, claims and victories were little talked of. The Emperor Napoleon III. was doomed to drift as does a wreck which is driven from shore to shore, and which is cast upon many a reef before it disappears forever into the depths of some great sea.

One glorious hour was, it is true, given him; one hour of peace and consolation, the hour, we might almost say, of his apotheosis. The hosannas and the *Te Deum* of 1867 were heard in the distance like the low tones of an

hymn, like the full, rich harmonies which fill
the great vaulting of a cathedral; they were
heard, too, with the noise of victory, ringing
with the notes of wild triumph, like those which
in the silence of night seem to pass from flag
to flag in the idle arsenal — those flags which
are never for a moment motionless, but ever
wave their tattered colours, eternal emblems of
a nation's glory, and also of the dire hatred of
man under the smoke of battle. The hosannas
and the *Te Deum* of 1867 rose in their loud
strains of praise toward the star of the Bonapartes, as of old the thoughts and the eyes
of the Magi were raised to the wonderful star
of Bethlehem. Claims and triumphs, however,
were henceforth silenced. Through hymns of
rejoicing broke the discord of a lie; the star
of the Bonapartes was about to set, the Emperor to perish, a desolate spirit, alone in all
Europe. To him whose heart was full of kindly
interest for all humanity, no affection was given;
to him who knew so well how to love, no love
was given. He died without a nation, he who
had ruled one of the greatest nations of the
earth.

V.

THE EMPEROR AND THE SALONS.

THE Second Empire, both during its period
of autocracy and during that of liberal government, awakened in the nation a spirit of implacable hatred, which no circumstances served to
lessen ; and this hatred was born and bred in
the *salons*.   I have, in my volume entitled " The
Empress Eugénie," and also in " The Court of
Napoleon III.," alluded to the animosity felt
by the leaders of the Faubourg Saint-Germain
toward Napoleon III.   These dislikes and pre-
judices, which the Emperor, in his excessive
generosity, feigned to ignore, will be dealt with
more fully in the present chapter.

It was, perhaps, during its period of autocracy that the Empire had most to suffer from
the *salons ;* in them were nourished the doctrines of absolutism and of aristocratic forms of
government, though they hypocritically affected
great sympathy with the republican opposition ;
the warfare which they waged against the Tuileries was continuous and without mercy.

There were, during the reign of Napoleon III., various distinct parties opposed to the existing government ; without entering into too minute analysis, we may at least recognise three such parties, which were animated by totally diverse principles, but united in their onslaught against the common enemy.

There were staunch royalists, disciples of the Comte de Chambord ; there were the Orleanists, who maintained the claims of the exiled sons of Louis Philippe ; and there were also the republicans.

The royalist party was led principally by women, and gave expression to a rather negative opposition by assuming an attitude of scorn toward the Emperor, the Empress, and all the court. The Faubourg Saint-Germain is not wont to express its sentiments in vigorous action ; a general appearance of activity satisfies its aspirations. In this instance it took refuge in the customs and the etiquette peculiar to itself, and in the regulation of its own enjoyments. Accounts of all proceedings at the Tuileries were received by it with most expressive frowns and pouts, which, however, were not dangerous. The women, in the strength of their recently emblazoned heraldry, set the example of these frowns and pouts as they mur-

mured, with all the sanctified manner of priests
pronouncing holy orisons at the altar, the word,
king. The men speedily adapted their views to
those held by the fairer sex.

The comparative respect shown the Emperor
and his family, and especially to the young
Prince Imperial, by Comte de Chambord, as
well as this nobleman's hatred against the
princes of Orleans, caused great annoyance to
the royalist opposition. If among the legitimist party, there were some who regretted such
respect and consideration, they nevertheless
acceded to it in public, and consoled themselves in private by directing against the Emperor and his court that ridicule which originated
in Coblentz. Their spirit was that of the
émigrés who made Robespierre the object of
their wit. It was not a novel game, nor was its
humour the most subtle ; it smelt of Spanish to-
bacco, of the musty face-powder worn by a ball-
room dame ; and it was not alarming. In short,
the royalist opposition under the Second Empire had in it less of political conviction than of
social sulkiness ; and the Faubourg Saint-Germain, in assuming opposition to the Tuileries,
gave expression to an extreme elegance, rather
than to any high principles of government.

The relations, therefore, between the court

and the Faubourg Saint-Germain were most
peaceable. The Emperor kept himself informed
concerning the exigencies of the royalist aristocracy, and was not ignorant of its tottering
position ; he quieted its claims by granting to
those whom he felt would be appeased thereby
favours and government positions with large
salaries, without requiring such persons to abandon their convictions. He invited to various
entertainments at the Tuileries those high-born
women who were eager to see once more, if
only for a moment, the palace which they had
never ceased to consider their rightful property.

It must be admitted that the men who distinguished themselves under the Second Empire
always maintained a deferential and a submissive attitude, and were guilty of no breach of
courtesy. The women, on the other hand, lacking in all sense of honour, envious of the radiant
beauty of the Empress, embittered because they
were given but a secondary place where they
would have wished to be mistresses, these
women, I say, who were by nature malicious,
and envious by instinct, preserved their dislike of the imperial family despite the kindness
shown them, and issued from the Tuileries with
derision on their lips and anger in their hearts.

In the intimate circle of their friends and rela-

tions they delighted to parody the conversation
and the gestures of the Empress and her court.
Such recognition as this of a truly delightful
hospitality is certainly open to criticism. Had
self-respecting plebeians been guilty of it, they
would have met with severe criticism from the
very classes which, as it was, committed the
offence; high-bred women of the aristocracy,
however, were greeted with praise for their wit
and intelligence.

From time to time, in order that the royalist
opposition should maintain a sort of dignity and
seriousness, a duke, a marquis, or a count of
good repute in the Faubourg Saint-Germain,
would leave Paris in the character of conspir-
ator, and hold conference with the king at
Frohsdorff or at Goritz. The best way in
which to conduct such interviews was carefully
considered in the Faubourg, and its probable
results discussed there with all the grace and
courtesy of long ago. After the nobleman who
had been charged with such a mission returned
to Paris, bringing with him that letter which
Comte de Chambord never failed to write on
such occasions, a letter in which he thanked
the messenger for his faithfulness, recommended him to the gratitude of his co-workers,
and expressed his faith in the future, there was

an unusual stir in the aristocracy; heavy carriages rolled through the streets drawn by horses
caparisoned with armorial bearings, and for a few
days Paris thought less of the Tuileries and more
of the splendour of times long passed.

These supernumerary *rôles* and parts for
comic heroes were well adapted to the members
of the aristocracy under the Second Empire;
great enjoyment was found in them, and the
Faubourg Saint-Germain had no wish to change
these pleasures for more perilous enterprises.
Caring little for the true interests of the country, they were at heart indifferent to the form
of government established; their thought, their
aspiration, their ideal, was but concerned with
the decorative element of the attitude assumed
by them.

The Comte de Chambord was in harmony
with their views on this point, and the princess
whom he had married sought in every way
to establish their æsthetic position.

I once had occasion to give a little sketch
of the Comte and Comtesse de Chambord; and,
believing my criticism to be in the main just,
I beg permission to repeat it here.

" The Comtesse de Chambord," I wrote, " who was an
Italian married to a French prince, exerted a fatal influence upon the spirit of European society; she not only

had strong power over her husband, but more than once interfered with the policy of France, both in its internal relations and in those with other countries. Anti-French in birth and feeling, she did not at all modify her prejudice when she married Comte de Chambord. This animosity was displayed in the most trifling concerns of life as well as in the momentous affairs of government. Possessing, as she did, complete power over her husband, she was able to conceal his true views. Thus blinded and deceived, this pitiable king without a crown obeyed her, regardless of the good or evil which might result therefrom. Much has been said concerning the noble life of Comte de Chambord, and many are the flowers of eloquence strewn before his memory. From a literary standpoint rhetoric is certainly fine, but it becomes objectionable in politics when it is but the expression of hypocrisy. The true cause of the admiration felt for Comte de Chambord is the fact that no one feared him. He was, in reality, a kind of heathen prophet, a god Buddha, a selfish man who preserved toward the interests of his country an haughty indifference; there is for him but one excuse, and this is brain weakness; he received impressions whose consequences he had no power to measure. He was a kind of king's effigy, a miserable man, occasionally arrayed, by his wife's orders, in the emblems of power; nourished by the delight of a barren dream, he lived on, a pitiable character, having accomplished nothing in his own interest or in that of the country which, in theory, he pretended to love and govern; he died, having bequeathed nothing to humanity or to history, not even that commonplace example of courage which has distinguished every other claimant to the throne, every other hero disowned by his nation."

There is a fact which should be noted in

regard to the opposition of the royalist *salons* under the Second Empire. Though this opposition had no effect on the internal policy of the Emperor, its influence upon his foreign policy was most disastrous. Through its relations with foreign diplomacy, the legitimist party had a large share in bringing about many disturbing events during the Second Empire, and can with difficulty exculpate itself. Led by the Comtesse de Chambord, this party continually opposed the imperial plans, and waged unceasing war against the Cabinet of the Tuileries. On one occasion, to cite an example of its mode of action, it obtained from Prince Metternich and the Austrian government a fatal interposition in the Roman question, and made use of this, and of the religious fanaticism of the Empress, as well as of its own authority, against the decisions of Napoleon III.

That noble feeling of patriotism by which a nation is exalted, by which it is led to the ruin or to the cruel glory of war, that high sentiment which fills all true hearts, did not exist among the politicians of the day or among the representatives of the aristocracy. To politicians, France was but a great table round which they gathered to play their game ; they threw down their cards with reference to a

certain stake, as a gambler throws down his
with an eye on the heap of gold before him.
The aristocracy, to whatever country it may
belong, regards patriotism as a kind of sport.
It is a bond between its members, be they
French, English, German, Italian, or Russian,
a bond which, like that of the Freemasons, for-
bids hatred. The aristocracy fights no less
valiantly upon the battle-field than do the
soldiers, yet a different ideal is ever before
it. It goes to war as it goes to the races,
and falls as willingly under a ball, a bullet, or
a stroke of the sabre, while wrapped in the
national colours, as it falls in the race-course
while taking a hurdle, arrayed in its costume of
jockey. Born and bred at a great distance
from the people, the aristocracy cannot feel
with the people; but as in the supreme moments of life, its acts are like those of the
whole mass of humanity, it is not well to cast
too much reproach on that somewhat original
philosophy which is peculiar to itself.

The Comte de Chambord was king of this
world, which, I repeat, we do wrong to condemn
and to stigmatise before having studied and understood. He shared neither the virtues nor the
defects of his race, but was an alien, an ingraft-
ment as it were, upon a different species of

tree, whose branches are unlike those of the tree itself. He was not, however, without refinement and kindly feeling, nor can we justly condemn him as a man altogether without noble sentiments. There is cause to believe that he disliked his mock-kingship of an idle aristocracy, an aristocracy unwilling to abandon the faultless conventionality of its convictions, and that decorum in which was no peril or disquieting element.

The *salons* of the Orleanists caused more annoyance to the government than did those of the Legitimist party. The former were not content to express vague theories, but held serious doctrines, and gave evidence of these in acts of more alarming import. They followed the leadership of men famous for their intellectual gifts, men renowned for their argumentative powers, and versed in the controversial questions of government; they thus rapidly became a power which the Cabinet of the Tuileries could not afford to overlook.

At the head of these *salons* stood the young exiled princes, who presented themselves, if not to the nation at large, at least to the lower classes, first under the prestige of misfortune, and later under that of a liberalism whose sincerity was, however, ultimately doubted. The tragical death of the Duc d'Orléans, father of the Comte de Paris, who was regarded as a possible successor to Napoleon III., was still fresh in all minds, and dwelt there, a kind of sentimental legend inspired by the popularity of this prince, who was indeed full of virtue and of charm.

The exiled princes by no means remained inactive, but added their influence to that of those who maintained their cause in France. They assumed an offensive position before the Empire; they made their voices heard in the discussions of the day, they supported journals which proclaimed the justice of their principles and of their claims. They reigned over the *salons*, which willingly bowed to their authority; nor was their rule that of the potentates of a comedy, as was that of Comte de Chambord over the Faubourg Saint-Germain; they governed with all the assurance of leaders certain of victory, and remind us somewhat of the mighty vassals of feudal days, who assigned the king his tasks.

Of the Comte de Paris little was said at this time. He appeared in the world as a young man of average intelligence, well qualified for the life of a parliamentarian, to which he was

destined, and inclined to support the theories
and the claims of his uncles, sons of the King
Louis Philippe. Of these sons, the Prince de
Joinville, the Duc de Nemours, the Duc de
Montpensier, and the Duc d'Aumale, much, on
the contrary, was spoken.

By a still-life deception, by a kind of sleight-
of-hand, the name of the Prince de Joinville was
always associated with the Napoleonic legend ; it
called forth the remembrance of the return of the
Emperor's remains from Saint Helena upon the
Belle Poule, which was accomplished through
the intervention of this nobleman. His nature
was contrasted with the ingratitude of Louis
Bonaparte, whose kingdom had been prepared
by the monarchy of July. The proud and high-
bred manner of Comte de Nemours, his personal
beauty, and his chivalrous nature, were constant
subjects of praise.

The Duc de Montpensier was also extolled,
and his intimacy with the Spanish princes was
made a source of rejoicing. Yet, of the four
uncles of the Comte de Paris, the Duc d'Aumale was undoubtedly the most popular. It
was he who inspired the Orleanist party in its
political acts ; it was he whose counsels were
respected and obeyed.

The Duc d'Aumale was more of a soldier

than were his brothers, and during his father's reign and his own exile had roused an enthusiasm which placed him on a somewhat higher plane in the eyes of the people. Acts of wild bravado were attributed to him, and escapades of love; this character of a Don Juan was most attractive to the masses, which in France are ready idolaters of any wild adventurer. The story which represents him at the head of his army waging furious war in Algeria was told and retold; nor did the *salons* ever tire of hearing how he passed in review in Courbevoie in the character of colonel, and how there rode by his side his mistress, Mlle. Alice O——, attired like him in a magnificent uniform of colonel. There was in the life of the Duc d'Aumale a resemblance to that of Henry IV., which procured for him a certain popularity. He was, moreover, young, brilliant, bold, and a devoted admirer of women, able in every way to justify the character with which public sentiment had invested him. He held regular correspondence with his partisans in France, studied the diverse questions which agitated the nation, watched carefully the course of events, and wrote letters which, when made public, assumed the importance of manifestoes.

The leading partisans of these princes in

Paris and throughout France, those who exerted influence in the *salons*, were men of true valour, or descendants of illustrious personages who had won renown in the monarchy of July. These were MM. de Broglie, de Rémusat, d'Haussonville, de Montalivet, Décazes, and de Montalembert. These men not only made their voices heard through the social world, but they wrote, and established newspapers ; their voices, joining with those of the republicans, sounded like the distant rumbling of a coming storm.

It was in the *salons* Thiers and Galliera that the Orleanist party usually held its meetings. It was here that the Duc de Broglie, young at that time, and imbued with liberal principles, communicated to his friends the somewhat vague ideals which filled his mind, and, with his eyes raised dreamily toward heaven, read to them the strange papers which he had designed for publication. It was here that M. de Rémusat proclaimed his royalist convictions, convictions which were, however, tempered by doubts and evasions in which an observer might have foretold the republican of to-morrow. It was here that M. d'Haussonville discussed, with his unflagging good-humour, the virtues of the princes ; and here, too, M. de Montalembert, of more violent temperament, hurled forth his

anathemas against the Empire, while the Duc
Décazes gave vent to his hatred of Napoleon
III. and of all which concerned him.

Duc Décazes, even after the war of 1870,
was one of the politicians of the National
Assembly who showed the most bitter feeling
against Napoleon III. It would have been
becoming had he remembered that his mother,
the Duchesse Décazes, had, in 1861, solicited
favour, and begged assistance of the sovereign,
and had met with compassion from him in her
misfortunes.

This incident calls for some mention here,
inasmuch as it proves, as I have stated in my
previous book, "The Empress Eugénie," and
in the chapter of that book which is entitled
"The Empress and Society," that, though
the Royalist party was in continual and fierce
conflict against Napoleon III., it did not
scruple, on convenient occasions, to make use
for its own ends of the kindness and the power
of the Emperor. Honesty and pride would
have seemed to forbid this party the use of
imperial favours; honour would seem to impose
silence on certain men who had been recipients
of these favours. To forget kindnesses received
is, however, too vital an element of human
nature to admit of much astonishment.

It was M. de Sainte-Aulaire who, in February, 1861, undertook to negotiate with one of the ministers of Napoleon III. for the assistance in behalf of the Duchesse Décazes to which I have just alluded. It was he who made public the letter in which the widow of that most popular minister, who had been compromised in the Restoration, solicited financial aid.

On March 7, 1849, Prince Louis Napoleon Bonaparte, President of the Republic, had granted the Duc Décazes a pension of six thousand francs. M. de Sainte-Aulaire, in his letter to the Emperor's minister, recalled this fact in support of the request which he transmitted.

" My dear Count," wrote M. de Sainte-Aulaire, " the enclosed note will prove the accuracy of the statements which I made to you a few days ago. That which we ask is the continuance of an act which has already given evidence of your great goodness. I can but feel that, setting aside all political considerations, this proof of sympathy bestowed on the widow of a man who occupied a position of importance in our nation will meet with universal approbation.

" Accept, in any case, my gratitude for your interest in this affair, as well as my most affectionate regards, which spring from a friendship of long standing.
" FRIDAY."

" Monsieur le Comte," ran the letter of the Duchesse Décazes, " In 1849 an annual and life pension of six thousand francs was accorded my husband, the Duc Décazes, to be paid from the revenues received by M. Odilon Barrot, at that time minister.

" The financial position in which I am left leads me to ask you, sir, to obtain from his Majesty, the Emperor, permission that this pension be continued to me.

" I shall receive this favour with a feeling of true gratitude, of which gratitude, sir, I trust you will be the faithful interpreter.

" I have the honour to remain, sir, your excellency's humble and obedient servant,

Dᴇssᴇ Décazes."

It is with no hostile intent that I publish these documents. Had not the Duc Décazes, son of the author of the preceding letter, assumed the offensive attitude which he did toward Napoleon III. after 1870, I should never have made them public. Such records as these, however, confirm too strongly my estimate of the Emperor's character to permit my withdrawal of them from the legitimate curiosity and the impartial appreciation of the reader. Facts of a personal nature like this, form, when accumulated, the philosophy of history; and if this philosophy presents to the sentimental mind only vain and awful cruelties, it, nevertheless, possesses for intelligent men certain claims which we have no right to neglect.

Unlike the Legitimist party, the Orleanists had few women in their ranks whose influence was

strongly felt. Men of courage, energy, and initiative were numerous among them; and their
opposition was dangerous because it manifested
itself not only in words, but also in deeds; because it organised a merciless war, at once
political, social, and academic, against imperial
institutions, and preached liberal doctrines at a
time when the government of the Tuileries was
opposed to all progress, all concessions, all relin-
quishment of its absolutism. The Orleanist
party, with an incontestable shrewdness which
it afterwards lost, foresaw the evolution of the
Empire, and checked its course by monopolising
prematurely its doctrine. In this act lay its
strength for the conflict which it had undertaken; the manœuvre would have insured its
success at the critical moment had the men who
represented the princes been at a less distance
from the people. These men were but disguised
aristocrats, and wore with little ease their *car-
magnoles* of fine cloth; in politics, they were
but dilettantes; they conspired in lace and perfumes; they hated the people, and were, in
return, if not hated, at least absolutely ignored
by them.

VI.

M. EUGÈNE ROUHER.

THE Second Empire is marked by two distinct phases : one is its power and absolutism, the other its liberalism.   If we set aside all personal prejudice in regard to governmental theories, and seek but to understand justly the true nature of politics at that time, we can hardly fail to acknowledge that the Tuileries knew marvellously well how to put its doctrine of absolutism into execution, or that it chose with admirable wisdom the men whose office it was to propagate its principles.   In its phase of liberalism Napoleon III. showed far less ability. This period of his reign seems less like a well-defined political era than it does like a transition period.   We feel in it a spirit of hesitancy ; its movement is clumsy, and shows lack of experience, reminding us of the work of an artisan in whose hands is placed a tool whose use he does not understand, but with which he is told to make an article whose manufacture is not included in his craft.   During its liberal period the Empire was like this artisan. Liberty was a new tool, which it did not know how to handle.

Setting aside M. de Persigny, who was a warm friend of Napoleon III., and who, as such, co-operated in all his schemes with more or less willingness and good humour, the authoritative Empire finds its personification in two men whom events brought continually into prominence, and who reaped rich harvests from such events. These men were MM. de Morny and Rouher.

I have already sketched the character of M. de Morny, and I will not repeat myself here. It is, nevertheless, impossible for me to write the name of this politician without recalling the indignation roused by my estimate of his historic *rôle*, at the time when I first made public my convictions. Friends who were somewhat too fervent sought to invalidate my statements ; they flatly contradicted the story which represents the Emperor's brother as involved, not only in all the financial problems of the day, but also in a thousand petty intrigues.

Despite the high regard in which his admirers and allies hold him, M. de Morny is, nevertheless, a man whose character justifies such a story ; the following letter which, in 1850, that

is, toward the close of his political career, as he
stood on the threshold of the great fortune
which was to be his, he addressed to M. de
Ruoltz, inventor of the famous jewellery, will
prove to the reader that I did not deceive myself in regard to him, or collect my data at
random.

In the margin of this letter was written,
" Received September 6th, 1850."

" WEDNESDAY."
(Here was affixed a count's coronet.)

"MY DEAR RUOLTZ," — the letter continued — "I
have seen the Devaux. They, together with myself and
Brown, propose to buy your business in thirds, paying
down now ten thousand francs, and in a year or two fifty
thousand more if the enterprise succeeds. You understand that you will, in this case, have the certainty of
said amount and the probability of one-third with me in
the English concern. I have been asked to lay this proposal before you. Let me hear from you directly. Reply
that, despite the arguments which I present, and the confidence which I feel in the power of the Maison Devaux
to make the scheme succeed, and the difficulties which I
have presented, you nevertheless feel that the success
obtained in France warrants great expectations in England ; that certainly you have need of cash, but are not in
such sore straits that you can afford to sacrifice an offer
like this. Say, in short, that you consent, out of consideration for me, to interest yourself in the English business, and to receive twenty-four thousand francs in cash,
while you leave to MM. Devaux, de Morny, and Brown,
permission to buy out the business here within eighteen

months at sixty thousand francs additional, or to give you twenty-five per cent of the net proceeds.

" You understand that by such a reply you reject my proposals and offer me new conditions. Write me such a letter as early as possible, that I may close up affairs with the Maison Devaux upon this basis. You perceive how necessary it is to settle upon some definite sum, for the interest which you retain through me is the same. Write a judicious letter and address it to me.

TULLY ALLAN,
Kincardine on the Forth,
Scotland.

" I shall show your letter to the Devaux, so be careful to say nothing in it which they should not see. If you have anything of a private nature to write, use a separate sheet.

" Good-bye ; I write you in great haste.

" Most cordially yours,

" MORNY.

" Keep this letter."

It will be seen that before placing one's confidence in M. de Morny, it was necessary to know him well ; nor was this easy to do. It will also be seen that none understood better than he how to betray those who trusted in his honesty ; that none understood better than he how to make use of an annoying associate, or one from whom gold was to be had. He knew, too, how to instruct his coadjutors when the question concerned, according to his own expression, " some definite sum."

The preceding letter hardly admits of further illusions regarding the personal morality of M. de Morny. It will, I trust, put an end to the efforts made by the public for his rehabilitation, efforts which, if persisted in, are likely to become grotesque or *naïfs*.

In this chapter I shall not, however, pause to consider M. de Morny, but rather seek to represent the character of M. Eugène Rouher, a man who, starting as a small lawyer in Auvergne, became vice-emperor ; a man whose broad mountaineer's shoulders were not yet strong enough to bear the weight of the many responsibilities which, in consequence of his own talents, devolved upon him ; a man who, gifted with tenacity of purpose, courage, and power, attained his heaven ; but, whether angel or demon, was one day hurled from Olympus by a mighty blast of that wind of which Victor Hugo sings, a wind which breaks the wings of the eagle, and interrupts the course of the most brilliant meteors.

When M. Rouher came to Paris to seek his fortune, it was not in the character of a local celebrity, or of an hidden genius that he appeared. He turned, however, with disdain from his lawyer's career, and directed his attention immediately toward politics. Of humble birth, his sympathies were called forth by the class to which he by parentage belonged. He proclaimed liberal doctrines and was a fervent democrat ; emperors and kings had no more ardent enemy than he. We should not be too bitter in our criticism of public men whose convictions change somewhat with the course of events. I mention the political revolution of M. Rouher's views as a simple fact, and add no comment on it.

M. Rouher's personal appearance remained for some years, despite the cares which filled his subsequent life, much as it was when he first appeared before public notice. He was a fine-looking man, with a stalwart figure and a much developed chest. His aspect would have been agreeable, had not his carriage been somewhat ponderous, and his manner in strange contrast to the dandified clothes which he wore. He was not elegant at any time. ' He was one of the few public men who were firm in their allegiance to the Empress Eugénie, and obedient to her every command, without having, as an excuse for submission, either a secret or an avowed passion. This is an historic fact of some psychologic importance.

At the time that he pleaded before the tribunal at Riom, M. Rouher held advanced principles of liberalism ; but when he established himself in Paris his feelings became even more emphatic ; and when in 1846, and later in 1848, he presented himself at the elections, his confession of faith indicated a marked progress in this direction, and a strong sympathy with the masses.

M. Rouher was defeated in 1846, but was elected to the Chamber in 1848, and became from this time a prominent figure in the world of politics.

Certain letters have been placed in my hands which were written by M. Rouher after his election as representative of the people in 1848. At this time the future Minister of State under the Second Empire was uncertain whether he should love or hate Louis Napoleon Bonaparte, and the letters show such a curious state of mind on the part of their author that I shall quote them here. The first of these was written in June, 1848, and is addressed, as is the subsequent one, to M. de Latour, mayor of Clermont-Ferrand.

> " FRENCH REPUBLIC.
> MAYORALTY-HOUSE OF PARIS.

" I am writing you," runs the letter, " in the Hôtel de Ville, during the few moments left before the departure of the post. My day has been spent in visiting the field-hospitals and the advance stations. What horrible butch-

ery! The victory, however, is ours, or will be ours.
The troops are arriving from every side. Of all wars a
civil war is the most hideous. All will be over this evening or some time during the day to-morrow. The custom-
house has been razed by Lamoricière with incredible
dauntlessness. The Faubourg Saint-Antoine, that mighty
fortress, has been taken after a long and brave resistance.
At this very moment —it is half-past four o'clock — news
of a complete victory is brought. The insurgents made
use of a frightful stratagem. The houses along the block
communicated with each other, and our captains were
secretly murdered. If they have done us much injury,
they have also brought upon themselves awful retribution.
At our very side fifty of these were shot, and it was but
by dint of great effort that we saved one of the wounded
from being thrown into the water.

" The killed and wounded on our side number about
seventeen hundred at the present moment. By close of
the day the insurgents will have lost an equal number.

" The firing continues in the city, and all about us, as
I write. The victory gained by our troops is announced.
The Garde-Mobile showed sublime courage."

Two months after these events — August 13,
1848 — we find M. Rouher's interest engrossed
by the external condition of the country.

" These questions," he writes, after having spoken of
the elections to the general council; "these questions
are, no doubt, of importance, yet they can but appear
secondary when compared with those which occupy our
attention in the Assembly. I do not know what will be
the issue of the Italian problem. War, that awful scourge,
seems to me imminent. Our course in the matter has
been most unfortunate. Instead of letting things rankle,

as we have done, the question should have been fairly
submitted to Austria. ' Your war in Italy,' we should
have said to her, ' will involve you in inextricable difficulty. Vanquished by Charles Albert, you will be forced
to abandon your rule in Italy; are you victorious, you
will win France as an adversary. Is it not better to negotiate?' Austria, disturbed in its interior, uncertain of
success, would in this case have accepted diplomacy.
To-day, however, the victory of the army is assured, if its
march upon Turin is not impeded. Our relations with
England will remain as they are for some time; but when
we begin to speak of liberty, she will grow indifferent,
and slowly withdraw, leaving us to face Austria and Russia, or else to beat an ignominious retreat.

" 'The debates on the subject are not of a nature to
help the situation. This struggle which to-day has become inevitable, unless, indeed, we purchase our escape
by an act of cowardice, will be one of great violence, for
it is at once personal and political. I fear, too, that the
vote will not show us to be the stronger power."

We find, dated during the same month, the
following lines, written in a somewhat bitter
spirit, and yet with a certain tone of satisfaction in them.

" The pretended conspiracy of Girardin has ended in a
liberation. In return, the executive power has decided to
repress the paper which is called the *Représentant du
Peuple*, and which is edited by our *dear* colleague, Citizen
Proudhon, who in a series of articles had resumed the
development of his anti-socialistic doctrines. How much,
however, can we hope to accomplish by these measures
when confronted by the immense evil which we are called
upon to overthrow? The government is acting as though

it were half asleep. This is a moment when, to encourage the outbursts of confidence which are making themselves felt, measures should be taken to increase the credit and the circulation upon public works. Twenty projects of different committees have come to a standstill through the announcement of yet another scheme which shall combine the advantages of all the preceding ones; but no conclusion is reached. It would be an act of strange self-deception to believe that order is fairly established, and in delaying its consolidation great danger is incurred."

We feel in these lines the strength of the man so soon to become a public authority. M. Rouher did not long hold the liberal views which he entertained at this period. One year after the Revolution of 1848 — on April 14, 1849 — he turned against the ultra-revolutionists.

" La Montagne," he writes, " grows more and more violent as we approach the goal. We stand facing each other, waiting for the enemy to demand leave-of-absence, that we may disband.

" Considérant is before the tribune. He has read us a tremendous socialistic discourse, to which we had the patience to listen. Indulgence and sympathy in this unfortunate country are only called forth by follies."

In July of this same year, 1849, M. Rouher again turned his attention to the foreign policy of France, and gave expression to most pessimistic sentiments.

"Our diplomacy," he cries, " has been strangely polluted by the revolution of February. Our present representatives to foreign nations, those, at least, who occupy subordinate positions, bring us far less honour than discredit. Should M. de Tocqueville cleanse the Augean stables, there would be numerous vacancies made.

"Politics are still in an unsteady condition. They lack air and horizon. Despite the storms which have burst over our heads, the atmosphere remains heavy, and I do not see what we can do to clear it."

This correspondence is curious and interesting, inasmuch as it gives evidence of M. Rouher's accurate and keen judgment of affairs. History will show us whether, having attained to power, he preserved in the execution of his political designs the same calm insight and practical intelligence which at this time distinguished him.

M. Rouher, despite the liberalism of his early life, and despite the Olympian mask which later circumstances forced upon him, was during the whole course of his career a plebeian living in constant fear of the Revolution. His private life, at least, reveals him as such ; and it is said that nature finds its truest reflection in our more intimate relations.

Of simple habits and a lover of old traditions, the powerful minister of Napoleon III. was wont, after public and parliamentary discussions, after hours spent in studying questions of government, to withdraw to his own fireside at the hour of curfew, and to resume there the game of cards interrupted yesterday. To see him then, one would have thought him a merchant, who, his warehouse closed, had come home to put on his slippers and rest, feeling well content with the day's sales. There was nothing in his bearing at such times to suggest the orator who a few hours ago had held, by the power of his language, the attention of a great audience; nothing to suggest the statesman who had united and severed nations, or the mighty functionary who had held vehement discussions with the sovereign. The doors closed, he dealt and shuffled the cards in his great fat hands. M. Rouher was like the good plebeian of the story, who, when evening came, locked himself within the house, fearing thieves; and who, if he allowed himself to speak at all, uttered only curses against the disturbers of public peace, who, he imagined, were constantly seeking means by which to rob him of home and sustenance.

M. Rouher's *bourgeois* temperament colours his whole political life. He strove for authority and he gained it; but was his motive that of most men who reach after riches and power?

Did he seek through these the accomplishment
of great things? Was his the spirit of the
artist who but sees in his advancement, in
the authority which he wins, the progressive
and the increasing power of his art? No; M.
Rouher had no ideal before him; he played
his part in the Second Empire with no trans-
port of feeling or subtle joyousness of soul.
He took a *bourgeois* satisfaction in power as
other men of his rank and temperament do
in commerce, or in a profession; with him
as with these the joy lay in amassing a fortune and in the selfish interest of a goal to
be attained.

As I have already said, M. Rouher was at
the outset a liberal; yet so dry and methodical
were the workings of his mind that he failed
to understand Liberty. The ring of the word
enticed him as it does all youthful spirits; but,
born old, his allegiance could be but of short
duration. The passionate words which Liberty.
breathed forth frightened him; her needs and
her claims filled him with dismay; and he was
glad to escape from her tight embrace, from
that fierce caress which had very nearly brought
ruin upon him. He trembled as a child trem-
bles on the breast of a stranger; he grew rigid
in her arms, and never ceased to feel that tight-

ening of the skin and quiver of the nerves
which her kiss had occasioned. It was like
a little spot of goose-flesh which never passed
away.

Having arrived at his goal, having attained
the legitimate kingdom of his personality, his
every step was now characterised by an almost
irrational hatred of liberty; his days were
passed in a routine of duties which flattered his
love of authority, and was in harmony with the
tastes which he had inherited by birth. This
hatred and this routine were indeed the well-
springs of his oratorical power.

Magnificently eloquent M. Rouher was, without a doubt. At the outset of his career, however, there was nothing in his speech to foretell
the power which was in him, to suggest that
marvellous gift of language which became so
mighty a factor in the influence which he attained. At the time when, without sincere
conviction or enthusiasm, M. Rouher advocated
liberty, his voice was without ring, his accents
fell cold and lifeless, and no voice was raised
in answer to his appeals. It was not until he
took up the campaign in favour of absolutism
that he developed his oratorical gift. From
this time, however, he showed himself a magnificent master of rhetoric. He had to combat

men of immense talent, such as Jules Favre,
Jules Simon, and Emile Ollivier. He was not
content to use against these men merely the
weapon of his own governmental endorsement
signed by an official majority; he resolved to
rise to their level, to crush them. In this
attitude he is magnificent, and the eloquence
with which he met them is superb.

His attitude was that of a wild boar before a
pack of hounds. Squaring his great shoulders,
he faced them, and stood there, an object not
to be moved, an impassable barrier between the
Emperor and the masses, between the people
and the throne; he stood like a living rock, in-
tercepting the paths which led to the Tuileries.
When he raised his great fist, and set free the
thunder of his voice, the world knew that an
enemy of the Empire was about to fall to the
ground, as though felled by the stroke of a
mighty Titan.

His eloquence was in harmony with his spirit
and his attitude. Violent and argumentative,
made up of anathemas and again of heart-stir-
ring sentences, it overpowered completely the
oratory of the enemies of Napoleon III.; it
held the attention of the public, it dramatised
the dictates of conscience, it exalted loyalty, it
carried imagination into realms where are built

the air-castles of the world, where are born those wild enthusiasms in which is no rationality, and which preclude all argument.

M. Rouher's oratory was, to speak justly, strong, but coarse and less intellectual than what is popularly called "taking." He sung the praises of the sovereign whom he served, he waved the red flag before the nation; and in his every harangue used this double-edged sword, which had been sharpened against the whetstone of rhetoric. At a period when the glory of the Napoleonic legend filled all minds, at a period when the masses hesitated on the threshold of a future which should have no Bonaparte as master, it was, no doubt, easy to win public sympathy by rousing the fear of a to-morrow holding no certainty, and by catering to those sentimental feelings which clustered round the names of certain historic characters. That M. Rouher, however, knew how to turn to good advantage the somewhat commonplace methods of oratory which he employed is indisputable. As he showed so much talent in the adaptation and use of these methods, it surely would be vain to discuss their intrinsic worth.

It was not till after the death of M. Billault that M. Rouher occupied a place of any great

importance in the Tuileries. M. Billault stood
before him in the relation of a rival, one who
understood the position which he wished to
occupy, and who remained an obstacle in the
way of his political development. When, however, he died, the power of M. Rouher declared
and emphasised itself. Confident of his own
abilities, assured of docile minds in the super-
numeraries who paraded the stage upon which
he had now stepped, he placed his great, nerve-
less hand on the shoulder of Napoleon III.,
and from this time forth never separated himself
from the Emperor. He mounted steadily, step
by step, toward power, and each day which
passed saw his influence increase. He was
helped, too, in his schemes by the Empress,
whose tyrannical ideas were in harmony with
his own. He became her habitual and loyal
counsellor; he organised not only in the political world, but in the court itself, a party which
swept everything before it, whose rule in the
Tuileries was absolute, and which later, when it
acquired the name of the Empress's party, and
adopting an almost official etiquette, plunged
the country into ruin.

The Emperor, whose ideals were higher than
those of his government, whose heart was nobler
than his absolutism, became uneasy when he

found himself thus taken possession of. Despite, however, the philosophical dreams by which he was haunted, he fell a victim to M. Rouher's charms. He still stood too close to the *Coup d'État* to discard the services of a man in whom the whole doctrine of December Second seemed to find its synthesis; he was still too widely separated from freedom to impede this man in his work. He placed the nation in the power of M. Rouher, and awaited the results of his own effacement.

From this time M. Rouher held the reins of government, and reminds us of a charioteer, who, regardless of the ditches which may intercept his road, drives his horses on at a mad speed.

The masses were full of discontent, and through them was felt a slight stir of revolt. They aspired toward a political state more conformable to public sentiment; M. Rouher refused to adopt the policy for which they longed, and received with haughty disdain the denunciations which made themselves heard round him like the distant roll of thunder when yet only an occasional flash is seen in the sky.

At a moment when the *rôle* which France had filled in the Roman question seemed to be approaching its end, he encored the act, and,

submissive to the wishes of the Empress, led
it on to its most tragic scenes, and nearly involved us in trouble with King Victor Emmanuel. Called to speak publicly concerning the
abandonment of Rome by the Cabinet of the
Tuileries, an action which was much desired by
statesmen, and also by the nation at large, he
pronounced that terrible word, he thundered
forth his famous " Never," which plunged the
Emperor and the nation into difficulties from
which they were not to emerge.

In analysing even superficially the course of
action pursued by M. Rouher, we can hardly
fail to ask ourselves whether this man were
truly a statesman or capable of directing a
government.

Though in doing so I place myself in opposition to the majority of those who have studied
M. Rouher in his long career, I do not hesitate
to reply that this all-powerful minister, this vice-
emperor, was not capable of ruling a nation
wisely, was not a statesman in the truest sense
of the term.

He marched toward power accompanied by a
pride unexcelled in the annals of history; that
same pride it was which torments the parvenu
when he has attained unwonted riches. He
marched toward power accompanied by the

martial strains of dauntless determination not
to be subdued. He broadened his own personality that there should be no place at his side
for another to occupy. Egoistic and avaricious
of authority, he appropriated to himself all
political benefits, and was unwilling to share
with others, whoever they might be, any portion
of them. He was like those who, having with
much difficulty acquired a fortune, no longer
take thought for others, but fear to spend one
penny of their hard-earned savings.

His politics were personal ; his enjoyment of
power lay in no wish to bring his country glory,
or to ward from it threatening harm. As some
men are selfish in their love, looking upon its
object simply as a means of personal gratification, and having in their heart no wish to share
their joy, so he was selfish in his devotion to
politics.

A statesman or a great ruler is moved by
motives other than these. To such, too, is permitted that consolation for the weariness, the
struggle, the bitterness of life, which is to be
sought but in one place, the holy of holies ; yet
his thought and ideals should be directed elsewhere. In them the destiny of the universe
should find its reflection. Born in the heart of
the mountains, M. Rouher had constantly before

his sight, like a gigantic screen, the towering ranges of his native mountains; his view had no horizon, no expanse, and he was one of those who measure humanity by their own shadow.

A day came when France found itself involved in disaster. Time rolled on, and brought in its train the memorable year 1870, the echo of whose voice was lost in the sound of lamentation. M. Rouher was, at this time, as I shall better explain in a subsequent chapter, President of the Senate, and less occupied than usual with political responsibilities; the hour seemed favourable for him to resume power; and, able to avert through his counsels the dangers which threatened the country, he promised to lead the people on to victory — a victory which to him meant the fall of the liberals who had checked his authority in the government, and the realisation of his own schemes. M. Rouher became henceforth the grave-digger of the Empire; he weaved with his own hands the funeral veil which now replaced upon the imperial brows the diadems and flowers of former days. He became a criminal, for he sought war; and to seek war for any cause but the one greatest and highest cause, is to commit a criminal act.

Though the authoritative period of the Second Empire seems to find its embodiment in M. Rouher, there were, nevertheless, others who co-operated with Napoleon III. There were in the Emperor's court men whose diverse but incontestable powers have brought them before public notice. Among these were such names as those of MM. Chevreau, Duvergier, Riché, Jolibois, Vuitry, Haussmann, de Parieu, Persigny, Walewski, Magne, Buffet, de Royer, Pinard, Piétri, Alfred Leroux, Segris, Devienne, Émile Ollivier, La Guéronnière, and others. M. Rouher amused himself one day by analysing the characters of these men. The paper on which he jotted down his estimate of them for the inspection of the Emperor has been found, but I will cite here only a few of his comments.

In M. Chevreau, M. Rouher saw "the justification of hope for true parliamentary ability;" but he accuses him of being too easily led, and adds that "*l'odor della femina* will lead him far from the true path."

In regard to M. Riché he inserts the following criticism : —

"He is a fine orator and a man of philosophical and fertile mind, yet lacking in decision and too much of a dreamer; he suffers from disorder of the stomach, which manifests itself in unnatural appetites.

" The nomination of M. de Persigny or of M. Walewski," he continues, " as ministers of the interior, could
only be accomplished by a reversal of the political views
at present held.   These men would certainly introduce
into the ministry elements of trouble and of dissolution.

" M. Buffet has the spirit of a doctrinaire, and yet is
always undecided, never willing to lend himself wholly
to any enterprise."

M. Rouher is more explicit in regard to M.
Pinard, who was a favourite of the Empress, and
whose influence he feared upon her whom he
had himself undertaken to govern and over
whom he kept jealous watch.   She sometimes
resented his tutelage, and tried on numerous
occasions, despite the sympathy of feeling existing between herself and the minister, to free
herself from it.

" M. Pinard," said M. Rouher, " is a magistrate and
an orator, who has won some reputation at the palace
and in the Conseil d'État, and will probably give evidence to the Legislative Corps of his oratorical powers.
As a parliamentarian I recommend him to the Emperor's
notice.   To launch so young a man, however, in administrative affairs" (he was alluding to the ministry of the
interior) " in a personnel, in labours unfamiliar to him,
to give him a voice of authority in a difficult problem,
before his moral sensibilities are thoroughly developed
and established, seems rather to injure than to serve him.
The choice of M. Pinard would involve great risks.   I am,
however, convinced that, should he follow a less danger-

ous and more gradual ascent, and hold himself aloof
from administrative affairs, for which he is generally considered incapable, he will in time occupy a prominent
place in the Conseil d'Etat and later in politics."

As our attention has been incidentally attracted by M. Pinard, I beg permission to devote to him a few words of a personal character.

M. Ernest Pinard, former Minister of the
Interior under Napoleon III., published only
a few months ago some memoirs, after the reading of which I am forced to conclude that the
anecdotal portions of my preceding works,
"The Empress Eugénie," and "The Court
of Napoleon III.," have not been altogether
without influence on the statements there
brought forth.

M. Pinard, however, not satisfied with having
drawn upon me for much material, directs an
attack against me on page 142, § 1, of the first
volume of his work.

" I hear," writes he, "that some old stories are being
re-edited to-day, and have been singularly changed since
1870. This is no matter of surprise to me. An enter-
taining narrative, one which its author colours to suit his
own taste, is pretty sure to find readers. It is well for
the author who wishes to coin money out of small scandals; for the Court of Napoleon III., so misjudged by
those who have not known it, possesses an ever fresh
interest for the public."

M. Pinard, one of the most powerful and most unwise ministers of the Second Empire, has remained faithful, faithful to the verge of blindness, to his comrades of past days. We can only praise so excellent a loyalty, but even this high quality of soul does not prove him able to correct the documents which I possess concerning the Second Empire.

M. Pinard, during his ascent to power, remained much at the ministry and did not frequent the court. As his views were puritanical in the extreme, he held himself aloof from the frivolities which pervaded the habitual circle of friends surrounding the Emperor and Empress. Though competent, except for his systematic indulgence of persons and things, to speak of the political world to which he belonged, he is in no way competent to discuss the attitude of the social celebrities of either sex which crowded the Tuileries.

I have for some years been in the habit of meeting M. Pinard at the home of the Comte and Comtesse de J——— D———, whose hospitable drawing-rooms, situated in Rue du Mont-Thabor, were open to their devoted friends, and which have been but lately closed on account of the tragic death of the Countess.

M. Pinard knows, being aware of my family

connection with one of the keepers of the seals under Napoleon III., that I am well informed concerning the affairs of the Second Empire. He knows also the authentic value of the documents in my possession. His attack is, therefore, but a conventional defence, inspired by feelings of gratitude toward his former co-workers.

Why, however, in the lines which he devotes to me, does he bring forward the question of money, which is certainly of an importance quite foreign to that of history?

It is no secret that a writer negotiates with his publishers, and receives from them the proceeds which, as an author, are due to him. Will M. Pinard permit me to ask whether, in his own case, he has refused all remuneration for his work? To suppose that he himself undertakes the expense involved in the publication of his books, would be to suggest a lack of confidence on the part of his publishers. His own attitude surely proves the foolishness of the argument, and I wonder that M. Pinard did not make use of a better one.

I return to the character sketches of M. Rouher.

M. Emile Ollivier is the object of severe criticism.

" M. Emile Olliver," says M. Rouher, " is full of enthusiasm, and labours heartily in the cause which he undertakes; his is a versatile nature, whose liberality is
checked by an unfortunate infatuation, and whose useful-
ness is impeded by certain hostile and advanced views
which he holds upon political questions. Far from con-
forming to my feelings, he has become more strongly
than ever partner of the hostilities directed against me by
M. Walewski. He singled me out for criticism in the
Chamber, at the time when the former President of the
Legislative Corps came out against me in a journal. I
know, however, that these are but straw fires, which a
few favours will serve to extinguish."

Of M. Guéronnière he speaks highly.

" His fortune is," writes he, " somewhat embarrassed."
He then advises the government to give him an embassy;
" for," he adds, " he is a man whose support the nation
cannot afford to lose."

These are the principal features of the criti-
cisms made by M. Rouher of the politicians by
whom the Emperor was surrounded, and whose
access to power he himself had cause to fear.
His scheme was to cast upon them no real discredit, but to place them, by this rapid analysis,
on a decidedly secondary plane in the estima-
tion of the Emperor. His *bourgeois* temperament was, indeed, consistent in all its parts, and
was characterised by prudence as well as by
excessive joviality.

In a chapter specially devoted to the declaration of war in 1870, I shall, as I have already stated, make known the *rôle* which M. Rouher filled at that time. He was one of the most fervent advocates of war; and it was he who, summoned before the Emperor after a first defeat, prevented his re-entering Paris, drove him toward the frontiers, and forced Sedan upon him — Sedan, where the Emperor met with political death, where he was crushed by the most cruel misfortune of modern times.

On the 4th of September, having returned from his travels, M. Rouher occupied the presidential seat in the Senate; ignorant of the troubles which were agitating the nation at large, blinded by the pride which always characterised him, he denied the disturbed condition of affairs, denied the revolution, and finally closed the session, despite the voices of the anxious dignitaries who surrounded him.

" Messieurs," said he in a tone of fine irony, which betrayed, however, startling ignorance, " Messieurs, we will discuss this question to-morrow."

Having pronounced these words, which have in them a certain ring of grandeur, and which are among those which history records with pride, it might have been deemed praiseworthy to present himself before the Senate on the morrow, and to force the door of the chamber of deliberation, which had been closed against him. M. Rouher, however, did not wait till the morrow, but rested his dignity on the words we have quoted, and on the very evening of September 4th fled, evading the search of the indignant people, that people which for so many years he had scorned and trampled on.

Why, however, should we dwell too much upon the failings of humanity? Do not these form the basis of the philosophy of empires? Is it not these which tarnish the gilt of thrones? The lion is glad to emerge from his den, the eagle to descend from his eyrie, and to rest for a moment on the dunghill.   In the palaces of emperors and of kings, crimes and shame are found as elsewhere, and we are foolish to be surprised or indignant at them.

After the war and the fall of the imperial dynasty, M. Rouher came up before the elections of the National Assembly, and was sent to Versailles in the quality of deputy.   I have already told a story relative to that memorable session, in which he dared with much courage to defend the sovereign whom he had served. His political *rôle* was, however, at its end, and he made no attempt in subsequent years to resume his former career. His voice was, however, heard in affairs of commerce and in economic questions ; and his true abilities in these directions secured him, despite the hostility provoked by the bare mention of his name, respect in parliament, and praise from his most bitter enemies.

He was at this period the chief counsellor of the exiled sovereigns, and became, when the Emperor died, the mouthpiece of the Empress. All his powers were directed toward the restoration of the Empire, and his energies employed in preparations which would make this restoration possible. For this reason he disapproved of the departure of the Prince Imperial for Zululand, and in his despair implored the Empress to oppose the scheme. Destiny had, however, cast the dice, and M. Rouher had no longer control over its ruling hand.

I have already given, with the independence and the impartiality by which I always seek to characterise my writing, my estimate of M. Rouher. It is, however, important to state that this man, through whose hands passed thousands of millions of francs, had a high standard of honour and was of unimpeachable honesty. Poor when he entered political life, greatness and power left him at the last without a fortune, and it was with empty pockets that, in the downfall of 1870, he sank with the Empire. It may seem strange to extol a man's honesty ; it may be deemed unnecessary to search his clothing lest, haply, there should be hid in its lining money dishonestly acquired, and to visit his home and force his safe, there to seek the source of his revenues. At times, nevertheless, of public agitation, at times when the clink of gold is accompanied by the sound of many disturbances, curiosity is natural, and the homage paid to an honest man comes to have a double worth.

Through the midst of the luxury and of the riches of the Second Empire, through the midst of that luxury by which so many were made dizzy, and of those millions which were showered on the nation's representatives, M. Rouher passed with uncorrupted honour, taking with him only his paraphernalia of *bourgeois* excellence. If his politics were not faultless, if his attitude before the masses was criminal, though by profession he was a slave-driver of consciences, and a bitter enemy of liberty, though in his blindness and in the final expression of his pride he failed, standing in the shadow of the Empress, to see the disasters which were threatening our country, he still remains, in the sight of history, unsullied by his contact with money, his character free from the stamp of the coin.

Through the sensual extravagance of the Second Empire he also passed calm and indifferent. Of Puritan principles, the license practiced in the Tuileries, which he only visited officially, met with his disapproval — or was he, perhaps, unconscious of it? Of an unimpassioned temperament, and unenticed by the pleasures of the flesh, it would not be strange had he been ignorant of the wild extravagances of love which pervaded every corner of the Tuileries. Is not, indeed, the very perception, the very condemnation, of sensuality, an expression of that same quality?

There are men whom death seems to exalt, whose graves one views expecting to see rise from them some mighty spirit. M. Rouher is not one of these. As an object is magnified in a mirage, so in triumph his personality appeared colossal. In the moral agony of the Empire it assumed its just proportions, which, in the years to come, are destined to shrink little by little.

I have said that M. Rouher remained a plebeian, even in the most vigorous expression of his authority. He was, in the midst of his power, like a jolly peasant, who, having on one

happy day gained an immense fortune in a
lottery, places it under lock and key, caring
little to put it into active circulation, or to find
for it an useful expenditure.   To M. Rouher,
who thus hoarded the power which was his,
history, scornful of vain enthusiasms and of
party exaggerations, accords but one luminous
ray in that firmament of suns where is reflected
the genius of those who have travelled over the
earth, and who, like flashing meteors, or else in
the calm course of their orbits, have crossed the
path of humanity.

VII.

M. EMILE OLLIVIER.

THE name of M. Emile Ollivier is among those which one can but write with fear and trembling; it provokes, even to-day, feelings of resentment and words of malediction. Those who judge men only by the external aspect of their lives, persist in associating the name of M. Emile Ollivier with the disasters of 1870; they hold him responsible for the horrors of that year; through the ignorant and foolish prejudice by which they are controlled, they make him the cause of their despair, the object of their hatred. It requires, therefore, some courage to present him in a true light before the public, and to state at the outset that this man, falsely judged, falsely understood, or else the victim of hypocrisy and of political lies, which in the parliamentary world are far too frequent, merits neither hatred, curses, nor resentment; that he is above every insult which has touched him; and that he was, and is still, one of the greatest legislators of our time.

It is known with what freedom from prejudice
I have studied the men and the affairs of the
Second Empire. The more dangerous my
subject, the more faithful to my convictions I
feel that I should be. I shall not, therefore,
on this occasion abandon my habitual mode
of treatment, but, holding myself aloof from recriminations as from excessive praise, I shall
express with all that impartiality which I have
imposed upon myself, my true feeling in regard
to M. Emile Ollivier. In so doing I not only
satisfy my sense of self-respect, but must hope
to win the confidence of the public as I could
not do by entering into an impassioned argument.

Before personifying the liberal spirit of the
Empire, M. Emile Ollivier was for a long time
the authoritative and eloquent advocate of un-
qualified liberty among the people. The opposition which he waged against the Empire was
of a peculiar nature. While his political co-
workers adhered to their former programmes
and to republican principles, M. Emile Ollivier
preserved his independence from any too dis-
tinctly organised line of conduct, and never
ceased to affirm that the war which at the present moment he waged against the Tuileries was

by no means without promise of happy termination, and that he was willing to relinquish it the first moment that the imperial government consented to modify its *régime* in accordance with the progressive ideas of the time. When, at a future day, M. Emile Ollivier expressed his satisfaction with the liberal policy adopted by the Emperor Napoleon III., he was accused of abandoning his former principles. Such an accusation is, however, a great injustice; he was at that time thoroughly consistent with his attitude in the past, and but put into practical execution sentiments which he had hitherto expressed.

The famous " Five," whose leader, together with M. Jules Favres, he was, shared his feeling at that time. MM. Hénon and Darimon were frequent visitors at the Palais-Royal, but felt no fear in appearing in the presence of the Emperor, while M. Ernest Picard, a man of intelligence, and ungoverned by prejudice, would not unwillingly have become a co-worker with Napoleon III. When, indeed, war broke out in 1870, he was nominated as senator, and his name presented to the sovereign.

It should, however, be stated that among these men M. Jules Favre alone maintained to the last the convictions of his life, and made no pretence of making peace with the Empire; he held firmly, under the new order of things, as in the old days of December Second, to his republican creed, and neither his words nor his public acts admitted of the slightest equivocation.

The voice of M. Jules Favre carried with it great weight in the parliamentary discussions of the Second Empire, and was one of strong influence in the opposition movement. Although this chapter belongs properly to M. Emile Ollivier, at one time his friend, but who afterwards became his rival and his enemy, it has seemed to me necessary to pause and consider him.

M. Jules Favre was an orator of true power, and the charm of his voice is still remembered. This voice was, however, capable of fierce tones in which a vehement and savage oratory found expression; at a time when men were still liable to parliamentary challenge, and when the enthusiasm of the masses was unroused by the course of events, his eloquence stirred them, and inspired their minds with hope and with ambition; their eyes magnified him who was thus their friend, as a child's thought magnifies the greatness of some fabulous hero whose wild adventures have been recounted.

Sessions of any solemnity at the Palais-Bourbon, sessions during which political questions

were exclusively discussed, were most rare under
the Second Empire; but when they did occur,
M. Jules Favre assumed a curious and interesting attitude.

This man, who knew so well how to address
the people, had an instinctive dislike of a multitude. On the days when he was to speak, he
hastened to the Legislative Corps before the
doors were opened, and withdrew to an ante-
room, where he sought to collect his powers.
Stretched on a lounge, or reclining in an arm-
chair, his large portfolio upon his knees, he
meditated upon his coming address. From
time to time an awful grimace would distort
his mouth — that satanic mouth, in which the
tongue of anger would seem to play, and at
the same time kisses to linger; that famous
mouth, which could express with equal force
hatred and love. With his right hand, white
and delicately veined like that of a woman, he
stroked gently his long beard, in which were
some streaks of grey. From time to time he
would shake back his long, thick masses of hair,
and then become motionless once more, absently
listening to the distant stir of life, cradled vo-
luptuously in his dream, in his power and in
his popularity.

He would then emerge from his retreat, and

proceed toward the assembly-room, to see if his audience were fully gathered. Satisfied as to this, and winning more than one admiring glance, as also more than one expression of hostility, he would slowly traverse the semicircle. The public responded eagerly when it heard that he was to speak. Ambassadors, statesmen, princes of the blood, electioneers, noisy financiers, the great women of fashion, women prominent in politics, enthusiasts from the lower classes, and the great courtiers of the day, alike bowed down before him, and cast upon him glances of admiration and smiles of favor as he passed. He heard every slightest remark which was exchanged; and under this rain of words and of tender glances, he drew himself up with a delicious sense of satisfaction, as if he would encore it all, his heart exalted by the force of pride. The perfumes which filled the room, the toilettes which were about him, the bated breath, the women who waited in eager expectation and with heaving breasts, intoxicated him. He breathed in the fragrance of the room, his lips quivered as under the pressure of a kiss, when he saw the approving smiles which were showered upon him; a sensual ecstasy took possession of his mind and body; he stumbled in passing out of the hall, and when he was once again in the ante-room, he sank down, exhausted, with a long, deep sigh.

He was superb when standing in the tribune. His huge figure commanded the admiration of the Assembly; his broad shoulders seemed to fill, nay, to outflank, if I may so speak, this tribune, which grew too narrow for him. His sleek white hands played along its edge in nervous unrest. He directed one glance toward the crowded benches of the hall, toward the galleries filled with those who had come to hear him, then gathered himself together, and in accents dull and monotonous at the outset, and vibrating with emotion as he continued, M. Jules Favre spoke.

Slowly and at length he unfolded the subject of his discourse, considering in its minutest details the subject which interested him. At times his mouth was distorted by that strange, characteristic grimace, and he would break out into violent expressions. He revelled in the sound of applause which filled the left wing of the room. His voice became more urgent, more bitter; and it was with a sort of death-rattle in his throat that he described the tyranny, the moral agony, in which he claimed that the country was dying. A smile would then return to his lips as he assumed a tone of mockery, and exchanged the dagger of hatred for the corded lash of sarcasm ; then, suddenly, he would break forth once more into fury. He walked up and down in the great tribune, which creaked under his steps. His arm extended as though to indicate an enemy, had an awful fascination ; his nostrils dilated, his eyelids opened and shut in a weird, grotesque way, while his chest heaved and swelled like a smithy's forge. Every now and then one of his strange, rough gutturals would interrupt a sentence, breaking into it like an hiccough. His body thrown backward, his hand thrust forward with a threatening gesture, none knew better than he how to curse and to imprecate. His dark face became purple, the blood mounted to his neck, his hair fell in tangled masses over his forehead, while the grimace on his mouth became convulsive.

His perorations were marvellous. His excitement increased toward the close of his discourse, but it was no longer anger or hatred which inspired him ; he abandoned for a moment the narrow radius of his subject, and generalised the whole problem which he was treating, his accents growing gentle as he spoke of liberty. He felt a thrill of voluptuous joy, he caressed liberty as does a man the woman whom he loves; he adorned it and made it beautiful, he depicted it under its most seductive aspects, he loved it as a serpent loves a bowl of milk. His audience listened to him astonished. Suddenly he raised a last cry, a shudder shook him, a spasm controlled his whole frame. He then brought his address to an end, and in his final sentences rang, as it were, prophetic despair and anguish. He forgot the great hall and his colleagues. The people, however, could hear him none the less, and it was well for them that he spoke. When at last he was silent, he still remained for a moment in the tribune as though riveted there, as though fascinated by the strange ecstasy which had taken possession of him.

There were few republican *salons* under the Second Empire; and the men of the opposition gathered for conference either in the offices of some of those few journals which were bold enough to oppose the policy of the Tuileries, or else at the home of one of the members. M. Jules Favre was among those who thus received his friends, studying with them the questions of the day, and determining their attitude in public debates.

He was the recognised and respected leader of the liberal party, to whom the heads of cer-

tain cliques and many parliamentarians came,
especially during the last days of the Empire,
to receive orders before giving battle. They
issued from such conferences armed and instructed, moulded according to his wishes,
submissive to his views, charmed, too, and
anointed for the battle like the athletes of
ancient days. Old and young listened to his
sacred words — the young for the sake of im-
buing their hopes with a new enthusiasm, the
old to strengthen their convictions, which,
through a continual course of disappointments,
at times wavered.

When the Empire adopted its liberal policy,
and when M. Emile Ollivier took direction of
the new movement, M. Jules Favre was filled
with both surprise and fear, — with surprise because his rival had outstripped him in the race
after power, with fear because new complications threatened, whose results he could not
foretell.

When M. Emile Ollivier, son of the pro-
script, became an advocate of the Empire, the
ranks of the republican opposition felt that they
had received their death-blow. He had a commanding figure, a large, thick mouth, and eyes
hidden by enormous glasses ; but behind his
cold personality lay a violent temperament and

terrible passions. His attitude in the tribune was as authoritative as was that of M. Jules Favre, who, from the outset, realised that he should sometime hate this man.

There was another obstacle in the way of M. Jules Favre's personal aggrandisement. On the horizon of the political world, or more properly of the republican world, a dangerous man arose, whose earnest and powerful words attracted the attention of the public, and gave birth to new hopes and enthusiasms. This man was M. Léon Gambetta ; and M. Jules Favre, though he received him with every appearance of joy, was frightened by the popularity which he won, and by the consequent lessening of his own.

M. Léon Gambetta was such a character as one calls a "type." He arrived in Paris from the south of France, where he was born ; and there, for a time lost in the crowd, he watched and waited. A Jupiter Tonans of breweries and of wine-cellars, he won the reputation of a statesman in the narrow streets and small hostelries of the Latin Quarter. One fine day, however, he went before the bar to plead in a political suit, and one evening he made his voice heard in an electoral reunion, where he exposed a complete programme of social re-

forms. He won on these occasions the approbation of the people, helped somewhat by his
southern bombast. He insured his nomination
to the deputation, and was at the end elected.
Despite his fretful voice and his emaciated
body, he acquired an immediate and a real
authority.

His manners in society were peculiar to himself. He walked on wax floors with his legs
wide apart to prevent slipping. When he perceived a friend or an acquaintance across the
room, he would call out, "Te!" He was very
familiar in his gestures, and would seize those
to whom he was talking under their arms, and
pull them about roughly, often playing with
their coat-lining, and tapping and thumping
their bodies. When he encountered a political
adversary, he had always at his command subtle
methods of changing his spirit to that of a friend
and partisan. He entrapped him in his bombast, in that never-failing southern bombast,
until at last one was ready to forgive his inde-
corum and his bad manners, and to excuse every
failing, conscious only of his kind spirit and his
good comradeship.

He was often wonderfully fortunate in his
choice of language; it was he who invented
that famous word "irreconcilables" to desig-

nate the militant element of the opposition; this epithet travelled through the country, and ensured his social success better than an hundred discourses would have done.

The world of Bohemia entered the Chamber together with him in 1869. This Bohemia, however, bore no resemblance to that of former times; it nourished neither love nor vague dreams, and had in it no spirit of sentimentality. It was the popular Bohemia which spoke through Léon Gambetta; and it became terrible, hip-shot and ragged as it was, when he made its voice heard in the parliamentary tribune. It acquired a rough vigour like that of a working-woman; it spoke with boldness, and in accents of intoxication, like those which are heard in the street, and became like a swarm of enraged hornets escaped from the hive.

M. Jules Favre was afraid of the boldness of Gambetta. He tried to keep him always in view, to make of him a sort of lion. He argued that his only safety lay in maintaining control over this man, in having him, as it were, under his thumb; for, did he escape, he would have everything to fear from him.

M. Jules Favre was ready to endure Gambetta just as he was, with his careless habits and his disordered hair. Gambetta did not know it; but

he was made to pass under the yoke by M. Jules
Favre, who awed by his aristocratic bearing this
rugged revolutionist, and who petted and caressed him, feeling it far wiser to be on his
guard, and to defend himself against this product of street-life, against his power and authority.   Gambetta, the Bohemian, would be
looked upon as a gamin in Paris, an object from
whom the social world would turn away, and
from whom there was little to dread; Gambetta
adorned with conventionalities would become a
rival, and M. Jules Favre had already as such
M. Emile Ollivier.

M. Léon Gambetta, nevertheless, became one
day just that power which M. Jules Favre had
feared to see arise; he became the controlling
voice in Parliament and throughout the whole
nation; it was his influence which caused the
downfall of the government which succeeded
the Empire, that ill-conceived and detested government of Marshal Macmahon.   Social and
diplomatic worlds were opened to him.   He
was no longer that colossal anomaly of former
days, no longer the intemperate politician, uncontrolled in word and in deed, and newly im-
ported from the south.   He was eminently
conventional; his hair, which of old fell over
his shoulders like a lion's mane, was now exqui-

sitely brushed and curled. He no longer called
" Te ! " when he entered the luxurious drawing-
rooms whose hospitality was freely extended to
him ; he was able to keep his balance on waxed
floors without spreading his legs apart. He
remained, however, enthusiastic and excitable ;
and it happened occasionally that, carried away
by his interest in a discussion, he would seize
his interlocutor by his coat-collar, which he
pulled and shook as though he would tear it to
pieces. Gambetta, however, was celebrated ;
Gambetta was powerful ; and his social lapses
were attributed to his fiery temperament, and
were tolerated. They were laughed at good-
humouredly, with a flattering sense of condescension and a blissful vanity on the part of
those who were his social superiors ; but Gambetta, perceiving the smiles, became suddenly
cold, assumed his polished manners, and would
have deceived the most careful observer. He
was a clever man, and one of true intellectual
calibre. Starting at the very base, he had
climbed the highest peak, and attained a power
not to be overlooked. From below, the world
might look up and salute him. His life was
certainly not commonplace. It had advanced
by means of long, high flights ; it was full of
charlatanisms, of cowardice, and again of cour-

age, and is an almost unanalysable compound.
Whatever the verdict of the past, whatever that
of the years to come shall be, it is worthy of
some degree of admiration and also of envy.
This democrat, this product of an obscure corner of France, had a subtle sense of distinctions,
and a statesmanlike foresight and judgment.
Europe and the foreign courts feared at the outset his flushed face and his imprecating voice
with its tones of martial command, its low
thunder like that of cannon, and, withal, its
irresistible magnetic power.   He had, however,
the good fortune to charm the Prince of Wales,
as, indeed, he charmed little and great who
came into contact with him.   His pride and
self-consciousness were calculated to reassure
those who were inclined to doubt.   He, on the
other hand, feeling himself obeyed, admired, and
applauded by his very opponents, hurried on
toward glory, intoxicated by popularity.   Gambetta was a patriot ; and France loved him, re-
membering that in hours of affliction he had
consoled, he had revived its courage, by telling
it falsehoods perhaps, but with a spirit of true
righteousness, and by giving to such falsehoods
the sacred character of dauntless resolution and
of noble hopes.   Gambetta was generous and
good.   His friends adored him ; and he, despite

the constant praise and approbation which were showered on him, was more gratified by their proofs of affection than by the voice of public eulogy, which made itself heard round him like the sound of a rising tide.

M. Jules Favre was unwilling to share with others any portion of his political success. He had earned, by the sweat of his brow, the position which he occupied, and he was jealous of its possession. He wished for himself its full and undivided occupancy, and would have protested to the very death against the participation of others in his privileges. He had been cast naked and unknown into the streets of a great city. His heart had often suffered from cold in the midst of his work; he had met with outrageous scorn from that great class of ninnies and of egoists by which the world is populated, a class made up of the rich and the fortunate, and whose stormy tide carries with it great blocks of gold which bar the way to thinkers and to ambitious men whose hearts are filled with longing to reach their goal. He remembered now with bitterness this phase of his life, and the remembrance furnished his heart with claws. What could modesty accomplish in the world of ease and luxury at whose threshold he stood? Nothing. It was through

work alone that he could attain the existence
for which he longed, and it was as a reward for
work that he claimed his share of life's pleasures.   He could have divided his time as others
have done, and consecrated one part to study,
the other to rest, to the joys of love, and to the
satisfaction of the senses; but he was among
those who make no false resolutions.   He had
crushed in himself every youthful aspiration,
all thought of pleasure, and had nailed mind
and flesh and nerves to his desk, resolving
neither to close his books nor to raise his eyes
till he had attained his object.   This self-
inflicted abuse embittered him; and now that
he had become a power and an object of envy,
he remembered with a feeling of resentment his
former isolation and his hours of moral suffering
and of hard struggle.   His life had been one of
unspotted chastity, and his determination that
it should be so rose like a lump in his throat
and choked him with rage and with regret.   It
was, however, through his purity of life that he
acquired his strength.   From the outset of his
career he exerted complete control over his
feelings, and was unflinching in this self-
imposed mortification of the flesh.   He had,
it is true, moments of feverish and passionate
revolt; his heart was touched by sensual

beauties, and his nature more than once breathed in the fragrance of some fair woman who passed him by. The burden, however, of his pride, of his studies, and of his ambition soon crushed in him the fugitive passion ; and it was with a steady and an even step that he entered his own door, and seated himself at his table which was covered with papers and books. The barrenness of his youth had given his face the pinched and bloodless look of an ascetic, and an expression of unrest like that of one who has suffered from poverty and disgrace. To see him walk through the streets with his great shoulders thrown back, his black hair hanging in profusion, his face wearing its expression of severity, was to be reminded of a wild animal seeking prey.

His hour came at last. He suddenly rose from the crowded and dirty streets and *salons* of Paris. Through the midst of the Empire's deep silence his voice was heard ; and its echo was carried far, like the howl of a hungry wolf prowling the forests by night. He saw ahead of him a multitude drunk with its pleasures, and this multitude sought to keep him back. He, however, elbowed his way through its midst, he raised his clinched fist and overthrew every obstacle. He understood that

there was a great work to be done at the beginning of this epoch of struggle and of visionary
dreams. The imperial sun shone in full splendour, and threw floods of light upon the past,
whose legendary spirit had been revived. The
sunrise gun of the Bonapartes saluted each
morning the dawn of new glories ; men shouted
the praises of the sovereign, and women laid at
his feet their hearts, which were woven of the
threads of worldly desire. The spirit of luxury
used its corded lash on reformers and on philosophers. From one end of France to the other a
great chain extended, composed of the fools and
extravagant pleasure-lovers who had been frightened by long years of austerity, but who rose
when the reveille sounded at the Tuileries.
Life was good ; humanity ate and drank and
made love. Wine and blood mingled ; and
bodies were made to dance to the music of an
invisible orchestra, the death-dance of voluptuous indulgence. Thought, however, was dead.
It lay far away in the corner of some cemetery,
buried in the common grave where are laid
misery and shame. Soul had flowed from the
veins of the nation, veins severed by the knife
of materialistic pleasure. The spirit of sensuality now stretched itself out, and fed upon the
lips of false love as a courtier upon those of a

fair virgin. Laughter was the order of the day. The world was made to laugh at any cost, and those who allowed themselves the luxury of weeping were sent away.

M. Jules Favre was conscious of all the benefits which he might reap from this half-mad world. It required some courage to seek to check a movement which was carrying the people with it. He had the necessary courage, however, and he rose before the nation. He turned toward the graveyard, where he found, in misery and the agony of death, thought and liberty. He descended into the grave where they lay not quite motionless, gnawed by the worms of oblivion; and taking in his arms what remained of the two bodies, he cast them one fatal day on the steps of the imperial throne. A strange terror took possession of the nation. The odour of the tomb, mingling with the seductive perfumes of the women, slowed for a moment the dizzying dance of the century. Society was astonished, and asked who this man was, this new Hamlet, who went by night to graveyards to play with the dead. Spirits of the past rose at the voice of M. Jules Favre, and through the nation there was felt the stir of life like the restless movement of caged beasts longing for liberty.

During the last days of imperial Rome, when the laughter of partricians was suddenly interrupted by the voice of a reformer, the nation sought out that voice, and took possession of the rising tribune, and cast him into the circus. The Cæsars, having fallen into an unwholesome sleep, did not wish to be disturbed in the satiety of their pleasures. Those who were content with life as it was, were surprised by the sudden apparition of M. Jules Favre, and tried to imitate the Cæsars of former days. They cried shame at him, for he was a revolutionist whom it was essential to suppress. Though there was no arena into which they might throw him, there was still the galley; it would be very simple to send him to the colonies. Every act of folly which anger can inspire was suggested and countenanced. The Emperor alone remained ignorant of public sentiment, holding himself aloof from all the follies which eddied round his throne. He left M. Jules Favre entire liberty to insure his authority and to attain his goal. M. Jules Favre, for his part, was little disturbed by the insults which the papers each morning heaped upon him and which in the evening were repeated in the drawing-room. He ignored, or feigned to ignore, the forebearance shown him by the sov-

ereign, and followed his straight path without
pause or digression. He spoke in the Palais
de Justice; he monopolised every political proceeding which attracted public notice, and his
power increased with conspicuous rapidity. He
had made a great leap from the bench where
he had once sat, and at the time of elections he now set his great body down in the
popular tribune of public reunions. His success had been tremendous. Having attained
the first halting-place in his career, he paused
for a moment and took time to consider the
best course; then, with a sense of assurance,
defied with renewed vigour the governmental
majority which rebelled at his advance.

The elevation, the triumph, of M. Jules Favre,
had certainly exerted no check on the enticing
follies by which the generation was led. Vague
anxiety was roused by his extraordinary success,
and the people realised that a new and terrible
power had risen; but so slight an event could
hardly serve to change the tide of life. They
even rushed on more rapidly than ever in their
race after joy, love, and largess; they raised
their laughter louder than before when this
great orator spoke, preferring not to hear his
voice, which sounded like the roll of thunder
rising above the orchestra of a dance-hall.

He, however, valued but little the praise
which he won, and was little disturbed by opposition. He counted, weighed, and classified
the feelings of hatred which he roused, not for
the sake of satisfying any feeling of anger or of
bitterness, but merely that he might understand
the conditions surrounding him, and be ready,
should necessity arise, to combat them.

Faith in virtue and in friendship seemed to
him, in this age of selfishness and of delirium,
vain and deceptive. To give one's love to any
human being, to consecrate to anybody the best
that is in one, without having even the satisfaction of believing that at death this person
will come to press the cold and rigid hand,
seemed to him an act which involved much
unnecessary suffering. M. Jules Favre was a
sceptic, and a pessimist in his methods of reason-
ing. In politics he would have demanded
nothing better than to belong to no party;
but such a line of action would have been dangerous; and it was necessary for him to choose
his side, whether he did so from earnest and
passionate motives or with a spirit of calm
indifference. He chose the former, and directed his sympathies — for he had thorough
control over his nature — toward revolutionary
doctrines. He became the advocate of liberty

through no heart-felt conviction, but because he found in liberty a mine not yet worked, or at least but insufficiently worked, and from which he hoped to gain some riches. Had austerity been the order of the day, he would, perhaps, have preached a life of pleasure, and with his soft and aristocratic hands have shaken the bells upon the jester's cap. Never having truly lived, M. Jules Favre was yet *blasé*. There was no hypocrisy in his nature. "Force is stronger than justice," was the motto of his life, the device which he had ever before him. He felt that logically and inevitably the strong must impose upon the weak. The success of his plans was largely due to the fact that he built on this basis, and to attain his purpose abandoned every prejudicial scruple. He was shrewd and far-seeing, and in this and in no other qualities lay his power.

Judged according to the social conventionalities which regulate our political and moral condition, M. Jules Favre was a dishonest man, capable of committing any roguery conducive to the realisation of his wishes and to the attainment of a fortune. Should we, however, on this account judge him severely? Should we not take into consideration the circumstances under which he was born, and by which he be-

came the natural product of a spirit of ill-will
and of vulgarity? The virus of hatred had
infected his blood; but was it not the long
period of mourning through which he passed
in his solitary, his ascetic life, and the battles
waged against his violent and passionate nature,
which had engendered this venom, or which, at
least, had determined the evolution of his nature? He was undoubtedly a philosopher; his
doctrines were based on ancient cynicism, had,
indeed, but cast off the mantle of antiquity,
and adorned themselves in that of an advanced
civilisation.

His authority had been long in developing;
he had the opposing force of the Empire to
overcome, but, once gained, his power was no
mockery; it rose like a threatening spirit on
days of solemn festivity, and it passed to the very
foot of the throne. From the top of the legislative tribune M. Jules Favre placed his authority in opposition to that of the sovereign, and
was master of a pack of howling rebels. He
was invulnerable from many sides, yet he was
not thoroughly consistent in his Jacobite severity. There was in his refined and sensitive
nature a sort of veiled mysticism which he
himself had never thoroughly analysed. This
quality, which his purity of life served to ex-

alt, led him toward a religious idealism, and
prompted a life of renunciation and of contem-
plation. Having denied himself sensual joys,
and believing that he had destroyed all fleshly
desires, M. Jules Favre still felt a need of the
extra-natural which takes possession of the ascetic with all the imperative force of a mono-
mania. He required a safety-valve for his
overflowing thought, and made the church a
confidante of his secret ecstasies, for he was sincerely religious. At seven o'clock each Sunday
morning he went to the Madeleine, where he
listened piously, his nose in a great prayer-book,
to the orisons of a priest. This curious trait
of character, which was universally recognised,
called forth no mockery from his political
friends. They were afraid of him, and well
knew that were he once irritated he would be
slow to forgive. Only one man, a Don Quixote
born of the Revolution, dared to criticise him.

"He is," said this man, "a Marat turned
Jesuit." This remark, which described him
most truly, had an immense success, and has
retained its celebrity.

M. Jules Favre of his own free will consecrated his whole being to the selfish satisfaction
of his political ambition, and yet politics made
of him an object of hatred. Unknown to him-

self, his weary soul sought to quench the thirst from which it suffered; it asked of the church the rest and peace supplied by its shadowy vaultings, and there it breathed in great draughts of life which he denied it. The spirit of sensuality, checked and restrained by a terrible will, groaned still within this pure man, in whom were yet many sleeping passions. The spirit of sensuality was not dead, but only bound, and it waged constant warfare with his self-interested ambition. A warfare such as this is both cruel and hideous. It is a monstrous thing to see a soul struggling in the tight embrace of an insatiable egoism. M. Jules Favre never spoke of the secret struggles of his life, of his nights without sleep, of the nervous sufferings by which he was tortured, or of those wild passions which interrupted the peace of his solitary hours. He kept such trials secret to himself. On the day succeeding a great moral crisis he was just as cheerful, just as calm and authoritative, as before. His heart was a sealed book, and it was in his excessive reserve that his power lay. He had truly cause for pride; for despite every failing, every weakness, he remained a great and an awe-inspiring man. He was, perhaps, a "Marat turned Jesuit;" but such an epithet seems still to say, "This is indeed a man."

I am, perhaps, allowing my thoughts to be carried far from the original subject of this chapter, but I repeat that M. Jules Favre occupied under the Second Empire a place of too great importance to admit of neglect. It has seemed to me equally natural to mention M. Gambetta here. My sketches of their characters will certainly not be unwelcome to the reader; for, if he has lived during the time of Napoleon III., they will call to his remembrance the physiognomy of the principal men who directed the liberal movement at this period; if he is too young to remember this reign, they will give him an artistic appreciation of the celebrated people and events which have now passed away.

I return now to M. Emile Ollivier.

Of all the men who, under the Second Empire, by their earnest language and their political activity, held the attention of the people, M. Emile Ollivier should rise in startling relief, should be granted an high place on the horizon of history. There was in his life an element of mystery and of fatality, which pursues him even now in the false appreciation which attaches to his name. It was, indeed, by a mysterious fatality that he was chosen as an instrument through which Napoleon III. should speak to the people.

M. Emile Ollivier was not a plebeian like M. Rouher, for his tastes were literary, and he was himself a writer of some little power ; nor was he, like M. Jules Favre, an ascetic constantly exposed to the danger of losing the fruit of his abstinence by a sudden and imperative passion, by a sudden revolt of the senses, for he had no terror of women ; yet he remained faithful to his home and family, only abandoning the field of political battle that he might enjoy the repose of his own hearth and devote his thoughts to the welfare of his household.

His political career began early ; and, by a strange coincidence, this career, which ended in sorrow and disaster, also opened with the noise of calamity. On the day succeeding the second of September, when he was hardly grown to manhood, he saw his father dragged from casemate to casemate, saw him barely escape banishment to Cayenne, which was the penalty imposed on many of his co-religionists. Thanks to the friendly intervention of Jerome, the old king of Westphalia, uncle of Louis Bonaparte, thanks also to the friendship of Prince Napoleon, M. Emile Ollivier was able to obtain the release of his father and to procure him a place of safety abroad.

Owing to his strongly philosophic spirit, his

memory of these days was mingled with no sense of bitterness, though they had brought such keen suffering to one whom he adored, and by whom he was intelligently and tenderly loved. His opposition to the Empire was in no sense due to the trials which he had suffered or to feelings of personal resentment ; and I am among those who, far from condemning this absence of bitterness as blameworthy or politic indifference to the claims of affection, find in it a spirit of stoicism which can but inspire admiration.

This man seems, in truth, to have thought little of popularity or power as far as these remained a mere personal gratification ; his aim seems to have been to attain a political ideal which should be as far as possible conformable to his convictions and to his theories of liberality ; never, however, did he, in seeking the realisation of his hopes, place himself in conspicuous opposition to the authority of the Emperor Napoleon III. His attitude before the public was never that of an irreconcilable enemy of the Tuileries, nor was his position before the Tuileries that of a candidate for any favour, or of a man hoping for a ministry ; he waited quietly, absorbed in the pursuit of his own purposes, the advent of a new order of things to which he would not be loath to give his approbation and his succour. Such an attitude as this was full of danger; and to maintain it required all the charm of language, all the authority which his name commanded.

From the time of his election to the Legislative Corps, and, indeed, from that of his entrance into the Palais-Bourbon, he was fully aware of its consequences. He wrote to his father, who was in exile in Florence, to ask if it were right for him to take the oath of allegiance to the Emperor, whether he could with a free conscience swear fidelity to a man who had taken from him that which was dearest on earth? If, in short, his duty were not to refuse an oath which seemed a violation of conscience, and whether by taking it he would not necessarily sacrifice his independence? His father replied that he was at liberty to take the oath which was required of him; that in so doing he would not abandon his independence or his convictions, but that it would impose on him certain consequences; that it would, for instance, forbid traitorous designs, and compel him to pursue his labours, though not under the patronage of the Emperor, at least without enmity against him.

Henceforth M. Emile Ollivier, strengthened

by his father's sanction and approval, saw
clearly the course which he was called on to
follow through life; and no circumstances led
him to diverge from the path which he had
chosen.

I feel it necessary to give here an impartial
account and explanation of the line of conduct
pursued by M. Emile Ollivier under the Second
Empire. My judgment is, I know, in opposition
to that of most who have studied the character
of this man. It will, perhaps, astonish those
who are the too violent partisans of a system
which grants no indulgence to the acts committed by mankind, and wound the unpropitiat-
ing faith of those who, having wept, have no
pardon in their hearts, no power to forget the
cause of their tears; yet it will, I hope, con-
tribute to a better comprehension of the personality of M. Emile Ollivier, and to a more
accurate observation of the phases of his political career.

The eloquence of M. Jules Favre was justly
the object of much pride during the Second
Empire, and its academic qualities much extolled. The eloquence of M. Emile Ollivier
was no less celebrated, nor did he have less
enthusiastic admirers; that faultlessness of lit-

erary quality, so rare among orators, distinguished him always.

M. Jules Favre advanced, as we have seen, toward the tribune in the strength of his commanding physique and of his deep voice with its vigorous and vehement tones; M. Emile Ollivier was, on the contrary, held back by the correctness of his person, by the preciseness of his sentences, by the sweetness and charm of his intonation, and by the musical accents which dropped from his lips. It was said of him, as it had been said of a famous tragedian, that he had a voice of gold. The description was accurate. Even to-day the voice of M. Emile Ollivier, despite a slight Provençal accent, which, indeed, adds a sort of beauty, like the lisp of a brook flowing over pebbles, has in quiet conversation a metallic sonorousness, a sound of ringing gold, thin, caressing, musical. The Empress, who was not fond of this man, and who, in contrast to her beauty, had a shrill and disagreeable voice, made fun of his tones, and vowed, with frank coquetry, that she was truly jealous of them.

It would, however, be a mistake to believe that M. Emile Ollivier preserved a constant sweetness of manner, that his language never departed from that special grace which characterised it. On occasion he lent to his language

all the heat of a fiery eloquence; and though his
gesture remained correct and elegant, though
his phraseology lost none of its literary quality,
he then rose to the very summit of oratorical art.

The present generation, which hears the public debates of the Chamber, which sees succeed
each other daily men well versed in the science
of language, in the art of speaking to the masses,
remains calm or indifferent at the mention of
those orators who triumphed before the war of
1870, and cares little to recall their eloquence.
It should, nevertheless, be remembered that the
Second Empire witnessed oratorical contests as
stirring and in every way as fine as those of
which the Palais-Bourbon is at present the theatre.   The eloquence, it is true, which moves
the public to-day is little like that which a short
time ago stirred it to passion.   It has changed
its tone: it has become violent, aggressive, and
malignant.   There was formerly more urbanity,
a more graceful setting to the attitude and language of politicians; there was less independence in their language; and the constraint
which, either by legislative regulations, or by a
regard for courtesy which was at that time less
scorned than now, had as a result a mode of
discussion more refined, and savouring less of a
street brawl.

When M. Jules Favre rose to speak to the Legislative Corps, the warlike attitude which he assumed gave to the debate on which they were entering a character which rendered its results uncertain and perilous. The governmental majority, stirred to opposition, if not at the very outset, at least before the close of the address, by the manner which the speaker adopted as he continued, entrenched themselves behind obstinate opposition, and listened, impassive, and with a spirit opposed to every modification, to the apostrophes of the speaker.

Through the gentleness of M. Emile Ollivier's language, and his lack of party prejudice, this majority felt itself touched, and a vague fear took possession of it. To repel by disdain the arguments presented by him was almost impossible, for they seemed to be offered in a spirit of friendliness; it was still less possible to drown his voice in insults, for he gave no cause for offence. In this mode of gaining the attention of adversaries refractory to conviction, lay for a long time the power gained by M. Emile Ollivier in the official Chambers of the Second Empire. He, however, abandoned this system at last; at the time, that is, when he took the power into his own hands.

After this he seemed to lose his self-control,

unnerved, perhaps, by the events which in quick
and disordered succession crowded on each other
and harassed his life. He was no longer content with a rhetoric which had undoubtedly
possessed much charm, but which had been
powerless to produce peace, or to prevent the
governmental dislocation which was now unavoidable, and he became irascible and almost
violent. He made short work of those who
battered in breach his authority. He raised
cries like those of an hunted animal, and his
spirit was full of revolt and of fury; his attitude became menacing; his voice, which seemed,
if I may so express myself, to mourn its lost
gentleness and grace, became harsh, and rang
out like the funeral-knell of his dreams and of
his hopes, like the funeral-knell of that freedom
for which he had sacrificed so much personal
feeling, for which he had undergone so many
unjust suspicions. He was, perhaps, very courageous at this moment, but he was certainly
most unfortunate.

The story, or the adventure, which is commonly called the conversion of M. Emile Ollivier, is most simple and easy of comprehension.

M. Emile Ollivier having entered politics free
from party prejudice, without thought of satis-

fying personal hatred or resentment, had no reason to avoid a change of opinion, or to fear an agreement with the men who governed in the Tuileries, or even with the sovereign himself ; it was in thorough consistency with the attitude which he had assumed that he finally reconciled himself with the Emperor.

It was through Count Walewski that his first interviews with Napoleon III. were arranged. I have already published conclusive letters on this point. It may, however, be affirmed that M. de Morny first dispelled in him any fear of an understanding with him whose authoritative government, rather than his own personality, he opposed.

Many years before he had held any intercouse with the Emperor, M. Emile Ollivier had talked with M. de Morny, who was at that time president of the Legislative Corps, and as a result there had arisen in his heart a sort of sympathy with this bold adventurer, who had played his part in the Coup d'État of December Second. In his book, *Le 19 Janvier*, we find that he does not forget M. de Morny, but presents him in a light not altogether unfavourable.

M. de Morny died ; and with him would, perhaps, have perished the projects which he had originated, and the hopes which he had placed in M. Emile Ollivier, had not Count Walewski availed himself of these plans and hopes, and given them a sanction.

Count Walewski, whose convictions were of the most liberal, liked M. Emile Ollivier. He admired his oratorical gifts and approved their nature. He took no pains to hide his admiration from the Emperor, and, indeed, easily persuaded him that in the more or less distant future this young deputy would be useful as one of his co-workers.

Napoleon III., who sought strong men attached to no political system, and who was glad to gain to his cause men formerly known as adversaries, who, indeed, with a charming coquetry, was rejoiced to run across an enemy for the sake of converting him and for the mere joy of making him a victim of his own charm and wit, received with delight the communication of Count Walewski, and arranged with him for the reception of M. Emile Ollivier at the Tuileries.

There then came to pass just that which was most in harmony with the temperament of M. Emile Ollivier. He talked with the Emperor, and he listened while the Emperor spoke, and was conquered. In this there is surely no for-

saking, no betrayal of principles; and I believe
that we may justly ascribe to false exagger-
ation and to party bitterness the reproaches
and the maledictions called forth by his reconciliation with the Emperor.

If examined calmly and philosophically, it is
impossible to gainsay the spirit of sincerity
which dictated to M. Emile Ollivier his conduct
in this matter. The same sincerity is notice-
able in the acts which followed his reconciliation with the Emperor, and especially in those
which lend a peculiar character to his short
ascent to power. He remained a liberal to the
last, and pursued liberty without causing any
disquietude to the governmental etiquette,
which, indeed, insured him the realisation of
his projects, and which protected that liberty
which he sought.

This attitude was one of apparent danger in
a country where the spirit of the men who
direct public affairs is not always understood
or treated with moderation; in a country, too,
whose nervous system is always in a state of
excitement, or at least in a state ready to be
excited, whose passions are not easily appeased,
and which is refractory to all change and adaptation, to everything which seems like an abandonment of the faith in which it was cradled.

M. Emile Ollivier called forth special bitterness
from those who sought to obey their own consciences and to keep themselves free from any
party. He saw arise that movement of revolt
which led France to renounce her old traditions.

It must, however, be admitted that his *rôle*
was that of a man active in government and
of a statesman ; it must be admitted, too, that
those circumstances which are necessary to the
development of the best leaders were lacking to
him, and that, having become a minister of
Napoleon III., he was far more the victim of
circumstance than of the weakness of his own
political system.

Having attained to power, he had to oppose
not only his old friends and the falsehood of
a legend which represented him as a rene-
gade, but also the authorities of the Empire
who grouped themselves round the Empress,
and a class of misguided men and women who
were pursued by the shadow of Napoleon III.,
and who, with a yet unsatisfied thirst, hastened
to recall a political era which had offered them
the unalloyed joy of existence.

Though he was never intimate at court, and
though he held himself apart from its frivolities, its intrigues, follies, and maliciousness,
M. Emile Ollivier was, nevertheless, cruelly

sensitive to the hostility shown him by the
habitués of the Tuileries, and a moment came
when he found himself fairly enveloped in this
hostility.

Such a detail as this may appear insignificant
in the life of a statesman ; but it has, nevertheless, its importance. It is necessary to have
lived among courtiers, and to have talked with
those who have been the objects of their
hatred, in order to appreciate the mighty influence that this little world of men and women
which moves round a throne has on the affairs
of government, and in order to understand the
many disasters which, in the destiny of nations,
are due to it.

When, therefore, M. Emile Ollivier became
President of the Council in January, 1870, and
when he wished to apply to practical ends the
policy which he had made his ideal, he found
himself confronted by a formidable opposition,
composed of those whom he was reported to
have abandoned, and also of those whom his
origin and theories annoyed. Even the plébis-
cite which followed his entrance into the ministry
had no power to calm the disturbance; and
after, as before, this appeal to the electors, he
had constant warfare to wage against resolute
and obstinate adversaries.

He had for some time been in constant oppo-·
sition to M. Rouher, and had condemned both
the words and the deeds of the vice-emperor.
When, therefore, M. Rouher seated himself
quietly in the presidential chair of the Senate,
M. Emile Ollivier understood that the most
violent attacks which were levied against him
proceeded from this man, and that it was he
who, with a power and influence encouraged by
the high approbation of the Empress and by
her overwhelming patronage, directed against
him the entire army of discontented spirits.
He accepted the battle which his rival offered,
he resumed the warfare of past years, and the
wounds were deep which these two men inflicted
on each other.

These were hours of storm and anguish ; and
M. Emile Ollivier, who had courage to assume
authority on the very eve of a revolution, at a
moment when the fabric of the Empire had
already begun to give way, had no chance of
victory. A mighty tempest made itself felt
from one end of France to the other; the
storm-bell rang through the air, and raised to
the very sky its loud notes of warning. M.
Emile Ollivier, because he had been unable to
check this storm in its course, because he was
powerless to master so mighty a force, fell as a

tree falls when struck by lightning; he was borne away, a shattered wreck, and hurled across space like some stray object seized by the wind.

The Empire assisted in his annihilation, public opinion seeking then, as always, some scapegoat on which to lay the burden of errors and crimes, glad to cast on him the responsibility of an Empire's death and of the disasters which France sustained in its heroic struggles against Germany.

In a subsequent chapter, entitled the "Declaration of War," I shall show the true attitude of M. Emile Ollivier at this period, and I shall name without hesitation, basing my statements on fact, the authors really responsible for the campaign of 1870. It will not be difficult to render to him the place which is due him in history, and to remove from his name the accusations and the anathemas of which he has been the victim. The task is made more easy by the fact that the prejudice which, till a short time ago was absolutely implacable, has to-day been somewhat modified; there is accorded to him, as to the memory of Napoleon III., not only absolute freedom of vindication, but also an attentive interest, a feeling of sympathy, and a tardy justice, toward which he may still look, not for rehabilitation, indeed, for such an expression is hardly appropriate, but for consolation and for peace, which will add serenity and pride to his gray hairs.

I write these things, and am not afraid to do so, because I know that they are true, because falsehood repels me, because I am glad to pay homage to misfortune when that misfortune is unmerited.

After that fatal hour in which he disappeared from the world of politics, M. Emile Ollivier remained in almost absolute isolation. The Academy, which had received him with joy at the time of his success, and which is usually little influenced by the spirit of the people at large, declined to authorise his inaugural discourse, because there was in it an eloquent and a courageous eulogy of the sovereign whom he had served and loved. He resigned after this fresh affront; and his voice was henceforth seldom heard except in private gatherings, where he spoke to a select audience, of diverse religious questions which he was thoroughly competent to discuss.

Silence had fallen, or nearly so, on his name, when an incident provoked by Prince Bismarck recalled it to all lips. He then appeared before the public, happy in the absolute and unexpected justification which he had received.

Will, however, this hour, which has put an end to his unpopularity, be followed by those in which M. Emile Ollivier will triumph over the evil stories which have attached to his memory? Will it be followed by a time when he will once more enter the world of politics and make the nation hear again his voice, that voice of gold?

I do not believe that he will ever resume active work in the problems which agitate France. I do not believe that he will become the partisan of that liberty which betrayed him. There are some men who never forgive an unfaithful mistress, and M. Emile Ollivier impresses me as a man of this nature. Old to-day, in years if not in capabilities, he will remain the impassioned spectator, for passion flows in his blood, and the melancholy spectator, too, it may be, of our struggles, our failures, and of the subsequent recovery of our power. His voice, if it is ever raised again, will be but like the soft tones which, according to the faith of mystics, come up from the tombs to console those who still live on the earth, and who are usually unable to understand their message.

VIII.

THE APOTHEOSIS.

WHEN a great drama is approaching its close, when the curtain is about to fall on the heroes and the heroines of a world of imagination, or on the splendours of a ballet, a last scene suddenly unfolds itself; it is in this that is found the synthesis of all the words, all the acts, all the charms, which have previously moved and amazed the public; it is in this that is found the symbol of the idea which was the inspiration of the entire play. This supreme revelation of a thought fraught in moral agony has its name; we call it an apotheosis.

The year 1867 had just opened. The luxuries, the loves, the follies, and the glories of the Second Empire were about to die. Before passing out, however, from the great gates of the Tuileries, never to return again, before issuing thence as a swarm of bees which has lost its queen issues from the hive, and fills the air with stragglers, which beat blindly against trees and walls, — these follies, loves, and spirits of slothful luxury raised a loud cry toward heaven and toward mankind, giving the world a last proof of their vitality, inviting it to the final scene of that comedy which night after night had been acted in the great theatre of kings and nations.

The year 1867 had just opened. The curtain rose on the apotheosis of the Second Empire, and revealed, like so many living lies created to conceal the great darkness which was about to succeed the brilliancy of the past, and the storm which was to follow long years of peace, men with crowns on their heads kneeling at the feet of Napoleon III., offering him their homage and that of the droves of humanity, which, like themselves, were prostrate before him and were part of that gigantic and dazzling picture which had the universe as an admiring spectator.

The year 1867 had just opened. The Second Empire, like a great drum-major, marking time with fife, clarion, and drum, marched before the kings and the emperors of Europe, and bade them sound their trumpets and call the roll of their glories ; then the emperors and the kings sounded their trumpets and called the roll of their glories, as though they had been poor trumpeters, or humble sutlers measuring out the rations of a regiment. The apotheosis was complete and dazzling. The Second Empire seemed to fade away within it, to vanish and give place — itself a thing too paltry for so great a spectacle — to an enormous shadow, a formidable spectre, a spectre which was not unsightly but which rose bright with the glories of the past, and, standing in the soft haze, assumed the figure of that Power which with one thrust of its sword scarred forever at its birth the brow of the century. It seemed as though all the splendours and the glories of the present moment were but the uninterrupted splendours and glories which had filled the reign of Napoleon I., of him who remains for all ages The Emperor.

The year 1867 had opened. The imperial legend was revived. History was made to lie, and the past was proved a forger ; for that legend which had stolen the voice of fame, hovered now in the air with the sound of stirring wings, and the buried glories of the past rose in triumph. The snow and the ice of Russia had vanished, for Alexander, who was their master, is here, bowing before the Emperor ; the duke of Reichstadt was not dead, was never buried alive and taken from his father by Austria, for Francis Joseph is here smiling before the Emperor ; Waterloo is a nightmare, and Blücher a

fabulous character, for William of Prussia is
leaning on the arm of the Emperor; Saint-
Helena is a melodrama, a product of the fancy,
for England sends the son of its queen to lay
his youth at the feet of the Emperor. The
century belongs to the Empire; and the Empire
fills it with its power, for the nations now, as of
old, are the vassals of the Emperor.

The year 1867 was at its birth. Its dawn
made bright an apotheosis. This apotheosis
was, however, a mirage, an illusion. If the year
1867 seems to be the synthesis of the reign
which it celebrated, it was, nevertheless, powerless to efface the gloom which preceded it. The
disasters which it sought to envelop in oblivion
had, nevertheless, known actual existence. An
abyss was between it and the events which it
wished to expel from history. These facts are
real and fearful, despite the painted scenes and
the bright lights which for a moment concealed
them. The chain of continuity between them
and the events then in evolution was not
broken. When the curtain falls on the last act
of the Second Empire, they will come out from
the darkness, and once more step upon the
stage of the world, and crowd it with their great
numbers, sweeping all before them, and strew-
ing the boards with ruin, casting at their feet,

before the foot-lights, the Emperor, the Empress, the Prince Imperial, and the whole court, carrying away the eagle from the nation's flag, administering a death-draught to light loves and to laughter, — to the glory and the joy of a nation's existence, — plucking out the very heart of this people, and displaying it, a bloody trophy, in a desolate place.

There was certainly much falsehood and vain glitter in the imperial magnificence of the year 1867, magnificence which had the Exposition as its pretext. We cannot, however, remain true to history and yet doubt that, despite the superficiality of that splendour which characterised the reign of Napoleon III., and gave to its events an appearance of strength and of vitality which in truth they did not possess, he who reigned at the Tuileries had yet a certain power and renown, that he won the respect of emperors and kings, and inspired with real fear the nations of Europe.

It is possible that King William of Prussia and Prince Bismarck had even at this time a wish to lessen the authority of the Empire and to involve Napoleon III. in some imprudent enterprise; it is not, however, likely that, confronted by this Empire which seemed to rest on foundations which could not be moved, and by an Emperor who defied destiny, they had any feeling of certainty that a day would dawn when the sovereign whose master they had then become would fly from their attacks, a vanquished power.

King William and Prince Bismarck had no friendly feelings toward France, and would have asked nothing better than to disarm its authority ; but they, like the whole world, were deceived by its appearance of strength, and, like the whole world, yielded to the influences of its imposing personality.   They made their plans with a spirit of fatal hesitancy, for it was impossible for them to estimate accurately the state of our military resources.

The Emperor Napoleon III. was not ignorant of the sentiments, more or less sincerely affectionate and kindly, entertained for him and his government by foreign monarchs, and he felt that a great display of his army would tend to increase the prestige of France before the nations of Europe.   This display took place at Longchamps on the sixth of June, when there gathered on the plain of Boulogne, under the scorching rays of the sun, about one hundred thousand men.

A review, the great review of the masters of

the earth who now assembled round Napoleon
III., gave the world the assurance of power, and
filled it with the honoured glory of a military
force at the very zenith of its power. Magenta
and Solferino, though now in the background of
contemporaneous history, gave to the wild notes
of the clarion the flourish of victory, and under
the flaming sky the blackened gold of the
ancient flags shone with the scintillations of
powder. The entire Guard was there, and all
the regiments from the various departments of
France. In front of the tribunes, where the
voice of the crowd was heard like the humming
of bees round a hive, the long line of grenadiers
and the light companies waited. From behind
and toward the right, in the direction of Saint-
Cloud, the heavy cavalry emerged, and, made
restive by its stationary position, gave vent to
its impatience by the neighing of horses and by
the clanking of swords. In the centre of the
panorama the stern and motionless artillery stood
in symmetrical line, a great mass of black. At
the left, half lost in the chaos of gilt braid, of
plumes, military coats, and cuirasses, the infantry, with grounded arms, gave to the plain
of Longchamps, which for a day was like the
many-coloured palette of an artist, a note of
sombre colour and also the austere moral of

humility. A hundred metres from the tribunes lay a long expanse of yellow and trampled grass, spotted with dry mud.

The open fields of Suresne looked like one enormous ant-hill; and the railroad station, with its wild eddies of smoke and the roaring of engines, let the people rush in as a sluice-gate when opened leaves waters free in their course. High up on a narrow and perpendicular cliff Mont Valerien rose and lowered over Paris, expanding its great brass lungs, that at the right moment it might shout forth the glory of the sovereign.

There was the stir of eager expectation in the crowd. Every one held his watch in his hand, trembling with feverish joy. Seats were brought, arranged, and fastened to the ground. People elbowed and pushed each other, eager to see more; men cried out to the women to shut their parasols; and there was a Babel of tongues and voices, of laughter and oaths, an uproar like the tuning of the instruments of an orchestra. Suddenly a cloud of dust rose to the sky, the sound of a cannon-discharge filled the air and echoed far over the the plains of Suresne, and the people, silenced by the vibrating air which had been rent by powder, waited with bated breath. A great silence reigned over the plain of Longchamps. Then, like a mighty whirlwind, with the sovereigns of Russia and Prussia at his side, the Emperor appeared on a black horse whose gilt trappings glittered in the sun. It was a wonderful moment. From above the cannon resounded, cleaving the air, thundering forth its hundred and one salutes, while, as though electrified by the same command, the hundred thousand men upon the plain presented arms and shouted loudly. The skin of the drums grew tense under the beating sticks, the clarions gave forth their metallic notes, and the shadow of the flags, lowered in salute, slowly stretched itself out along the ground. Trotting rapidly on his black horse, the Emperor passed before the grenadiers and the light companies. He was preceded by Spahies, who caracoled in Oriental disorder, and who, enveloped in the flowing folds of their mantles, seemed to advance through a snow-storm. Behind him came the staff, made brilliant and imposing by the marshals, generals, and foreign officers who escorted the Cent-Gardes. As it passed before the tribunes, the Empress, who was in the central loggia, rose, and with her the whole court. The three sovereigns then raised their caps and thus passed in front of the troops. These three men traversing the plain, their heads bowed low, as though in homage, over the necks of their horses, never knew a more glorious hour. The crowd, sceptical and scornful a moment before, now drew itself up in wild enthusiasm ; heads were uncovered, and great cheers rose from the people, mingling with the hurrahs of the army. Alexander and William grew dim and faded away in the aureole which expanded round the passage of the Emperor. They seemed but taken in tow by the glory of this man, who, according to the expression of his very enemies, had plunged into the flood in the midst of a storm, and sought to recover his name from the depths of those waters whose waves bathe, and lap with their tongues, the rock of Saint Helena.

Mont Valerien was silent, reposing for a moment before again shouting forth the hosannas of war. The long line of troops trembled in mute expectation. The Emperor, after having visited all the ranks, had described a semicircle and taken up his place in front of the official loggia. A marshal left for a moment his escort and approached him ; then, having received his orders, in a voice ringing with enthusiasm and with authority, made the field resound with the command of the sovereign. A low, volcanic rumbling ran over the seared plain of Longchamps. The hundred thousand men, tired of their stationary position, proud of the victories written on their torn flags, began to move, happy to live for a day the life of a Napoleon.

Like a ball of twine, the troops unwound themselves and drew out like one long thread, ready to pass before the Emperor. Six horsemen of Saint-Cyr advanced ahead of them, and were followed by the battalion from the military school, whose automatic and admirably regular step called forth much applause. Suddenly a cloud of hot dust rose, and a loud noise was heard. A chaos of red turbans, black faces, and blue jackets rushed pell-mell on the field, running in savage or childish disorder, crying and gesticulating, and filling the air with their rough and uncivilised voices. The Turcomans, those gamins of the East, those spoiled children of the Empire, obtained that day a place of honour, and took their position immediately behind that of the Saint-Cyriens. How proud they were, those emigrants from a limitless desert, to traverse with their free and undisciplined steps the great fields of Longchamps! It had been told them in the morning that they were to see the Emperor, that they were to speak with him, and now that the moment had come they rushed on in feverish hurry. The Emperor, who was touched by the childlike joy which hastened toward him the steps of those adopted children of the French fatherland, seemed to caress by his kindly regard their tumultuous onward march; and when, with an outburst of heartfelt enthusiasm, they leaped toward him, waving their guns and their black arms, he saluted them with a long, low sweep of his hat, a salute which seemed to carry with it an expression of comradeship. Deeply moved, he then followed for a moment with his eye the hellish crowd which yelled his name: "L'Emperour!" . . . it cried, "l'Emperour!" . . .

Beyond the enclosure reserved for the privileged public there arose, where were assembled the common people, great shouts and cheers. They pushed and elbowed each other with terrible force, and the guards were obliged to cross their bayonets in front of the on-pressing mass of plebeians. All at once the crowd spied its favourite colours, and with a movement of sympathetic curiosity people stretched their necks and rushed forward toward those who were seen advancing on the run. "The soldiers!" they cried, "the soldiers!" Voices were raised in loud exclamation and in song. The crowd joined in the airs played by clarion and drum. "Did you see the cap?" was the oft-repeated

question, "the pretty cap?" Every one wanted
to see and to salute the little red breeches
which the labourer's child had made famous
through Paris. The line had drawn up abreast,
and now stretched from one side to the other of
the field, beating with its mighty tread the hard
ground. In unbroken silence it passed, receiving the bravos which greeted it, with the same
stoicism with which it had received the balls of
the enemy, while over the whole plain the sound
of human voices and the neighing and stamping
of horses was felt, and served to excite more
and more the crowd, which was already half
crazy.

It was a beautiful sight. The sombre colours
had retreated to the background, and now the
entire Guard, grenadiers, and light companies,
advanced, followed by the cavalry, which flashed
its steel across the fields, making them glow like
beds of live coals.

The full glory of the Empire laid itself down,
alive and trembling, on the yellow verdure of
Longchamps, like a beautiful woman stretched
out upon her couch. The Empire showed to
the world its flashing breast-plate, and drew itself up proudly in the dazzling light which
enveloped it, trembling in every nerve through
its imperious need of the joys which it had

made its own. Women went to the reviews at
Longchamps with spirits weary and rebellious
at the poverty of existence, and returned full
of undefined desire, their eyes kindled by the
brightness of those golden spangles which
shone on the officers' coats, their hearts aglow
with newly born passions, while they breathed
through dilated nostrils the unknown delights
of life, and passed gaily through the streets.
Their thought was little for the victories whose
story the flags told. They wore their gloves
out in clapping, but their bravos were addressed
far more to the beautiful uniforms than to the
renown of the great army. The supernatural
spirit of the Empire stood there in marvellous
draperies. A legend took root and began to
grow round the Guard, which waited in splendour and magnificence ; and it seemed as though
even the sun cast on this Guard its brightest
rays. It seemed as though the star of the
Bonapartes, which had set on the day which
followed Austerlitz, had risen now on another
Napoleon, and would follow the voice of his
wishes as faithfully as it had done that of his
great ancestor. Confronted by the huge bear-
skin caps of the grenadiers, sweet memories
were revived in the minds of the old, and hopes
kindled in the hearts of the young. Over the

field of Longchamps, where little by little the vision faded away, eyes travelled far, far into the distance, till, rising above the Bois de Boulogne, they sought the dome of the Invalides, under which the crowd remembered that "the other" slept his eternal sleep. The glory and the mighty thunder of those days resounded like echoes of war in the ears of those who were assembled there. The legend expanded, it crossed the field at a giant's stride, and men, forgetting their political dissensions and bitterness, accompanied its echoing step by the rhythm of their enthusiastic cheers.

A noise of rattling iron and lead suddenly rose over the plain, accompanied by the sound of rumbling wheels crunching the ground. From the direction of Saint-Cloud a black mass became visible. It was the artillery, which in its turn had begun to unwind. The cannons, with their yawning mouths, advanced through a flood of sunshine, and the low crackling sound of grape-shot was heard. Some of the waggons were drawn by pure white, others by dark horses, and this harmony of colours pleased the spectators. It was truly a monstrous exhibition of murderous machines! The brazen pieces cast reddish reflections and left behind them the lurid light of a stormy sky. The long ramrods hung over the flanks of the carriages, and were knocked up and down on the bruised and battered wood. Behind these came the powder and bullet-carts, and following them strange carriages with top-awnings, which serve as kitchens in time of campaign. This long line passed on rapidly and disappeared on a full trot, its noise dying away like that of a sudden clap of thunder.

For a moment the troops paused in their onward march. The silence which had preceded the arrival of the Emperor was again felt over the field of review. It was thought that the exercises were finished, and the crowd prepared to scatter, when it was checked by an imperious command. From far in the distance ten thousand cuirassiers rushed forward in a furious charge upon the tribunes, then, facing about, they described a semicircle and passed like a hurricane before the imperial staff, making savage leaps and bounds like Titans. This was the final moment, the climax as it were, of the whole. A nervous tremour passed through the crowd; skin and muscle were felt to tighten, and with cries like that of wild animals, people rushed on the barriers, which gave way before them. It seemed as though the tribunes must sink under the cheers and hurrahs. A world was there, which watched with pride and satisfaction this frightful charge. The cuirassiers bore with their flags the true spirit of war, and this spirit passed from them to the people. If the grenadiers had awakened memories, these men evoked legends. The dire story of Waterloo rushed onward with them, and its awful name was repeated over and over as though it recalled hymns of victory. The imperial epic was revived by these regiments of steel. The glories of the past pressed forward, at once bloody and radiant as though they had issued from the colossal womb of some menacing chimæra, and with their metallic cries cut the air, which was thick with smoke and warm with battle.

When the last cuirassier had disappeared, the staff reassembled in its turn, and the three sovereigns, taking the field, advanced slowly till they were within ten metres of the official loggia. They then paid their homage to the Empress in a salute, and, followed by the escort of princes and marshals, wheeled about, while Mont Valerien once more took up, in its *basso profundo*, and brought to its close, the hymn of war.

This, then, was the review of Longchamps, which will remain famous in the annals of

France. Though it commenced under a brilliant sun, it nevertheless closed in darkness. After Napoleon III., the King of Prussia, and Emperor Alexander of Russia, had dismounted, and were returning in a carriage across the Bois de Boulogne, a shot resounded which had been directed against the Emperor of Russia, who was seated by the side of Napoleon III., and a ball struck the head of the horse which M. Raimbaud, one of the equerries of the Tuileries, was riding. The poor animal fell ; while the two sovereigns, covered with blood and very pale, insisted that they had received no injury.

This event is well known, and I shall not describe its dramatic circumstances. It had as an almost immediate result, however, an interview between Napoleon III. and the Emperor Alexander. It is this interview, an account of which was given by Napoleon III. to Count W——, but which has as yet never been made public, that I am about to reproduce here.

A few days after the review of the sixth of June, Napoleon III. and Alexander II. shut themselves in a little study in the Tuileries, and there conversed together alone. After having discussed the attempt on the life of Alexander, which had taken place in the Bois

de Boulogne and which was occupying the
mind of the public, they began to speak of
liberty, that liberty which at this time was
struggling for supremacy in certain parts of
Europe. Alexander II., who was by nature
liberal, approved of the movement, of which
he was, indeed, one of the promoters. He,
however, approved of it with a practical real
isation of the dangers which it would necessarily create round him, ready, nevertheless,
through his generous spirit, to face these dangers. Napoleon III., also a socialist at heart,
rejoiced in that current of public opinion which
was destined to change the present policy of
his government ; but in his rejoicing he denied
the presence of peril, his heart filled with the
fervour and the mysticism of a believer. A
dialogue therefore ensued between the two
men, which Alexander opened.

"We live," said he, "in an age when it is
said that we must love freedom ; and I do, as do
those who believe that freedom will regenerate
the world, that is, I love it. What benefit have
I to reap, however, by being liberal ? It will
result for me in the constant fear of assassination on the street corner. I should like to
forget the attempt made against my life only a
few days ago in France, but how can I ? Does

not our very conversation recall it fatally to my
mind ?   It is in vain that one seeks to attenuate
the horror of assassination under the false pretext of an exalted patriotism.   Berezowski was
led by no race prejudice when he took his aim
at me ; he but yielded to that mighty spirit of
liberality which is rising against us who are
emperors and kings, and, as it is believed, open
and unflinching enemies of all progress.   What,
however, does regret avail ?   The people claim
their independence, their freedom, and I am
among those who are ready to give them what
they ask.   I will create a liberal Russia, and I
shall hope to make it as strong under the *régime*
of liberty as have my predecessors under that
of autocracy.   My purpose, however, ceases
here ; I see too clearly the dire condition of
affairs to raise any air-castles for my own
future.   I hope to gain nothing either for myself or for my people by liberty ; and were I
called upon to express my whole feeling in this
matter, I should say that I expect but evil to
result therefrom.   The new spirit, Sire, will
kill the old.   Liberty will lay on us the hand
of a master, and who knows but that I shall be
the first among the sovereigns of Europe to fall
under the stroke of the fanatic ?   The ball which
to-day swerved from the path toward which it

was directed will to-morrow hit its mark ; this ball is speeding along my way, and I feel it in the air."

Napoleon III. was somewhat surprised by these words.

" Our political education," he replied, " has not been the same. Yours, having diverged from its source through a love of humanity, is yet influenced by early anti-liberal tendencies. While hastening toward it, you still fear liberty. Comfort yourself, nevertheless. The people are good, and by no means ungrateful. Though the populace hides in its ranks a few such monsters as he who lately attacked your life and outraged the hospitality which I have extended to you, it is not just to feel that, on this account, it must be entirely made up of monsters. Alms appease the bitterness of the poor, and liberty will cast oil on the resentment and the enmity of the people; it will be to them a consolation in the midst of their sufferings. A day will come when I shall grant freedom to France ; and on that day I, who, as well as you, Sire, was exposed to the assassin's ball, shall no longer fear for the safety of my life. The people will bless me, and I shall lead them with a strong hand toward new destinies."

" Your Majesty may be right," replied Alexander II., "but despite myself I can but doubt and fear. I have, moreover, no faith in the agglomeration of races and in the unity of nations."

"Are you alluding," asked Napoleon III., "to the theory of national unity?"

"Does not this very theory, Sire, to which I was indeed referring, and which is the broad and illimitable consequence of the principle of liberal government, seem to you like the supreme consecration of our effacement, as the acme of that danger which is destined to fall on our thrones and to crush them?"

"Italy and Germany have established their unity, and I see no evidence that their sovereigns suffer from the political and social system which they have adopted. Were nations gathered together in an universal confederation tending to destroy in them all spirit of patriotism and all race feeling, they would then, of course, have little interest in creating emperors and kings. Such a stage of progress is, however, far in the future. Nations are like children who, when they emerge from swaddling clothes have need of leading strings, and of strong arms when they try to take their first steps. As the years pass they will increase in strength, and learn to move firmly on their feet.

They will advance without ceasing toward a better condition, toward an era of certain progress. An hour will then come when they shall have no further need of being guided in life, through which they will pass free and strong into the future. In that hour, Sire, our end will come. We shall have to appear in the public places and to mingle with the masses; we shall be required to blend our thoughts and personalities with those of the community; we shall be required " — here a mischievous smile appeared on his face — " to descend from our thrones and to take up our seats in the chimney-corner."

Emperor Alexander shook his head sadly.

" Your heart is kind, Sire," he said gently, with an expression of affectionate pity, " your heart is kind; may it be rewarded by an opportunity for so much resignation."

His tone then suddenly changed.

" Why," he continued, " why can we not at least march together toward this future which you evoke with a spirit of assurance and of serenity, and whose advent I dread because I do not believe in the virtue of national unity; because I see in the results of this theory dangers which God alone can reveal to us in their entirety? Why, ah, why have not politics made us allies? We should have loved each other."

Sincere emotion took possession of Napoleon III. A little pale, he raised his head and looked into the face of Alexander.

"As it is, Sire," he said with a smile, "as it is, do we not love each other?"

Emperor Alexander did not reply; but he rose and went toward Napoleon III., and taking his two hands in his, he pressed them warmly.

This was a solemn moment, born in the first hour of a crisis which was destined to bear the dynasty of the Bonapartes far from the throne. Napoleon III., however, waited unmoved, and let it pass him by. Having returned the pressure of the Emperor's hand, he directed the conversation into channels which lay wide apart from those problems which were dearest to him.

IX.

THE DRAMA.

THE year 1867 having closed in joy and brightness, the politics of the Second Empire suffered a change, and its private and public life were transformed. The drama which was to cast darkness over its last hours now opened.

In the years which were past, events had rushed rapidly upon each other, as waves on a day of storm hurry toward the shore, and hurl themselves upon each other, eager to spread out along the land, or else to tear themselves on the rocks. In those years events had arisen and succeeded each other with a logical continuity; forgotten facts, of which I spoke in the preceding chapter, emerged from the shadow, and reappeared with a menacing expression in the face of joys and feverish excitements which have not yet ceased to be like revengeful spectres.

Since the year 1867, and even during the festivities of that year, political revolutions had been accomplished, to which little attention was given. Stirring debates had taken place in the

Legislative Corps, as well as in the Senate,
concerning certain works which were judged
licentious by the authoritative moralists of the
Second Empire. The prosecution of the authors
was demanded and penalties attached ; and not
satisfied by this appeal to extreme severity
which was opposed to the spirit of the Emperor,
the authors were traced and found.

A revolution had taken place around Napoleon III., and a formidable opposition had arisen
against him in the very Tuileries, whose purpose was to check the fulfilment of his plans
for liberal reforms. The Empress had resolutely taken direction of this movement, and
had, by aid of intrigue, won her cause on several occasions. By such means, and through
the intervention of M. Rouher, she succeeded
in expelling from the presidency of the Legislative Corps, Count Walewski, whose chair was
offered to M. Schneider.

It was also found necessary in this year, on
account of the attitude assumed by Prussia, to
abandon the annexation of Luxemburg, which
had been declared, consented to, and amicably
arranged for with the Netherlands.

A fearful thunderbolt had made itself felt
in the midst of the gaiety and the folly which
succeeded the Exposition. The tragic death of

Maximilian, Emperor of Mexico, had filled with momentary horror the royal guests of the Tuileries. The blood of the unhappy man of Queretaro had seemed to spurt across the seas, and to stain the gay faces of those men and women who lived in thoughtless enjoyment of the imperial festivities.

Finally, the volley fired at Mentana, a volley arranged in order to meet the exigencies, the superstition, and the resentment of the Empress, had provoked a rupture between France and Italy, had separated forever Napoleon III. and Victor Emmanuel, and prepared the claims and the neutrality of the *Re galantuomo*, which the future was to make manifest.

Day followed day, and events succeeded each other rapidly.

The year 1868 lighted the *Lanterne* of Rochefort, and cast from her throne Queen Isabella of Spain; dissensions, too, among the masses, both in Paris and in the provinces, caused some disquietude. New men with unheard-of names rose daily and spoke to the people, inspiring them with bitter hatred of the Empire. The old, who in the past had kindled in the people a spirit antagonistic to tyranny, fell now, exhausted by battle and by the weight of years; but the young rose up in their places, carried on their discourses, and assumed with even greater boldness their attitude, while the crowd listened and applauded.

In 1869 a priest, Père Hyacinthe, fell from the pulpit which he had occupied with renown, and to which he had drawn the attention of the court and of the people at large, and his fall had an ominous sound. His renunciation of those things which he had hitherto venerated, stirred all souls and filled many hearts with terror.

The Emperor having succeeded, despite the difficulties occasioned by his campaign, and despite the party which had sprung up as a result of this campaign, in putting to a practical test his ideas of liberalism, political reunions took place every evening, where violent and abusive language was heard, whose echoes reached the Tuileries with messages of lugubrious warning. Words, too, were soon exchanged for deeds ; and the streets were invaded by uproarious bands from the outskirts of Paris, as well as by the silent patrol of the soldiers.

There were riots. The boulevards were thronged with a half-crazy people, and the troops made furious charges, killing without mercy.

The people made their onslaught against the Empire with the revived fury of tragic and revolutionary days experienced in the past. The soldiers, cradled in the imperial legend, humoured and flattered by power, both by instinct and profession enemies of peace and rejoicing in warfare, prepared, with all the enthusiasm of prætorians, for massacre.

Regiments quitted their garrisons and came to Paris as they would have marched on a foreign city ; and they were seen to pass, the war-cry on their lips and a menacing accent in their steps, behind the captains who commanded them.

The Guard in a state of agitation awaited in its quarters at Versailles, at Saint-Cloud, at Saint-Maur, and at Saint-Germain, the command which would interrupt its peace, and anger and drunkenness entered its ranks.

This was a precursory period. The Legislative Corps and the Senate, seized by the moral agony which had taken possession of the whole nation, were unfortunate in their deliberations, and lingered over futile and harmful discussions, exerting their strength in volleys of words which increased the nervous exhaustion of every one, and accentuated in disturbed and hesitating minds an innate lack of equilibrium.

Despite this overthrow, however, of all which had existed under the Second Empire, of all which had constituted its glory, there yet lingered round it a sort of radiance. The inauguration of the Suez Canal brought a moment of repose to the follies and furies of the Second Empire; and the Emperor, who had sent his consort to represent him on Eastern soil, had reason to believe that the truce afforded him by destiny would have a glorious morrow.

From such a dream he awoke in sorrow; but, always a fatalist, he watched the steady development of events with surprise yet without fear. The liberty which, after proclaiming the edict of absolute power, he had sought to establish, disappointed his hopes. The ideal, however, had grown to be a part of him, and he believed in its excellence. He did not argue with himself that a return to those prerogatives which he had at one time enjoyed might save his throne from threatening danger. He resorted to no violent act of authority in order to recover the prestige and power which he had for a long time enjoyed. Resigned or, more properly, confident of the justice of that mission which he had undertaken, and of the immutability of destiny, — that destiny which, according to his faith, no circumstance could

serve to modify,—he faced with philosophical
calm the new and strange events which transpired round him, and watched them with impassive mind.

The festivities and magnificences which
accompanied the opening of the Suez Canal
brought a smile of contentment to his pale lips.
He raised his voice with a cry of joy, he
stretched out his hands toward the little spot
of blue which had appeared in the heavily
clouded sky, a gleam of brightness kindled by
beams from his own reign. He forgot the
injuries dealt his throne by the repeated attacks of his enemies. He forgot the bitterness
which life had brought, life which is the same
for king and plebeian, which tires of happiness,
and ordains that tears shall succeed joy.

The Emperor Napoleon III. was good and
believed in goodness. Strong in the greatness
of his name, strong in the consciousness of
deeds of kindness freely performed by him,
he had, during his reign, the conviction that he
was loved by the people, nor was he in error
here. When men whom he did not know rose
before him with hatred on their faces, he was
filled with astonishment, but did not for a
moment dream that their anathemas could find
a ready echo among the people. He looked

on these men, and on the events which they
created, with a feeling of sadness, with the
sorrow of a person who hates evil and who yet
feels its hand laid upon himself.   It would certainly have been possible for him to respond
to the attacks and insults of which he was the
victim, by an implacable exercise of his authority, by the abandonment of the humanitarian
dream which had inspired his liberalism.   He,
however, never conceived of such vengeance.
He felt that he owed the people and the government the consolation and the mitigation
which he had promised them.   He felt now
as he had done years ago when, after a long
exile, he set his feet on French soil, that he
was Napoleon, that he was a man predestined
by a legend, and that no force could cast him
without the pale of history.

The inauguration of the Suez Canal, whose
glory belonged to him, and the success of the
plebiscite in 1870, confirmed this assurance.
Despite the physical infirmities of age, despite
his moral suffering, he held himself erect, and
was filled with a fervour and an enthusiasm
which urged him toward the future.   Neither
the voices of praise, however, which came to
him from the East, nor the last cheers of the
nation which saluted his name, could give back

to him the bodily and mental force of past
years. The strength which had enabled him to
take possession of the throne was no longer at
his command ; he tottered as he advanced
toward the future for which he longed, and,
like a wounded duelist who lets the sword fall
from his stiff fingers, he relinquished his own
personality, and watched events stoically, while
men in whose bosoms were hidden the invisible
and the unknown, passed on. He was crushed
by them, as some poor victim fallen in the
streets of Paris would be crushed by the heavy,
rumbling carts.

The Second Empire perished. All the hours
of its glory were dead, and over their remains
Destiny chanted its *De Profundis*, while the
drama which was to fill with terror its last
days slowly developed.

It might have been expected that in the presence of events which fell on the world with all
the ruinous rapidity of avalanches, the one on
the other, the *habitués* of the Tuileries would
lay aside their enticing follies. It might have
been expected that before those threats which
rose clear on the horizon, the court would grow
sober, and seek to evade the danger which was
marching implacably toward it. It was not,
however, so. Politicians who frequented the

Tuileries made no allusion at this time to the future of the imperial dynasty, while the worldlings and *habitués* of the palace remained alike unconscious of the people's claims and of the hostility shown by foreign nations.

In their ignorance of the public agitation, they continued to enjoy the easy existence which they had made for themselves; they abandoned none of their diversions, but, on the contrary, plunged deeper into the flood of pleasure.

The feeble opposition of the "Five" was far in the background. To this little group of adversaries had succeeded a legion of men who were resolved to overthrow the Empire. There were daily dissensions in the Legislative Corps, and discussions which slowly but surely took from the government of the Tuileries what authority and prestige still remained to it.

The court mocked the men who assumed a violent attitude before the government. It denied the power of the rebels who advanced toward it with hatred in their hearts. With a complete absence of moral courage, it turned disdainfully from those who tried to warn it of the danger, and in a profound egoism it deplored the apprehensions of the Emperor, and sought to destroy them by multiplying the

frivolities and enjoyments which existed round
him. The court was at this time, as I have
already said, an assembly of fools of both sexes
which nothing served to quiet.

In the face of the disturbing prophecies
which passed lugubriously through the days
of the Second Empire, it experienced no emotion, no sadness, no fear. It believed, perhaps,
lacking as it was in all just appreciation of
the nature of affairs, that this was but a
political disturbance of weak vitality which one
word from the Emperor would destroy. At no
time did it dream of the dissatisfaction with
which its own philosophy of life filled the
nation. It even found in the opposition raised
against the Tuileries a source of some amusement, and a new diversion was added to the
many which were enjoyed by the Empress.
When the elections of 1869 appointed to the
Legislative Corps unknown men who were to
overthrow the Empire, the court made sport
of these men. Caricatures were drawn of
them in the Tuileries, and their eloquence
parodied, their attitudes aped with a spirit of
mockery, and the *Lanterne* of Rochefort became a favourite journal among the *habitués* of
the palace. The Empress did not resist the
popular follies, but, while feigning indignation,

became the assiduous reader of this paper.
This fact may seem improbable, but it can be
affirmed by those who knew the Empress in
her private life.

The years 1867, 1868, and 1869 are characterised by the death agony of a society which
perished from the excesses of life.

I do not wish to appear in the light of a
morbid writer who is opposed to all enjoyment.
It is, nevertheless, evident that the conduct of
the men and women of the Tuileries, in inspiring the masses with discontent, and in wounding
the half-hypocritical puritanism which foreign
nations had at that time assumed, — and which,
indeed, they still assume in our presence, —
had alienated from it the sympathies which in
the hour of political crises and revolt would
have been helpful to it. The frivolous life,
too, of the men and women of the Tuileries
must have had a fatal influence on these men
and women themselves. Weary and enervated
by so many days of uninterrupted gaiety, they
remained without physical force or power of
moral resistance when misfortune overtook
them. There was no alternative but resignation ; they were like men who, rising from a
feast, find themselves in a state of intoxication,
and can but lean against some wall, powerless

to regain their bearings, and who watch with vapid mind and soul the passing mockers and those who toss encouraging words to them as they stand there helpless.

When the men and the women who had filled with their laughter, their gallantry, and their beauty the reign of Napoleon III., fell into the gutter, other men arose, who, young and healthy in body and mind, made their claims heard, and urged the duty of humanity. The nation listened to them, the nation followed their lead with applause on its lips, and enthusiasm in its heart, and anger, as well, that it should so long have maintained an allegiance to this decaying society; it grew strong in the hope of seeing arise on its misery and bondage a new day bright with promise.

When the year 1870 initiated the old government into a new policy, — as young blood is sometimes transfused into the veins of an old person, — there was a great stir in the faubourgs, and the symptoms of a fever, sure to cause delirium, became evident in the crowd. Some believed that the liberal Empire would conduct France peacefully toward a period of happiness; but those with the most foresight and the boldest spirits only smiled and shrugged their shoulders when an era of political prosperity was announced. Their thought travelled far beyond the present which the world forced itself to receive with the appearance of joy, and in the mysterious darkness of the future it discerned objects which filled it with terror.

These objects — revolution or war — took up their place at the end of a long line of follies and chimeras ; they pursued the Second Empire, and soared high among its clouds, as yet invisible, flying like the flocks of crows which follow an army. When destiny struck the hour of supreme struggle, all things were in readiness to serve this destiny. They fell upon the Second Empire, which, weak and bloodless, had not the power to throw them off. A great noise filled the air and shook the ground like the expiring groans of some great monster ; and those who dared henceforth glance back at the Tuileries saw but a desolate solitude, in the sepulchral silence of which a woman swathed in black, the Empress Eugénie, wandered in terror. Those who dared henceforth look out on the frontiers of France saw there but one lonely shadow, the Emperor Napoleon III., bending under his load of sorrow, a shadow so small and so pitiable that it appeared smaller and more pitiable than the shadows of those beggars who weep along the wayside.

X.

THE DECLARATION OF WAR.

PRINCE BISMARCK has given the world some information concerning the war of 1870, and diverse theories have been formulated concerning the originators of this war, and opinions formed as to who were probably responsible for it. It would take long to cite these theories, to analyse, approve, or condemn them ; but I shall, nevertheless, consider one which has seemed to be expressed with more exactitude and with more violence than have the others.

Without pausing to study details or to consider those attendant circumstances, which, in truth, are of great importance, there are many who unhesitatingly affirm that the disastrous results of the war of 1870 are due to the men at that time belonging to the liberal party, and are almost ready to declare that this war should in its very genesis be imputed to them.

No statement could be more false than this ; and if the reader will allow me to volunteer information upon the matter, I shall find no

difficulty in setting forth the true causes of the
war of 1870.

There is a question of some importance to be
answered at the outset. Did Prussia seek in
1870 to involve France in war, and was the
candidacy of Prince Leopold of Hohenzollern to
the throne of Spain arranged for the purpose of
discontenting us and of provoking a rupture?

We answer firmly, No. In the question of
Hohenzollern, no more than previously in that
of Luxemburg, did Prussia endeavour, systematically and with fixed purpose, to excite our
warlike spirit and our hostility. We continually deceived ourselves under the Second Empire, and especially during the last years of the
imperial reign, concerning the sentiments entertained by Europe toward us.

Misled by the external policy adopted by
Napoleon III., public opinion stood in constant
distrust of Prussia. It is, however, to be noted
that this country, interested by the humanitarian dream of the Emperor and by his theory
of national unity, was not content with the
rather negative friendliness of him who reigned
in the Tuileries, but, less egotistical, less hypocritical, or more practical, than certain other
neighbouring States, proposed, and even urged,
an alliance. The bearing of M. de Goltz, Prus-

sia's ambassador to France, is marked by such
sentiments ; the visit of Prince Bismarck confirms them ; and it is only by the repeated
refusal of Napoleon III. to involve his name
in a policy of conquest, that the chancelleries
and the government of Prussia and the cabinet
at Berlin abandoned its project, and consoled
itself with new hopes. Prussia, though certainly wounded by the almost scornful attitude
of the cabinet at Paris, did not, properly speaking, desire present war with France, when in
1870 an incident arose which rapidly assumed
the importance of a *casus belli*. It had in
reality no idea that it was so close upon a conflict with us, and was as much surprised by the
fact as were we.

Prussia, indeed, despite its preparations for a
campaign against us, and despite its perception
of the difficulties in the way of an international policy which was visionary and ven-
turesome, was more honest in its relations with
France than were Austria and Italy, upon
whom not only the nation at large, but also the
court of the Tuileries, were accustomed to rely.
M. de Goltz in saying as he did : " Europe is
old, too old ; it is slowly dying for want of
blood to nourish it. Its book is closed, and
those who shall open a new one are born. Tell

the Emperor this; he will perhaps realise that there is yet time that we should understand each other, and that the destiny of nations may be accomplished without endangering the peace of the world"— M. de Goltz, I say, in speaking thus, had far more thought of reconciling the interests of his country and of ours, than had Austria and Italy, who provoked so much enthusiasm in the persons of their representatives, MM. de Metternich and Nigra, those two sly and cruel enemies of France, whose one inspiration was the thought of our abasement, though this wish was prompted in each by a different motive.

When in 1869 and 1870 the Liberals assumed a position of importance, and when the Emperor declared openly his wish to reform his internal policy and to confide its direction to M. Emile Ollivier, a clique rose in the court and in the Chambers composed of men devoted to the Empire, but opposed to the new order of things, and called "the party of the Empress," because its leaders received their inspiration directly from her.

At the head of these men, among whom were deputies, senators, chamberlains, and simple *habitués* of the palace, stood MM. Rouher and Chevreau. All their efforts were designed to check the Emperor in the pursuance of his liberalism.

It has been said that the plebiscite of 1870 was undertaken for the purpose, for a long time nursed, of bringing on a war which as a result should give back to the Emperor the authority which at the outset of his reign he had possessed.

It has also been said that the ministry of January Second invented the plebiscite in order to adorn itself, under the shadow of the imperial name, with a prestige that would enable it to launch out in warlike enterprises by which its tottering power should be made firm, and its policy, as yet little understood by the masses, be strengthened. These assertions are not conformable to truth.

After the plebiscite neither the political world nor the court, which was submissive to the tyranny of the Empress, conceived the project of war with any nation. The incident which determined the campaign of 1870 was born of spontaneous circumstances of which it was a necessary consequence. After the plebiscite, however, events transpired at court and in the circle surrounding the Empress, which are worthy to be related.

A plot was formed for the purpose of destroying, in the mind of Napoleon III., those ideas by which he was at present led, and the thought was for a moment entertained of directing against the men of January Second a sort of *coup d'état* which would make the continuance of their work impossible. The plebiscite, which came to consecrate once more the name of Napoleon, might have served as an aid to this intrigue, and with the help of some resolute persons have smothered all protests. In a word, a project was formed by the party of the Empress, and in direct opposition to the will of the Emperor, to take possession of the ministers of January Second, and to imprison them during the time necessary for the re-establishment of absolute power.

When this plan for a policy contrary to his desires was cautiously suggested to Napoleon III., he, already feeble in body and mind, revolted ; and in the earnestness of his liberalism, in the sincerity of his purpose, he foiled the designs of his too zealous friends.

The party of the Empress, however, though baffled in this affair, was not at all discouraged, and in its extreme hatred of the liberal counsellors of Napoleon III. sought but an official pretext by which to oblige them to retire from the government, and to revive in the Tuileries the bright hours of the authoritative Empire.

At the time of the Hohenzollern incident this party raised a cry of joy, and prepared to avail itself of the opportunity which thus offered, happy to attain at last the object which they had with so much eagerness pursued.

The Empress, and with her the whole court, which in its blind adoration approved of her attitude in the affair and was obedient to her least word, rejoiced in the incident, clinging to it like a drowning man to a buoy, and had henceforth no thought but to avail itself of the opportunity which had offered so unexpectedly, and to pursue once more their plans of long ago, to build up their fallen hopes and restore an authoritative Empire, in the accomplishment of which the Emperor should himself help them.

The Empress immediately summoned M. Rouher, who, together with certain persons belonging to the party in open conflict with the Liberals, appeared before her, and it was agreed that regular council should meet to offset the official council of the Emperor.

After this time conventicles were held by the Empress and her faithful followers; and it was then that the famous question of "guarantees" was raised and presented as a supreme

and decisive argument against conciliation with
Prussia, and against the possibility of an understanding with that country.

When, indeed, M. Emile Ollivier, who had
succeeded in restoring peace, and who had
received satisfaction from Prussia, whose king
approved the retirement of Prince Leopold of
Hohenzollern from the candidacy of the throne
of Spain, presented himself before the Chamber rejoicing that he was the bearer of such
good news, the party of the Empress was filled
with stupefaction, with discouragement, and with
fury. Once again power had escaped it, that
power of which it stood in imperative need.
A war would almost certainly ensure it the
possession of authority ; and it was essential that
this war should take place, and that its pretext
should be one of such weight that no discussions could arise to delay its accomplishment.
The question of guarantees saved the situation.
This question, presented before the council of
ministers and the Legislative Corps, imbued
the conflict which had risen with the spirit
which it needed, and permitted Prince Bismarck to give free rein to his hatred of France.

The Empress had, unfortunately, in the Cabinet itself, if not partisans of her policy, at least
admirers of the extreme enthusiasm which she

showed at this time, and which she called by the name of patriotism. Despite the efforts of M. Emile Ollivier to calm over-excited minds, despite the wise advice of the Duc de Gramont, which was, however, somewhat moderated by his obedience to the wishes of the Empress, the nation deferred to the desires expressed by her; and in the face of the accusation of cowardice brought by the authorities against the Liberals, who opposed all further negotiations with the king of Prussia, Count Benedetti, ambassador to Berlin, received the order to present more positive claims.

The events which followed are well known. The king, who was at this time at Ems, was accosted by M. Benedetti during his promenade, and as our minister presented to him, for the second time, the question of guarantees, he showed some impatience, though he did not depart from a perfect courtesy and correctness of bearing.[1]

Prince Bismarck then entered upon the scene. He falsified the message of Prince Radziwill, which related the interviews of the King and M. Benedetti, and thus war became inevitable.

[1] Count Benedetti related this incident to a dear and intimate friend of his and mine, M. Eugène Bazin, who lived at Versailles, and who himself told me of the circumstance.

I have spoken of the cabals arranged by the Empress and M. Rouher, whose purpose was to check the pacific policy of the Emperor and of his ministers. Among the important men of whom were composed these secret councils, the Duc de Persigny cannot be forgotten. Though he belonged to the absolutist party, and though he held all liberalism in horror, we must yet do him the justice to say that he did not wish war.

In 1866, when, after the defeat at Sadowa, Prussia found her forces weakened, he counselled the Emperor to oppose the unification of Germany, and the strengthening of a power which might become in the future a danger for France. In 1870, however, he feared a war for our country; and, as he was well aware of the hypocrisy of those feelings of affection expressed for us by Austria and Italy, it was not without alarm that he saw the Emperor engaging himself in a problematical conflict, whose results, judging from private documents and from official correspondence, remained doubtful in the extreme.

Perceiving that no attention was paid to his advice, he declined to sit longer in the councils of the Empress and M. Rouher, and he informed the Emperor of the grave and perilous events which were taking place. The Emperor, however, much broken in health, and placed between a domestic scandal and the frenzy of Parliament, — a frenzy which had taken possession of the whole country, and especially of Paris, — had attached little importance to the revelations made by M. de Persigny, and contented himself by watching the phases of the drama which was being played out before him. At the last moment, however, he opposed the declaration of war ; and when, after the incident at Ems, he was obliged to admit that a duel between France and Prussia was unavoidable, he resigned himself sadly to the hard fate which had visited him.

We have seen that the war of 1870 was desired by the Empress and by the party which, receiving its inspiration from her, was called by her name. It was desired with the express and clearly defined purpose of destroying the liberal Empire, and of expelling from the government those men who aided Napoleon III. in the task which he had undertaken with a sincere conviction of its justice ; with the distinct purpose, too, of bringing back the hours of joy and of absolutism, which had now escaped them, but whose existence had given so much happiness to a few ambitious spirits and to a few courtiers.

The Emperor, ill and suffering, was forced into the most atrocious enterprise which can be imagined; and it cannot even be said in excuse that either the Empress or the court was ignorant of his physical infirmity, for it had been decided in 1870 that the court should remain at Saint-Cloud, and that any change of residence should be avoided, lest it might fatigue the sovereign, and increase his suffering.

Neither can it be denied that the Empress desired war from the very motives which I have ascribed to her; for she herself, when at Florence after the downfall, said to General Moceni that this war could and should have saved the Empire and the papacy.

In regard to that which concerns the papacy, I have already told how the Emperor, urged by his consort not to abandon Rome, rejected the proposals of Victor Emmanuel, who promised an armed intervention, on the condition that he should himself be free to adopt whatever policy he chose against Pius IX.

Political interests, perhaps, require us to turn our attention away from these facts; but history has its rights, and is above rivalries, selfish greed, and hatred. It registers events with an unerring wisdom and justice; and humanity sins in travestying the facts which belong to it, and in appropriating to its own interests and preferences what is rightfully the property of history.

If in 1870 the sentiments entertained by Prince Bismarck toward us admitted of no equivocation, the party of the Empress gave by its actions free play to these sentiments, and rendered possible both their expression and their practical application; while in persisting in its determination to see in the question of Hohenzollern a premeditated outrage on the dignity of France, it furnished Prussia with a formidable pretext to enter into war with us, and produced very strained relations between Paris and Berlin after the refusal of the Emperor to meet the advances of this body.

In regard to that which concerns the despatch from Ems, Bismarck has said all that can be said. It has always been known that a certain despatch was falsified; but the public, labouring under an error, accused the ministry of January Second of this act, of this crime, we may better say. Truth has, however, exonerated the men who were innocent.

The despatch from Ems, nevertheless, and the avowal made by Prince Bismarck, seem to me to give rise to some doubts, and to provoke inquiries which I am astonished that the press has not brought forward.

Prince Radziwill addressed to his leader, Count Bismarck, by order of the king of Prussia, a telegram relating to the interviews which our ambassador, Count Benedetti, had held with William I. ; and Bismarck, considering that this telegram was likely to foil his own designs, cynically misrepresented the message, and, thus falsified, communicated it to the European States.

How did it happen that M. Benedetti, confronted by this falsehood, which was to involve two nations in war and to place his country in a position of great danger, allowed the ministers to declare in the Chambers that he had received an insult at Ems, without hastening to contradict the statement made by Bismarck ? Why did not M. Benedetti inform the minister, the government, the Emperor himself, of these events, and proclaim loudly that the assertions made by the opposing diplomatic party were false, that the king of Prussia had never insulted him, and that he had never had occasion to offend the king ?

Such a declaration as this would have reached many ears ; and though it might, perhaps, have been a slight violation of official courtesy, it would still have saved the lives of more than five hundred thousand men.   This might, I think, have atoned for a breach of that etiquette which is observed by the diplomatic world.

On the other side, if M. Benedetti, contrary to the statements of M. Emile Ollivier, who says that he had never in his hand the original telegram, informed the government of the affairs which concerned it, how is it that the men who at that time made their voices heard through France did not announce to the Chambers, to the nation, and to Europe the abominable expedient resorted to by Count Bismarck ? How does it happen, furthermore, that, if our government was not informed by our ambassador, it omitted to demand explanation before declaring war ?

One is truly lost in a multitude of conjectures on this score, and frightened by the weight of responsibility which attaches to the circumstance, as well as by the absence of conscience and of intelligence shown throughout.   If Bismarck, in the loquacity of his old age and in the bitterness of feeling which he entertained toward his sovereign, appears a man somewhat less noble than that genial leader of nations on whom we have been wont to look, it must also be admitted that his adversaries fell very short of their duty, and in becoming his prey showed themselves to be both short-sighted and ignorant.

One man alone, I believe, and this was Napoleon III., understood the true cause of the war, and realised, though he may have been ignorant of the falsehoods involved, what its results would be.

"Who knows," wrote he to General Lepic at the moment of his own departure, "who knows that we shall ever meet again?"

It was he alone who had power to turn from himself and from the country those evils which had risen. In 1870, however, Napoleon III. was a dead man whom his crew cast into the sea, and of whom, after the body had disappeared beneath the waves, it no longer thought.

I have based the statements made in the preceding pages on data furnished me by one of the persons whose relations with the Emperor and Empress were most intimate in 1870. I have also substantiated them by an interview with one of the former members of the Privy Council of Napoleon III., a man who is distantly related to me by marriage, M. Charles A——, who has very recently died, and whom I met some years ago, not only in the Chamber where he sat in the quality of deputy, but

also in the drawing-rooms of the Comtesse
d' H——, niece of a general who filled an important *rôle* in 1871, at the time of the capitulation of Paris, and also at the home of one
of my aunts, the Comtesse D——.

The information which I have thus received
concerning the war of 1870 seems to me authoritative ; yet, in a question such as that with
which this chapter is concerned, one cannot
refer to too many documents, and I have decided to make public a letter which a former
diplomat, Comte de V——, has sent me, and
which reveals this affair in an aspect which,
though not thoroughly satisfactory, is yet
interesting.

Comte de V—— seems to be among those
who remain assured that the war of 1870 was
undertaken purely in the interest of the dynasty. About this time a discussion rose in
the Legislative Corps concerning an abrogation
of the laws of exile relating to the Princes
of Orleans ; and he, basing his conviction on
proof, which is certainly plausible, unhesitatingly believes that the Bonapartist party and
the *habitués* of the Tuileries, frightened by the
suggestion of the return of these Princes, provoked war for the purpose of rendering this
return impossible, which, had it been accom-

plished, would without doubt, in the present state of affairs, have given rise to political dangers whose seriousness it would be futile to deny.

The account given by Comte de V—— is curious in the extreme, and it is for this reason that I repeat it here. His argument, however, still allows me to believe that the sudden power attained by the Liberals who had won a place in the councils of the Emperor, caused the Empress and her party more anxiety than did the claims made in behalf of the Princes of Orleans. I cannot but feel, too, that if war was desired for the sake of restoring, in the strengh of new and glorious victories, the authority and absolutism of years past, such a war could not have been accomplished upon the plea of a possible dynastic rivalry in the future.

However this may be, the letter of Comte de V—— merits attention. I therefore commend it to the attention of historians, and to the public in general, having already volunteered some information designed to uphold my own convictions in the matter.

"I have read," writes Comte de V—— to me, "your various publications upon the private life of the Court of the Tuileries, and upon the close of the imperial reign. I have, however, been surprised that you were not led to reveal the hidden motives, the true motives, which forced upon the Empire that fatal line of conduct whose last step was Sedan.

" In order to do so, it would, it seems to me, have sufficed to read the account of the session of July 2, 1870, during which a demand for the abrogation of the exile of the Princes of Orleans was presented, and to consider the excitement produced by this demand, and the comments which it called forth.

" What would have been the most fatal blow which the imperial *régime* could have received ? A movement, surely, which would have confronted this *régime* with a dynastic opposition, with a royal family, which had left France in the possession of profound and sympathetic affection. Memories which are now forgotten clustered thickly round its name during the Second Empire ; and it was easy at this time to swell the expressions of sympathy, and, with the concourse of all the discontented spirits of France, to raise loud voices of cheer. This was, indeed, just what was done in the session of July 2, 1870.

" After the discourse delivered by M. de Montalembert in 1852, not once during twenty years of the imperial *régime* was the name of the Princes of Orleans pronounced in the French Chamber. Suddenly the astonished Legislative Corps resounded with the name of Orléans, of de Joinville, d'Aumale, and de Montpensier, and tears were seen to flow, under the influence of sincere emotion, from the eyes of deputies who had become Bonapartists from necessity, but who had almost all served under the government of July, either in the army, the navy, or the administration, and had with few exceptions sustained it with their votes, only rallying at last round Napoleon III. in the absence of anything better to do and in the fear of something worse.

" I was present at the session of July 2, and was seated in the tribune of the diplomatic corps, to which I then belonged. The hall was crowded, and excited scenes were expected.

" Arriving at the Palais-Bourbon, I met a senator, Baron de H——.

" ' The session,' I said to him, ' is likely to be an agitated one, is it not?'

" ' Bah,' replied he ; ' the young Estancelin will set off a cracker, M. Emile Ollivier will put his foot on it, and there will be some noise.'

" Events did not, however, carry out this prophecy. With power, and with an emotion either real or feigned, he who has been called the ' young Estancelin,' a personal friend of the Princes in time past, and who doubtless recalled the words of Lamartine, ' It is not to the voice of reason that France responds, but to that of the heart,' pleaded the cause of the exiled princes, though he evoked neither the claims of law nor justice. He resuscitated, if I may thus express myself, the young exiles, who had been in a measure forgotten, and presented them to the Assembly.

" The former Orleanists remembered their enthusiasm in past years, when the Prince de Joinville, at the head of his marines, brought to Paris the ashes of Napoleon ; their applause, when the Duc d'Aumale, with his regiment, bronzed by the sun of Africa, crossed the capital, accompanied by cheers from Vincennes to Neuilly ; and the emotion after the attempt made against his life.

" When the old general Lebreton, a Bonapartist, and at that time questor of the Chamber of Deputies, raised his strong, peremptory voice, and added his ringing words to those of M. Estancelin, it seemed to me, in truth, that it was the voice of the French army which spoke. I remember well his last words.

"'I have served the government of the Emperor,' he said, 'in the days of hardship, but I have also served the Duc d'Aumale in Africa. I have often had cause to admire his military talents. I should be happy to restore to my country one of its best and greatest citizens.'

"'Those are fine words,' a member cried to him as he closed. 'The Duke is a man of parts.'

"Esquiros, Jules Favre, and Picard treated the question in its legal aspect. The old Marquis de Piré, a furious Bonapartist, joined his voice with theirs.

"Kératry, also, attacked the ministers with his habitual spirit and energy.

"One member of the opposition, too, M. Jules Grévy, without defending the Cabinet, came to the same conclusion, and met with the scorn of his colleagues of the left wing by whom he was surrounded when he pronounced his famous words, 'I will be neither a dupe nor yet an accomplice.'

"The government, therefore, found itself suddenly confronted by a great body of enemies, which had drawn up on common ground, and stood united by a single thought, which was both popular and anti-dynastic. It saw even its friends hesitate to take up its cause, so moved were they by old reminiscences. So true and so apparent was this, that at one time the Swiss minister, who was seated behind me, gave expression to his surprise.

"'In this Bonapartist Chamber,' he exclaimed, 'there seem to be but Orleanists.'

"In thus speaking, this diplomat but expressed the thought which was in the minds of all.

"In issuing from the Chamber I gave my arm to the Duchesse de G——.

"'Ah, my dear Count,' she said to me, 'it is not a political, but a dynastic session which we have attended to-day. I cannot tell what will be its consequences, but I believe that they will not be unimportant.'

" ' I share your feeling,' replied I.   ' A terrible blow has been dealt the Empire.'

" These events took place on the second of July, 1870.

" On Sunday, the third of July, the first cry of war was raised by M. Chevandier de Valdrôme, minister of the Interior. Emile de Girardin gave us, some months before his death, an account of this incident.

" Emile de Girardin dined that evening with M. Chevandier de Valdrôme. After they had risen from the table, the minister went toward him.

" ' You know the news?' said he.   ' We shall certainly have a prince from the house of Hohenzollern on the throne of Spain.'

" ' In what way,' asked the publicist, ' is that going to affect us?'

" ' What!' replied M. de Valdrôme, ' do you not see that this is a danger for France, a threat against her? We shall not allow this candidacy ; we shall be compelled to make it a *casus belli.*'

" ' Such an act would be most foolish.'

" ' Not at all ; and you must write an article to-morrow to prove this very necessity.'

" ' Never!'

" Despite this exclamation, the desired article appeared. It is true, however, that Emile Girardin pleaded in his own excuse that it was not written by him.

" On this same day Prim received at Madrid a telegram announcing the protest of the French government, and its opposition to the candidacy of Prince Hohenzollern to the throne of Spain.

" One of my friends was with him when he received this message. After having read it, Prim crumpled the sheet and threw it upon his desk.

" ' This,' he cried, ' is a little too much, and it arises from a misunderstanding of the circumstances. *Our relations with the Tuileries were most harmonious.*'

" You will understand clearly from the preceding facts the hitherto unknown causes of the war of 1870.

" It became necessary to turn the mind of the public away from the question of the Princes of Orleans, and to parry the stroke which had been dealt against the imperial dynasty. War was the result of these efforts.

" Was it the clearly defined purpose of the Tuileries to urge matters thus far, and to necessitate hostilities? This I do not believe, and the hesitancy and blind groping of those first days would seem to confirm my disbelief. When, however, one is fairly launched on a dangerous course, it is often difficult to turn aside; and when the dynastic interests of a government are at stake, when a court acts against the decrees of a sovereign, it becomes impossible that the head of the government should control events and retrace his steps."

This is the remarkable letter written me by the Comte de V——.

The statements made herein seem, I repeat, despite their clearness, to give rise to some inquiries. They are, nevertheless, in accordance with my own account, in so far as they firmly establish the fact that the intrigue which originated around the Emperor was designed for the purpose of turning to the advantage of the government the threatened war between France and Prussia.

Despite the sentiments still entertained by

the old Orleanists who had now rallied round the Empire, the sons of King Louis Philippe were, even in 1870, little deserving of fear. The Liberals, who, under the leadership of Napoleon III., were beginning to assume power, were objects much more to be dreaded by the party of the Empress ; and I think that I am not too bold when I state that history holds decisive proofs that the whole hostility of the Empress and of her partisans was directed against the men of January Second.

If, therefore, the question of the Princes of Orleans is laid aside, it remains undeniable — and the letter of the Comte de V—— confirms the statement — that the war of 1870 was but desired and undertaken with the purpose of substituting the influence in the government of men hated at the Tuileries for the authoritative rule of men who were liked by the Empress and her partisans — of substituting, indeed, for the will of Napoleon III., who was old now and feeble, the wishes of the Empress, who was still in the full glory of her woman's beauty, and at the zenith of her political power.

After the Hohenzollern affair was made public, the Empress Eugénie not only used, as we have seen, all her influence, together with that of her following, to hasten a conflict be-

tween France and Prussia, but she also became
very nervous and irascible, and gave evidence
of her ill-humour to all who approached her.

She seemed more than ever unbalanced, and
controlled by thoughts and feelings which made
her wholly incomprehensible.   At times she
would lapse into meditative moods, and absorb
her mind in thoughts which she did not reveal; at others she would fall into the delirium,
as it were, of some wasting fever, whose secret she also guarded sacredly.   She had her
crises of gaiety, which were suddenly followed
by crises of tears, of doubts, of spontaneous
effusions and caprices, and was possessed by
an imperative need to affirm her own personality.

This condition of mind became most emphatic in the conversations which she continually held with her partisans, and often resulted
in painful scenes, in which her most devoted
friends were made to suffer.

Such exhibitions were usually childish in the
extreme, and were only the expression of the
mercurial temperament of a pettish woman.
There was one, however, which assumed almost the importance of a political act, and which
filled with terror those who witnessed it.   It
took place at Saint-Cloud, and in the presence

of some of the most intimate friends of the
Empress, one of whom, indeed, told me the
story.   It certainly confirms the assertions
of history as contained in the documents to
which I have referred in writing this chapter,
and it is for this reason that I feel myself
called on to relate the incident.

The Hohenzollern question had, as it is
known, become most bitter, and a rupture between France and Prussia was imminent, when
the Liberal opposition in the Legislative Corps,
by requiring from the ministry the communication of the diplomatic documents on which
the nation relied to legitimatise the declaration
of war, retarded the close of the relations between Paris and Berlin.

This adjournment of hostilities, as is to-day
clearly realised, was not at all in accordance
with the plans of the Empress and her party;
and she, much excited and wrought upon, did
not in any degree conceal her discontent, which
was shared by the courtiers.   There were,
nevertheless, among her friends some who,
without openly opposing her attitude, saw with
apprehension the development of a conflict
which they might certainly by prudence, tact,
and calm, have succeeded in averting.

One afternoon while these questions were

being discussed in the presence of the Empress, one of her friends, the Comte de ——, had the courage to speak, not this time as a courtier whose one desire is to please, but as a brave man, on whom danger has imposed frankness. The Empress attacked with great vehemence the deputies who had shown themselves refractory to projects of war, and then she paused, as usual, to receive the approval of those who had heard her speak. The Comte de ——, after a brief silence, ventured to make his reply.

"Your Majesty speaks truly," said he. "If Prussia has outraged France, and if M. Thiers and his friends do not oppose the idea that the Emperor avenges the country from purely political and party interests, their *rôle* is odious. We should not, however, be unjust toward those men who, at this moment, seek to avert any rupture between King William and Emperor Napoleon III. If the opposition, without lessening the prestige of France, could accomplish a reconciliation, an understanding, between Paris and Berlin, I believe that the government and the nation — and I respectfully submit my observation to your Majesty — would owe it strong gratitude."

When the Count ceased speaking, stupefaction was written on all faces, and the Empress,

amazed and nonplussed, remained an instant
without replying.   It was only a moment, however, before she recovered consciousness of the
situation.

"What," she exclaimed, turning brusquely
toward the speaker, her tones full of anger,
"What, is it you who speak thus? We see
how you, too, pass to the Left.   Ah, what will
become of me if my friends abandon me and
adopt the cause of the Liberals? Such men
are but cowards who seek unforeseen popularity
under the guise of false patriotism.   In inter-
fering with war they seek, in this instance,
to foil the designs of the Tuileries, as they
would have sought to hasten hostilities had
the Tuileries shown themselves pacific.   Do
you not see that the men of the opposition
are liars, and that the hatred with which we
inspire them is their sole inspiration? It is
me, beyond all, whom they hate; it is on me
rather than on the Emperor that they wish
to be avenged.   They know that, had the Emperor listened to me, they would never have
set their feet in the Legislative Corps, and they
cannot pardon me the intervention which,
unhappily, was futile.   They detest me, but I
return their feeling in like measure."

She paused for a moment in her violent

harangue; but no one replied, either to applaud her, or to calm her excitement, and she resumed her discourse.

"I can hardly think," she continued, "that any are so foolish as to accept the arguments which they present, or to follow that retreat. which they counsel. When the campaign is at an end, and when the victorious troops re-enter France, we shall see if they have still the impertinence to offer us advice, and to put obstacles in the way of our projects. I will meet them there, and we will sum up our accounts if they wish to do so.

"All good things," she added, with increasing irritation, "are dying in this country; yes, all good things. The government, the respect for authority, religion, patriotism, are all disappearing, to give place to, I know not what ideas of independence and of revolt. It is time, truly, that we should meet these conditions."

Turning toward the persons who were listening to her, she supplicated them, evidently much moved and very impatient, like a child who asks for a thing which is accorded it with hesitation.

"You will help me, will you not," she continued, "to restore to the Emperor the authority of which he has been robbed? You will aid me

in the difficult task which has been laid upon
me? Say that you will help me, say it, for I
want your co-operation."

Angry and exhausted, she clenched her fists,
and began to sob; then crumpling her dress
with her fingers which she opened and shut
convulsively, her force passed away, leaving her
motionless and without strength in a state like
that of a faint.

She was humoured and cared for by those
round her; and the Comte de ——, sorry to
have provoked unconsciously such a scene, left
the room, shaking his head sadly.

Great fear, as I have already said, had taken
possession of the court at the news of the
Hohenzollern affair, and this fear reached its
maximum when the declaration of war was announced to the country and to Europe. The
Empress, however, exerted an imperative will,
and was filled with an enthusiasm which could
but be contagious. Under the influence of her
bearing, the men and the women who held
their court round the sovereigns and gave free
rein to their pleasures and frivolities, were
reassured and inspired by new hopes for the
future — a future which should not deny them

the joys which for so many years had been theirs.

They did not accustom themselves at all to this unusual state of disturbance, to the noises which rose from the street, and, echoing through the air, reached even the imperial dwelling. These were strange things, truly, which had come to pass ; they interrupted the even course of existence at the Tuileries, and for this reason were to be regretted. The campaign, however, which was about to begin had been represented to them in so bright a light that the *habitués* of the court had at last calmed their anxiety and resumed their good spirits and their careless bearing, which was like that of demigods whose creed is invulnerable.

There was, it is true, a murmur of terror when the Emperor commanded that the band of the Guard should play the Marseillaise under the windows of the palace at Saint-Cloud ; the people ventured a few remarks of scorn and irony when they heard the echo of the revolutionary hymn ; but as Napoleon III. had exerted his authority on this point, they deferred to his wishes, in appearance satisfied.

A few words spoken by the Emperor at this time in regard to the Marseillaise, which was played by official sanction, are important.

One of his chamberlains expressed astonishment that he should be willing to listen to music of Rouget de l'Isle, and that he should command its public hearing.

"We should to-day," replied the Emperor, "neglect nothing which is French, nothing which can quicken the pulse of our throbbing hearts. The Marseillaise, whether its spirit is true or false, will embue the people with enthusiasm. It is for this reason that I tolerate its performance."

"If the old royalist cry," he added, "that of ' Montjoie et Saint-Denys,' could gain a victory for France, I should command my troops to give it. There are circumstances when it is important to understand the French."

The life at court hardly changed after the departure of the Emperor for the army of the Rhine, but continued much as it had been before all these events had transpired. The courtiers continued to enjoy their frivolities and to encourage their self-interested hopes. The enthusiasm of the Empress knew no abatement; and we may safely affirm that she was truly happy, for she could now practise her authority without check and establish it beyond discussion. She reigned, and she reigned truly, in all her grace of womanhood, and with the

respected authority of a sovereign, while the
frontier remained silent and deserted. When,
however, the sinister echo of our reverses
reached her, when she had a vision, like a
nightmare, of those masses of humanity which
were moving round the fields of Alsace killing
and wounding each other, she gave a cry of
distress ; it was not a cry which rose from the
heart of an Empress who sees her dream van-
ishing, but that of a miserable and wounded
woman. She began now to waver.

She understood that for her everything was
lost ; that all those sweet flavours of life which
she had tasted with such delicious enjoyment
would in the future be denied her. She knew
that her hope was gone, that her hatreds, as her
affections, were at an end ; she knew that the
Empire, in falling, must crush her. She then
seemed to suffer a transformation, and was
exalted by truly humanitarian principles ; instead of allowing herself to be mastered by
sorrow, she rose superb in her affliction, and
with that intuitive sense which lies at the core
of the feminine character and which exerts
itself in supreme moments of danger, she met-
amorphosed herself and was, what she had
never before known how to be, the Empress.

She held councils, she inspired courage, forgot bitterness, and sacrificed sympathies, that France might better recover itself and again attain happiness. If it is true that a single hour of nobility and of generosity effaces in the life of a human being the hours consecrated to frivolities and to selfishness, history will not hesitate to render its homage to the Empress Eugénie in this crisis of terror through which she passed; history will not hesitate to salute her in the midst of the loss and affliction which she supported with so much dignity, in the midst of those rapid and tragic days during which, in pitiable loneliness, away from her friends and separated even from herself, she reigned — that is, she suffered and wept.

XI.

SEDAN.

HAVING arrived at Sedan, the Emperor Napoleon III. established his residence and that of
his quarter-general at the *sous-prefecture.* On
the evening of August thirty-first, he was caused
some disquietude by news of the battle at
Mouzon ; but, assured that the troops were
gathering around Sedan, and, in obedience to
the command, were preparing for battle, which
it was believed must take place in a few hours,
he was somewhat reassured.

He was unable, nevertheless, to calm entirely
the agitation which on that evening, August
thirty-first, had taken possession of him. He
paced his room in feverish anxiety, demanded the
details of the army's operations, and informed
himself concerning the material and moral condition of the regiments. Long and doleful silences would succeed his words, and a sudden
immobility transfix him to his place, while he
lapsed into reveries from which he only issued
to resume his steps up and down the apart-

ment, and to pronounce at intervals short, sad sentences.

There were round him generals, orderlies, and aides-de-camp. He had, however, brought with him no functionary of his civil establishment, and the story which represents him as surrounded by his ordinary chamberlains is false. Two of the quartermasters who were included in his military household had accompanied him, and received as salary for the campaign the sum of ten thousand francs each.

These persons were with him on the evening of August thirty-first, and but responded to his rather incoherent remarks in monosyllables. It was already late, and the Emperor and his retinue were preparing to take a little rest, when he spoke with great effort and with a prophetic realisation of affairs.

"We shall never recover," he said, "from this."

Napoleon III. had been, since the first defeat of his army, possessed with the idea which he expressed on many occasions, of commanding the retreat of the soldiers and of recalling to Paris those who still remained to him, thus separating the French and Prussian armies, and making an offensive return possible to his generals. When Marshal Mac Mahon had re-

formed his regiments, now materially decreased
in number, and added to them new and young
recruits, the Emperor raised his voice in favour
of a backward march on Paris. The minister,
however, influenced by the Empress Eugénie,
begged him not to carry out this project.
M. Rouher sought to prove to him that only
a movement eastward could save the country,
and the poor sovereign, dispossessed of his
authority, did not feel it right to assume the
responsibility of a command which was open
to so much criticism. He claimed but the
satisfaction of remaining in the midst of the
soldiers whose captain he had been, that he
might rejoice in their triumph were they victorious, and suffer with them were they vanquished. This privilege being accorded him, —
the expression, alas! has too much truth when
used to describe the relation of the Emperor
to his government, — he came to Sedan, where
he was terrified by the vision of a horrible
drama.

"We shall never recover," he said, " from
this."

He was filled with regret that he had been
unable to withdraw the army from the frontiers,
and this ejaculation was called forth by his
despair.

As those who surrounded Napoleon III. made no response to his words, he let them pass without comment or explanation, and wishing to retire to his own room, he saluted his officers with the same words which he was wont to use to his friends in the Tuileries.

" I will bid you good-bye, gentlemen," he said, " until to-morrow."

When the Emperor found himself alone, he paced his room up and down, till exhausted, he fell into a chair. Weary and discouraged, he then undressed himself and went to bed. He did not sleep, however, and those who stood guard at his door heard him moan, for at this time he suffered much from his kidneys ; he muttered, too, indistinct words during the night, and at times threw himself from the bed.

At half-past three the next morning he abandoned all thought of repose, and, making a rapid toilet, summoned Captain Fiéron of the Cent-Gardes, who did not leave him again ; he then dressed himself carefully and waxed his moustaches as was his custom.

An engagement with the Bavarians took place in the neighborhood of Bazeilles during the day of August thirty-first. It was here, indeed, that the battle of Sedan commenced.

The Emperor had scarcely finished dressing

when, at about four o'clock, he was startled by the noise of a fusillade. He inquired its cause, and was told that Bazeilles was again attacked by the Bavarians, confronting whom stood the division of the marine infantry which was commanded by General de Vassoignes, and which was to support the Twelfth Corps commanded by General Lebrun.

The Emperor seemed satisfied by the reply which he received ; and after having commanded the officers belonging to his private service to assemble, he issued with them from the *sous-prefecture* and commanded them to mount their horses.

Those who saw him at this time noticed the extreme difficulty with which he himself mounted, and the expression of horrible suffering which passed over his face as he arranged himself in the saddle. It was only a moment's weakness on his part, however, and, reins in hand, he appeared, though greatly careworn, with all his accustomed grace and dignity.

A thick fog hung over Sedan and its environs on this morning of September first, 1870, and it was through a thick mist that the Emperor and his officers left the *sous-prefecture* on their way to the field of battle.

As little by little they approached Bazeilles, the noise of firing increased, mingling with the ominous detonations of the artillery and the sounds of distant uproar which were brought nearer by the echoes, and which the undulating waves of mist seemed to cast back and forth upon each other.

The Emperor and his escort rode, silent and with hearts downcast, through this unknown region. It was not long, however, before the sun dissipated the vapours and allowed them to watch the engagement.

The battle, which had begun at Bazeilles, travelled gradually northward, till it surrounded Sedan, and arrived at the Fond de Givonne.

The German artillery turned its death-dealing machines against the French lines, which, intrepid, fought hard and thinned by tens the ranks of the enemy which had drawn up too close. It, however, became necessary, in order that the Twelfth Corps, which was in the thick of battle, should come to a decisive stand, that our artillery should advance to its aid. Unfortunately our pieces, put to the battery and replying to the fire of the Germans, proved a disastrous fact ; proved, that is, that their range was insufficient, so that the projectiles did not reach the desired point.

It was now half-past six, and Marshal Mac Mahon, who commanded in chief and who had gone to reconnoitre the position of the troops, was seriously wounded by a volley of shells ; he fell from his horse and was carried to Sedan, where he transmitted his authority to General Ducrot.

As he was half way between Sedan and Bazeilles, the Emperor met the lugubrious *cortège* which was bearing the Marshal away from the field of battle. He paused, and bending over the wounded man, spoke to him a few affectionate words, and then continued his route.

Having at his side General Pajol, General Courson, Captain Guzman, Captain D'Heudencourt, Captain Fiéron, his aide-de-camp, Ney de la Moskowa, Captain Trécesson, and various other officers whose names escape me, he directed his course toward the right upon Bazeilles where the infantry of the marine and the Twelfth Corps, commanded by General Lebrun, were engaged against the Bavarians. He, however, faced about with a sudden change of resolution and hastened toward the Fond de Givonne, where the battle was equally fierce.

When the Emperor reached this place, it was swept by storms of canister-shot, and, ac-

cording to the description of one of the witnes-
ses who took part in, and escaped from, this
conflict, the horses which the sovereign and his
officers rode, with an instinctive realisation of
the danger to which they were exposed, trembled and swayed so that it was necessary to
hold them with a firm rein.

As, however, he looked out over Bazeilles, it
seemed to the Emperor that the French had
the advantage, and he was filled with rejoicing;
but suddenly a movement of retreat puzzled
and disquieted him. He immediately sent one
of his officers, General Guzman, to ask an
explanation from General Ducrot, who made
known the new disposition of the troops, and
his command that they should retreat upon Illy,
which lies to the north of Sedan, in order to
avoid the danger, feared since the preceding
evening, of being hemmed in by the enemy.
Napoleon III. received this message silently,
expressing neither approbation nor disapproval.

Suddenly an unforeseen incident plunged
the Emperor into his former state of dejection.
Toward ten o'clock the retreat began and was
duly accomplished under the command of General Ducrot. The troops paused, and then began to retrace their steps, with an apparent
desire to assume again the offensive attitude

which they had abandoned. This action had a cause foreign to all calculation. General Wimpffen, furnished with a letter from the minister of war, came to dispossess General Ducrot of his command, and now traced for the army a plan of battle entirely contrary to that which it had till now followed. General Wimpffen, confiding his desire to " throw the Germans into the Meuse," commanded the obedience of all. Without realising the consequences of that disorder which a change of tactics must occasion the troops, he assumed supreme authority and forced the submission of the regiments to his will.

The Emperor, who for more than an hour had remained exposed to the fire of the enemy's artillery at Givonne, undoubtedly understood the danger of the position in which the army was placed ; but, and this was perhaps unfortunate, he was ignorant of the discussion, or rather the dispute, which had arisen between Generals Ducrot and Wimpffen concerning whose authority in the decisive moment should be exercised. It was only at Sedan and after the battle that he learned of the rivalry between these two men, and could analyse its results.

Who knows but that, had he understood the irascible claims of General Wimpffen and the

patriotic sorrow of General Ducrot, he might
have abandoned his *rôle* of simple spectator, and
used his sword against this criminal rivalry?
Seizing again the authority which had been
taken from him, he might, perhaps, have
given to this day of Sedan, which was powerless to procure victory, at least a less fearful
ending.

The Emperor had seen, while he stood at
Givonne in the face of the German batteries
hurling forth their volleys of shot, several men
of his escort fall at his side mortally wounded,
and also a few of his officers.

Some moments before General Ducrot yielded
the commandership to General Wimpffen, Captain d'Heudencourt, to whom the sovereign dictated a message, was struck by a shell and fell
to the ground instantly killed. Horses, too,
had fallen round him, their bodies ripped open;
and, as each man died, as each poor horse ex-
pired, the Emperor turned his head sadly toward
them with an expression of despairing grief, and
then resumed his attitude of spectator.

Leaving at last the Fond de Givonne, he
once more directed his course toward Bazeilles,
halting for a moment on the plain of Moncelle,
also covered with shells. During the retreat
commanded by General Ducrot, the Germans

had advanced and now occupied Bazeilles, which our troops were resolved to reconquer.

The Emperor remained for a long time on the plateau of Moncelle, where General Courson and Captain Trécesson received many wounds at his side; followed then by his escort, which inspired admiration by its calm intrepidity, he descended to Bazeilles, where he crossed the line of action. Turning, finally, his back on the battle, he proceeded to Sedan.

It was now half-past eleven, and the Emperor had been on the field for five long hours. During this time he had remained almost silent, inspecting with his field-glass the various points of battle, and suffering horribly from the disease of which he subsequently died; suffering so horribly that, as I have stated in my book, *The Empress Eugénie*, and in the chapter which is entitled "After Sedan," he held his two hands on the pommel of the saddle and refused to dismount, as he was begged to do, fearing that, did he yield, he would not be able again to ride his horse.

When the Emperor re-entered Sedan, forcing a difficult passage through the thousands of soldiers who, driven from the field of battle, sought refuge in the town, it was one o'clock in the afternoon, and the day was lost for the French.

A blazing sun had succeeded the early morning fog, and now cast its rays on the last efforts of the French army, seeming to throw an ironic light on our sorrow.

After a campaign of some weeks, startling in its progress and in its fatal results, our regiments, disorganised and demoralised by a course of murderous and futile engagements, returned to die in Sedan, the old frontier town, whose fortifications, unprepared for a defence, but offered them false and traitorous protection. Drawn up before the city, they sustained the attacks of the Germans, who, moment by moment, hemmed them closer in by their formidable artillery. The greater part resisted still, but signs of disorder made themselves felt in the ranks; already entire battalions, despairing of victory and fearing the threatening massacre, abandoned the field and fled into the town.

Papers and documents lay strewn among weapons and corpses on the ground, while horses and beasts of burden, in some cases fearfully mangled, rushed wildly between the trees and among the *débris* of waggons, powder-carts, and fallen breastworks, mingling with the combatants, and following each other in endless procession, like the waves of some bloody sea invading the land.

The sun gilded the scene, lending its irradiation to the humid, acrid, and sticky crimson which flowed from yawning wounds and fertilised the ground, bearing away the life and soul of the bodies which by thousands lay stretched out in the dust. The enormous disk stood high in the heavens, and kindled with its fire this red September afternoon, piercing the thick smoke of the powder and irradiating the opaque atmosphere, reminding one of the many-coloured bottles which in the cities shine through the darkness of night upon the passers-by from out the chemists' windows.

The French had made a final effort to repulse the revolving lines of the Germans. A charge had been made and the struggle was terrible ; there had been great butchery round Sedan, human butchery, so full always of madness, of suffering, and of terror, the sinister forerunner of deep silences, long periods of repose, and of a final awakening.

It was with his mind full of this monstrous vision that the Emperor re-entered Sedan and proceeded toward the *sous-préfecture*. As he approached the postern, M. Ney de la Moskowa, who followed closely after him, was again wounded in the arm by an explosion of shells.

The town presented a spectacle never before witnessed, and had become an awful counterpart of the field of battle.

The streets and public places were full of soldiers, in the midst of whom rose up great heaps of weapons, over which, regardless of the noise of objects crushed to powder, passed with oaths and the noise of thunder, the powder-carts, waggons, and cannons of the artillery, while broken teams without drivers rushed past at a furious gallop.

Projectiles began to fall in the town, and spread indescribable confusion among this mass of people and things. The inhabitants took refuge in their cellars; and the soldiers, drunk with powder and blood, treated the city as though it had been taken. They entered the houses and broke the furniture in their search for food and wine, issuing thence with a staggering gait, their eyes brightened with the purpose of crime. Cries of "Treason, treason!" rang through the streets and alleyways. People became crazy in their desperation, and the city was filled with the abomination of assault and pillage. The Emperor saw at a glance the horror of the scene, and resolved that the massacre should be checked.

Having returned to the *prefecture*, he, together with the officers who were still left him,
retired to the room which served him as an
office. He had scarcely entered his apartments
before he braced himself with one hand on the
edge of a table, and then sank exhausted into
a seat.

"This is too much," he murmured in a voice
full of sorrow, "this is too much. Why was I
not killed upon the field?"

He then lapsed into silence, and let his forehead sink on his right hand, his chest heaving,
his frame shaken by convulsive movements.
Those who saw him at this moment believed
that he was crying, and were deeply moved as
they watched the sorrow of this man, who
scarcely knew what it was to shed a tear.

The battle, however, continued round Sedan;
and the rumbling of the artillery, like the noise
of thousands of carts rolling over pavements,
indicated the nearer and systematic approach of
the German lines.

At each new and louder crash the Emperor
raised his head and listened, his frame shaken,
the muscles of his face contracted, his fingers
playing nervously on the table with all that
agitation which is usually peculiar to a dying
man.

It was two o'clock.   Suddenly a fearful explosion shook the air.   The German artillery
had succeeded in surrounding the town, and it
now gave fire from all its guns on the *débris* of
the French army.

The Emperor rose, looking very pale.

" O friends," he said, " what an awful thing
this is !   Will it never have an end ? "

He then sank back into his chair, horribly
broken, his tangled locks of grey hair falling
confusedly over his temples.

He had eaten nothing since he left Sedan on
his way to the field of battle.   According to
the command of an officer a plate of sand-
wiches, a little cake, and some Madeira wine
were now brought him.

General Wimpffen, who elsewhere renders
homage to the courage shown by Napoleon III.
during this journey, has been pleased to state
that the unfortunate sovereign on his return
from Sedan took a hearty breakfast, while
those who remained on the field of action, and
the generals who commanded their troops in
the face of the Germans, could only obtain a
few raw carrots to appease their hunger.

General Wimpffen was not at this moment
near the Emperor, and I have based my statements on those of a man who did not leave

him during the day. I affirm that Napoleon
III. declined the dish which was offered him,
and, indeed, scarcely noticed it, so absorbed
was he in gloomy thoughts, and but poured out
for himself a little water, which he swallowed in
feverish thirst.

The continuous detonation of the artillery
seemed to increase the mental suffering of the
Emperor, and a moment came when he felt that
he could no longer endure it. He rose suddenly, looking as though he had recovered his
old strength.

" This must end," he said, " it must! Of
what avail is so much bloodshed, so much
slaughter ? "

It was almost three o'clock. The Emperor
summoned one of his orderly officers, and commanded him to go to the citadel, there to hoist
the white flag.

This order having been executed, the battle
still did not cease, and the Emperor was unable
to control his impatience.

" My God," he muttered over and over again,
" my God ! "

He could no longer remain in his chair ; and
as he asked, for perhaps the tenth time, the
inexplicable motive of the continued firing after
the white flag had been raised, General Le-

brun entered his room. Eagerly the sovereign hastened toward him.

"Why is it, my dear General," he said, "that the fighting continues? More than an hour ago I commanded the white flag to be raised on the citadel, that this useless battle might be brought to an end. There has been too much bloodshed, and I wish for no more. I want an armistice."

General Lebrun then offered the explanation which Napoleon III. had demanded of his officers before his arrival. He made known to him that, according to the laws of war, the white flag did not require the cessation of fire; and that, in order to obtain the armistice, it was necessary that the general-in-chief of the vanquished army should dispatch to the general-in-chief of the victorious army a messenger, bearing a written demand for the cessation of hostilities.

"In that case, my dear General," said the Emperor, "return to M. Wimpffen and beg him to do that which is requisite to the realisation of my wish."

General Lebrun obeyed the Emperor's request, and rejoining the general, transmitted to him the message of the sovereign. M. Wimpffen, however, grew very angry, and declared that he would in no wise check the battle, and wished no armistice. The firing was not, therefore, suspended.

Awful hours were yet to come and to run their course. It was with great anxiety that the Emperor awaited the result of the message which he had sent to General Wimpffen.

Sedan became untenable. The fire, far from abating, increased, and the city was filled with shells which killed and wounded the unhappy victims confined within it. Ambulances became necessary, and sinister fires broke out in several parts of the town.

Finally, toward eight o'clock, General Wimpffen presented himself before the Emperor. Offering his resignation as commander-in-chief, he refused to arbitrate for what was no longer armistice, but capitulation. He was, however, compelled to assume the terrible mission which he had sought to evade, but which the attitude of his colleagues forced upon him.

He presented himself before the Prussian quarter-general, and the battle ceased. All was, however, lost; and the Emperor Napoleon III. remained henceforth without crown or sword.

Strange things were heard and seen on that evening, whose shadows fell on so many desolate hearts, on so many mutilated bodies. One army, that of the Germans, was seen lifting its face toward heaven, where the stars shone, and consecrating to God its victory. Thousands of soldiers raised loud hymns of praise, while captains and chaplains stood by. Through the night, whose darkness was illumined by the tremulous light of the bivouacs, were seen to pass troops of men with torn hair and red with blood, who, after the barbarous yells of the day, now shouted forth the liturgy of their faith ; for these men were good or evil according as destiny cast them, irresponsible and unconscious, toward good or evil.

XII.

THE CLOSE OF A REIGN.

I HAVE already told how, on the day of September fourth, the Empress Eugénie, abandoned by all, fled from the Tuileries, accompanied by a few faithful friends, among whom were Metternich and Nigra. I have already told the story of the sad hours which the Emperor Napoleon III. survived after Sedan; and the public will doubtless recall the curious and tragic incidents which characterised his trip across Belgium, when he was on his way to Germany, there to give himself up as prisoner of war.

The account of the departure of the Empress has, however, never as yet been made public; and the world is ignorant of the experiences which she underwent before embarking at Trouville, on her way from France to England. I am about to give the reader an account of this journey.

Much has been said concerning the conduct of the Empress on September fourth, and during that which is commonly called her flight, which

is wholly false, and but the product of the admiring, or else the unfavourable, prejudice with
which she is regarded by false and biassed historians. The truth is most simple. Surrounded,
I repeat, by a few of her friends, among whom
were Mme. de la Poëze and Mme. la Maréchale
Canrobert, she placed herself, when she saw
that the Tuileries were shortly to be invaded,
under the protection of Prince Metternich and
Signor Nigra, and left her apartments, hastening to the gate of the Louvre, after traversing
the lateral galleries of the palace.

Finding herself at last in the street, opposite
the church of Saint-Germain l'Auxerrois, herself thickly veiled, and having with her only
Mme. Lebreton and Signor Nigra, she remained
fixed to the spot in a state of great anxiety,
leaning against the railing of the gardens which
extend in front of the colonnade, waiting for
Prince Metternich, who had gone to fetch his
coupé, which had been stationed on the *quai* at
a point where now the tram passes to Louvre-
Passy.

It was while she thus stood waiting that a
small urchin recognised her.

" Ha, ha," he cried, pointing to her, " that is
the Empress !"

As Prince Metternich still did not come, and

as the crowd increased and became more noisy, she hailed one of the cabs which was passing quietly through the streets, and drove directly to the house of a friend. This friend was away from home; and the Empress, for a moment disconcerted, gave the coachman the address of Dr. Evans, her dentist, who lived on what is now the corner of the Avenue du Bois de Boulogne and the Avenue Malakoff.

Hardly had she entered his house, where she happily found him at home, before the Empress fainted; and the doctor, seeing that she had need of care and sustenance, for she had eaten nothing for twenty-four hours, gave her a little bouillon, and persuaded her to remain in Paris till the next day. It was, therefore, on September fifth that she started on her journey to a foreign country, accompanied by Mme. Lebreton and her host.

They travelled in a carriage with four seats, drawn by two horses, and on the box were two valets in the livery of the doctor.

As they crossed the Square of Courbevoie, where is to be seen on a pedestal the profile of Napoleon III., the Empress leaned slightly from the window. This was an act of imprudence; and a passer-by recognising her, as the gamin had done on the preceding evening, shouted out the news. The populace pursued the carriage ; but the coachman lashed his horses, and they were able to gain rapidly on the crowd, and soon reached open country, leaving Paris far behind, wrapped in its mist and possessed by feverish unrest.

This handsome equipage, however, on passing through towns and villages, attracted the attention of the inhabitants ; and, owing to the unusual state of excitement caused by recent events, this notice was far from reassuring. It was most important that the social rank of the travellers should be disguised ; for, were their identity suddenly revealed, the most serious dangers might result to the Empress. This flight might then become like that to Varennes, and its results be as lamentable. Dr. Evans understood the danger of the situation, and resolved that it should be averted.

It was important that they should first dispose of the carriage in which they were travelling, and continue their journey in a vehicle which could attract no attention. As Dr. Evans was explaining his ideas to the Empress, chance came to their rescue. With the sound of rusty springs and rattling windows, an old coach passed the stylish turn-out in which they were driving in the direction of Evreux.

Dr. Evans ordered his carriage to stop, and alighted hurriedly to bargain with the hackney-man for this conveyance, in which, as he said, he wished to take his family as far as Trouville. Arrangements made, he helped the Empress and Mme. de Lebreton out of one vehicle and into the other. They then resumed their journey, while the compromising carriage returned to Paris.

An unforeseen difficulty, however, arose to disquiet the Empress. The horses which they had hired were miserable beasts and unfit for a long journey, so that on the following morning they came to a standstill in a little village, and showed themselves incapable of farther service ; it, therefore, became necessary to replace them.

The travellers drew rein at a miserable inn which lay on their route, and which seemed to be propped up against a kind of barn. The Empress and Mme. de Lebreton passed into a strange little room on the first floor ; and, while the doctor went out in search of a new relay, the driver, a glum and silent peasant, gave himself up to eating.

Ill-luck seemed to pursue the fugitives. The sky, so beautiful on the day before, was now dark, and the clouds thick and menacing. A storm broke, and torrents of rain fell, inundating the roads.

The Empress in her impatience could not remain still. She paced the inn up and down, and finally went out-doors to watch for the return of the doctor. The rain did not cease; and she stood under the shelter of the immense doorway of the barn, holding but a tiny umbrella over her head and concealing her face uneasily behind it.

Dr. Evans at last appeared, having persuaded one of the villagers to rent him two horses; and thus equipped, they no longer lingered where they were, but hastened on.

Everything went well, or nearly so, till they reached Evreux. Dr. Evans was anxious to avoid this village; but as to do so would have involved the loss of much time, they decided to pass through it. This decision was unfortunate for the Empress.

They had traversed several streets without disturbance, when they came out on a square where people had assembled in evident excitement. Mounted police were there to keep order, and bands of armed men were drawn up in line as though for drill, while the notes of drum and clarion mingled with the sound of marching soldiers.

The carriage in which were the Empress and her friends had advanced too far for it to turn back or escape from the curiosity of the people. As soon as it was noticed, a rabble rushed toward it ; and the Empress now for a third time recognised and discovered in a flight likely to prove successful, Dr. Evans was obliged to face the danger squarely.

Resigned and ready for any emergency, he dismounted from the coach, requesting that he should be taken before the authorities, while the crowd gathering round him encircled the Empress. Cries of "Long live the Republic! Down with the Empire!" rose on every side. It was a critical moment, and one act of imprudence or one unfortunate word on the part of the Empress, or on that of any excited person, would have sufficed to give a tragic turn to the scene.

The Empress, however, remained silent, and there was not one among the crowd who thought of offering her an insult.

This condition of affairs could not, however, last long; and Dr. Evans, in his anxiety, was wondering how it would all end, when he noticed a man who he thought must be an official.

He hastened toward him, and explained the circumstances which had transpired.

This man proved, indeed, to be an official,

and was, I think, the mayor of Evreux. He showed himself to be, moreover, a gentleman, and expressed profound sympathy for the Empress, who was thus miserably leaving France. He approached the carriage, and, bowing low, gave the order that these travellers should continue their journey without molestation.

The cries which had risen on the arrival of the Empress had now ceased, and silence reigned in the square. When the carriage again began to move, it was not without deep feeling that the occupants passed through the motionless ranks of the people, who had drawn up in two lines and who had become voiceless.

From this point the Empress and her escort continued their sad journey, comparatively free from misfortunes. They had, however, one startling experience.

One night, finding themselves, as well as their horses, exhausted with fatigue, they drew rein in a village through which they passed a little this side of Trouville, and knocked at the door of a hut whose appearance was certainly not propitiating.

After much parleying, carried on through closed window-shutters, an old peasant woman opened the door, and still distrustful, despite the promises of munificent recompense offered her by Dr. Evans, she refused to grant them admittance till she had made a minute examination. A lantern held in the tips of her long, thin fingers, she inspected in turn the face of the doctor, that of the Empress, and of Mme. Lebreton. The driver himself did not escape her observation, and it was only at his injunction that she finally opened her door.

"Come, come, mother," he said, "you will be paid, and these are good people."

While upon the road the Empress, so it is said, found herself much inconvenienced by a severe catarrhal cold; and as in her haste at leaving the Tuileries she had failed to bring a supply of handkerchiefs, the doctor busied himself with drying by the door of the carriage, as fast as she used them, those two or three handkerchiefs which she had brought.

The embarkation of the Empress at Trouville had in it nothing of special interest. It is known that Dr. Evans secured a little pleasure-boat, in which he brought the unhappy woman over a tempestuous sea to Hastings.

To whatever party one may belong, whatever scepticism one may profess, it is impossible to feel no emotion in the thought of the fall of the Empress Eugénie, and of that Calvary through which I have traced her steps.

She passed away in an hour of passion and of moral suffering — in one of those hours which in history determine the evolution of nations, and the ephemeral grandeur of kings.

She is not alone in her fall ; she is not alone among the women who, having reigned, now weep for their power and their pride. The ground beneath her is strewn with smiles and with crowns which have abandoned those who once, all radiant with joy, believed themselves to be invulnerable and exempt from the laws of fatality.

In the evening of this century their image finds reflection, and the mystery of those melancholy nights when they fell from the stars is re-born. The sun sheds its last glory, its red apotheosis, on the world; the sky has grown dusky, and twilight has come. Queens fall through the darkness, but as faint stars now. They pass swathed in black, their heads still shining, as though their diadems had kindled an ineffaceable glory on the brows which may no longer wear them, and their hair sown with sparks of fire. They pass like stars, yet more like phantoms, and before this funereal proces-

sion of souls and bodies, which the people blessed
and cursed in the same breath, one watches and
wonders what poets shall arise to sing these
epics, these romances, these glories and trage-
dies.

Queens fall, as of old the virgins fell in the
circus, and the people, seeing them prostrate on
the ground, throw their stones ; yet this is the
same people which once kissed their skirts and
their feet. Wandering and phantom queens
are these, who seem condemned to eternal pil-
grimage. The love and the reverence of the
crowd are no longer theirs. Circling through
the whirlwind by which they are swept, they
sing the song which is sung by little girls as
they clasp hands and play their games : — "We
dance no longer in the wood ; the laurels all are
cut."

The public is familiar with the rôle played by
Countess de Mercy-Argenteau at the time of
the Emperor's captivity at Wilhelmshöhe, when
the Empress had taken refuge in England, in
carrying out the mission which Napoleon III.
charged her to execute with the king of Prussia,
hoping that conditions of peace less severe for
France might thus be brought about. It is
also known that it was Comtesse X——, who,
stopping at the time at the Hôtel de Flandre in

Brussels, directed negotiations for the restoration of the Empire.

Women had, during this time, considerable influence in the development of affairs ; and the days which followed the fall of the imperial dynasty are remarkable for the spirit of intrigue with which they imbued them, and by the undeniably intelligent aid given by them to the statesmen who were concerned in solving the problems of the delicate and embarrassing situation which had resulted from the war.

One of these women, Mme. de V——, sister of Mmes. de la Moskowa and de la Poëze, women belonging to the court of Empress Eugénie, found herself involved, like Mmes. de Mercy-Argenteau and X——, in the affairs which followed the cessation of hostilities ; and as her attitude at this time was most noble and patriotic, the public will be glad to have it recalled to mind. The story is most touching, and seems, indeed, like pure romance, or even like a fairy tale.

To begin, therefore, there was once upon a time at the Court of Prussia, a minister from France, Marquis de la Rochelambert, who had three daughters, one of whom, exceedingly beautiful and intelligent, was the godchild of the Prince Royal, afterwards Emperor William.

There was at this court a nobleman of high birth, a dashing cavalier and man of wit, who fell in love with the lovely child and sought her hand in marriage. Family ties and bonds of friendship united the Marquis de la Rochelambert to the court of Prussia; but having consulted his daughter, and assured himself that she had no attachment for this nobleman, he rejected his proposals.

The suitor was Count von Arnim, who at that time was in all the splendour of his youth, at the very height of power, and occupying an exceptional position.

The Marquis de la Rochelambert returned to France. His daughter did not see again the unhappy aspirant; and, as far as appearances are concerned, they forgot each other. Did they, indeed, truly do so — or rather, did the Count von Arnim forget his vain dream? If we may believe the word of the slanderer, he remained always faithful to that which he had once desired; and in the very bosom of his family — for he married and himself had a charming daughter — he still dreamed of the former object of his love.

Mlle. de la Rochelambert became a wife and then a mother; and it is probable that the years would never have brought her and her old lover

together, had not the dramatic events of 1870
and 1871 arisen, bringing misfortune to the
two.

When the National Assembly nominated M.
Thiers as head of the executive power, and invested him with a mission to discuss the treaty
which was to put an end to the hostilities between France and Prussia, this shrewd statesman surrounded himself with a few of his
ancient colleagues who during the Empire had
been members of the Legislative Corps, and
created of these ministers for himself, among
whom was M. Pouyer-Quertier, to whom he
gave the direction and the reorganisation of
the department of finance.

Before facing Count von Arnim, M. Pouyer-
Quertier was called on to recognise Prince
Bismarck. The Norman and the Teuton confronted each other; the fox and the dog exchanged courtesies.

The story by which it is sought to prove that
Prince Bismarck tried to intoxicate M. Pouyer-
Quertier at a dinner where they were in *tête-à-
tête*, is too well known to call for repetition
here. I am, however, familiar with another anecdote which has not been made public, and
which the reader will doubtless be glad to
learn. Before, therefore, continuing and bring-

ing to its close the romance which I have begun, I relate this circumstance.

By a singular coincidence, and one most
favourable to him in the position which he now
occupied, M. Pouyer-Quertier found that he
was bound by ancient ties to the family of the
Rochelamberts, and consequently to the daughter of the ex-minister of France to Berlin, who
since the abortive idyll to which we have referred, had become Comtesse de V——. This
friendship rendered easier day by day his relations with the heads of the German government.

One of his daughters, moreover, had married
the Comte de Lambertye, who had large possessions in Alsace, in the outskirts of Belfort.
This fact assumed some importance when it
became necessary to determine with Prince
Bismarck the boundaries of the new frontiers.

Bismarck was determined to take possession,
if not of Belfort itself, at least of parts of the
territory which surround it. After having opposed his pretensions, M. Pouyer-Quertier, despairing to move the Chancellor, saw with cha-
grin a moment come when he was forced to
own himself vanquished. At the final moment,
however, he received a sudden inspiration.

Dipping his pen in the ink with which he
was to sign his name to the fatal treaty, he

still hesitated a moment and paused to reflect. He then threw his pen vehemently on the table and turned to Prince Bismarck.

" Let him who will," he said resolutely, " sign this treaty, Prince ; it shall not be I who do so."

Bismarck made a gesture of surprise and displeasure.

" What does this mean ? " he asked. " You were ready to ratify my conditions."

" It is true," replied the Norman. " I did not, however, dream that in accepting these conditions I should deliver over to you not only some of my countrymen, but among these persons who are especially near and dear to me."

" Explain yourself."

" I shall find it easy to do so. My son-in-law, Count de Lambertye, owns almost the whole of those territories which surround Belfort (our ambassador sacrificed truth somewhat for the sake of his cause), and my name shall never stand at the foot of a document which will rob him of his nationality, and place me in the relation of a foreigner to him.

" Forgive my sentiments," he added, as he rose, " which are no longer those of a Frenchman purely, but also those of a father. I will report to my government the delay brought about in our negotiations, and will ask it to accredit you a man unhampered by personal feelings, and who will thus be able with greater freedom to submit himself to your conditions."

In praise of M. Pouyer-Quertier, we may state that Prince Bismarck had a great admiration and liking for our plenipotentiary, and was attracted by his easy and unconventional ways.

Without replying to the words which were addressed him, he rose and paced the room. He then suddenly paused before his interlocutor, and looked him well in the eye.

"You do not wish, my dear minister," he said, "that your son-in-law and your grandchildren should be Prussians. That is certainly a natural feeling. Where are the lands of Count de Lambertye? Show me their approximate position."

Seizing a map which was used by the staff, he unfolded it before the minister, who, as he has since avowed, could scarcely believe what he saw. He did not, however, allow himself to become agitated, and taking up a red pencil, he traced out boundaries as extensive as he dared of territories partly real, partly imaginary, which he said that his son-in-law possessed round Belfort. He then showed the map to the Prince.

Bismarck examined it slowly and carefully,
too much so, indeed, for the equanimity of his
adversary.   Placing it on the table, he then took
up the document in which were set forth the
conditions of the treaty, and there inserted the
special clause which left to France Belfort and
its territory, and remitted to M. Pouyer-Quertier the act thus modified.

"There," he said, in tones half serious and
half mocking, "there, are you satisfied?"

The emotion felt by our ambassador was profound.   The tract which he had retained for
France against the exactions of our enemies,
was, it is true, small; but it seemed to him at
this moment immense, and in itself a great empire.   Objects acquire in the minds, and especially in the hearts, of men the proportions of
those sentiments, be they of joy or sorrow,
which attach to them.

This anecdote has been supplied me by M.
Pouyer-Quertier himself.   It will, I am sure, be
of interest to those who read these pages on
the frontiers which were then under discussion,
and who will learn from it of the circumstance
by which they escaped being Germans.

I will now return to my romance.

When Mme. de V—— learned that M. Pouyer-Quertier was appointed to arrange for the

payment of the indemnity of war due to the Germans, in concert with Count von Arnim, nominated as representative of Emperor William in France, she sought an interview with the old friend of her family.

"Count von Arnim," she said, "is to all appearances gentle and courteous in the extreme; but he is exceedingly obstinate and austere. Whatever may be said to the contrary, he is imbued with hatred of France, and will be implacable in the mission which he has accepted. You know that through my former relations with the court of Prussia, I am somewhat familiar with men and affairs beyond the Rhine. I know M. von Arnim by heart. Do you want me to bring him to an agreement with you? Do you want me to serve you at the same time that I serve the interests of my country? If so, give me free use of my own methods. Count von Arnim at one time wished to marry me; and though it is many years since we have met, I know that he has not forgotten me. Shall I see him? I am sure that such a meeting will result in circumstances which will favour and facilitate your task."

M. Pouyer-Quertier knew Mme. de V—— so well that he felt assured she was not speaking without wisdom and forethought.

"Where," he asked, "could you, or would you, see Count von Arnim?"

"Here."

"Here, at the ministry?"

"Yes."

"That is impossible."

"It would become possible were you to authorise the interview."

"In what way do you plan to conciliate him?"

"That is my secret till the new order is established."

"Your secret?"

"Yes; but a secret which everybody knows, and which you will doubtless divine. It will result in one of two things: either, as I have been told, M. von Arnim has not forgotten me, in which case I will use my power over him; or else he has forgotten me, and all my diplomacy will fail before his firm purpose. In what way, however, do you risk, under either circumstance, the success of your negotiations or the good of the country, by introducing me to his presence?"

"Let it be so," replied M. Pouyer-Quertier, himself coaxed and persuaded by this woman, who spoke with so much authority, with so just an appreciation of political and personal affairs;

"do as you think best. Count von Arnim is expected here to-morrow at about two o'clock. Be at the ministry, as though by chance, at the same hour yourself. I will put everything in your hands."

The next day, a little before the hour appointed, Mme. de V—— arrived at the ministry; and, after a hurried interview with M. Pouyer-Quertier, she took her place in the vestibule of the building where is the staircase leading to the official cabinet.

M. von Arnim soon presented himself; and when the Countess saw him alight from his carriage and come toward the vestibule, she placed herself erect on the first step of the staircase, as though, having had an audience, she was about to pass out. She was, therefore, the first person on whom the eyes of this diplomat fell.

Mme. de V——, though no longer young, had retained the features of her youth, and was still very beautiful, and consequently easily recognised as the woman whom he had known in the full glory of her girlhood.

At her apparition, Count von Arnim paused and took a step backward.

"I am lost," he muttered, as though divining the cause which had placed this woman be-

fore him at the decisive moment. " I am
lost."

These are the actual words which he spoke.

Agitated and filled with emotion, which he
took little pains to conceal, he came toward
her and clasped both her hands in his.

Count von Arnim had indeed spoken truly
when he said that he was lost.   Mme. de V——
took him with her and went up a few steps;
then seating herself on the staircase, and making
him sit by her side, she spoke to him rapidly
and earnestly in German.

What did she say?   We can divine the burden of her words.   M. von Arnim listened with
out speaking, his head bowed, his hand still in
hers.

"I will obey you," he said with a great effort,
as she ceased; and then he repeated the words,
" I will obey you."

Mme. de V—— rose and released him.

"Remember your promise," she said, as she
left him; "the minister is waiting for you.
You will become a German again when you are
with him, too much of a German.   I, however,
shall be in a little room opening from his office,
and shall hear your conversation.   If I find
that you are playing me false, I shall enter and
remind you of your pledge."

She did, indeed, just as she said. During the interview which took place between M. Pouyer-Quertier and M. von Arnim concerning the liberation of territory and the conditions relative to the payment of the war indemnities, she remained in a little room opening from the ministerial cabinet ; and when the discussion between the two seemed to take an unfavourable turn, she shook the door which she had previously opened part way, and thus imposed on the ambassador the moderation which she had exacted from him.

Count von Arnim accorded us conditions less severe than he had been instructed to do by Prince Bismarck. A love-story written in the past procured for us comparatively easy conditions ; and the Chancellor, greatly displeased, reproached him severely for the concessions which he granted us. Did he ever learn the romance of his ambassador and its unforeseen epilogue ? However this may be, he did not pardon his delegate for having failed to execute his orders, for having placed his sentiments in positive opposition to his rigorous and austere resolutions.

Mme. de V—— retained after this hour feelings of tender gratitude to the man who had not only remembered her through all the years, but who also blended with his personal affection a voluntary and unconscious compassion for our country. When Count von Arnim fell under the hatred of his former captain, she mourned him compassionately.

Does not history offer strange truths, and is it not worthy to be told ?

This book has conjured up many beings, many events, whose existence was in the past. The Emperor Napoleon III. is dead, his son has joined him tragically in the tomb ; and of the brilliant society which scattered joy and folly through the reign, there are now but a few waifs left.

Did the Emperor, living in exile, have sincere faith in a restoration of his dynasty in France? He, indeed, did all that could be done to make such a restoration possible, that his son, whom he loved and cherished, might rehabilitate him before the people ; yet it would be too bold to affirm that he felt any real assurance that his name would acquire the glory of another triumph. The Emperor remained during his reign a silent spirit ; and when he took up his abode on English soil he remained that which he had always been, and none knew how to read the thoughts which were in his heart.

Before his sun set, he saw many legends fade

and pass away with his own. He saw the indifference and the scepticism of the people deal
their blow against kings. If we may be allowed to ascribe to him a philosophy consistent
with the dream which filled his whole life, with
his humanitarian ideal, we may perhaps venture
to state that his own effacement and that of his
race caused him but little sorrow when viewed
as an expression of that spirit of social equality
which should rule in the generations to come.

The reign of Napoleon III. was full of bitter
disappointment ; but, as I have shown the public, there was in it also much that was great
and good.

Despite the origin of his sovereignty, despite
the Second of December, despite, too, the follies
of his court and the bloody hecatombs of 1870,
the Emperor Napoleon III. was never hated by
the people ; and in the calm with which to-day
we look on his memory, the feeling of affection
concentrated to him in the past is reborn and
finds its way to the mausoleum where he re-
poses.

The ultimate justice of the world is far more
than a vain theory. Mankind preserves this justice in its love of truth and in its tenderness of
heart ; and when anger and bitterness are appeased, those who have been most iniquitously

condemned turn to humanity for refuge and atonement.

The people, exalted by a moment of patriotic sorrow, cast their anathema on the Emperor Napoleon III. As the years have passed, however, and as the strength of the people has been restored, they have had time to think ; and the man whom they cursed at a moment when he was represented to them in the light of a monster indifferent to their sufferings, calls forth in his sorrow their affection and their pity. He has at last appeared to them as he truly was, kind, eager to aid whom he could, saddened by the hard conditions of life among the masses, and filled with a constant desire to ameliorate their lot ; and, in his benignity as a sovereign, they have learned to see the reflection of his native generosity of heart.

Hatred and anger are never disarmed before the memory of a man like Napoleon I., whose awe-inspiring and egoistical genius was unmoved by the consciousness of human suffering.

Hatred and anger, however, cannot hold their place eternally before the memory of a man like Napoleon III., always so gentle and compassionate to the humble ; and history cannot record such sentiments, even where they would seem in a measure justified by his failures and his errors, as the changeless expression of a popular verdict.

There were troublous days in the reign of Napoleon III.; but does not the hour in which this book is offered to the public imbue it with a realness and vitality, both political and philosophical, for the period, too, in which we are living is one of terror and disturbance?

Let us admit that there were, in the eighteen years of the reign of Napoleon III., unwholesome joys, errors and deceit, shame and crime. The Emperor, however, was a stranger to these things; the Emperor remained unassailable before them all, a sad dreamer and a sacrifice to the follies of the world. The inconsistencies and the faults of those whom he favoured, and who turned to their own profit his infinite kindness, should not reflect on his name. His memory rises above insult and condemnation, as, in the present hour, the Republic rises above the ruin of a past, above the afflictions of those who, born of it, yet have given it no hearty love.

FINIS.